DANIEL, DECONSTRUCTED

Books by James Ramos
available from Inkyard Press

Daniel, Deconstructed
The Wrong Kind of Weird

favorite people, which is profoundly ironic given that half the reason I'm here is to support Mona Sinclair, our top varsity soccer player, who just so happens to be my best friend, and one of my favorite people on the entire planet.

She's goaltending right now. Her face is flushed and her dark curly hair is done up in two French braids that whip around her shoulders as she jumps and dives. Her Under Armour tank top is covered in dirt and grass stains, and her tawny brown arms are glistening with sweat. While I know the opposing practice team is trying to kick the ball past her and into the net, it seems a lot like she's what they're actually aiming at, which is probably a testament to how good she is. It's like she has a sixth sense about where the ball is headed next. If her athletic prowess wasn't enough to make her a great subject, there's also the fact that she's ridiculously photogenic. Just like she can always somehow sense where the ball is headed, she can always tell when someone is snapping a photo or recording video.

The other half of the reason I'm here is to get footage for the school broadcast.

I've attended Frederick Jones High since I was a freshman, but there are a lot of new faces here today. That's because of *The Merger*. Basically, the Tri-City District couldn't afford to keep all three of its high schools open, so after eight whole months of deliberating, negotiating, and finally, voting, it was decided that Carl Sandburg High, our rival school, would be the one shutting down, and half its students would be transferred to us. I'm grateful we weren't one of

CHAPTER 1

Generally speaking, I don't do crowds. Which means the Frederick Jones High School stadium is totally *not* my scene. Crowds, to me, are a lot like horror movies: I can watch them, I can enjoy them sometimes, but I wouldn't want to be caught in the middle of one.

It's mid-August and the air is humid and thick. The breeze carries the sweet scent of pollen and fresh-cut grass. I'm leaning against the water cooler station next to the soccer field, and I am literally surrounded by Athletes™. The tennis players are going at it on the courts behind me. The football team is running drills to my right. Cheer squad is working through a routine next to me. All the while the track and field team are sprinting laps all along the perimeter of the stadium. If I were to close my eyes, it would sound like a battle scene from a swords-and-sandals epic—all grunting and shouting and huffing, punctuated by the occasional clash of bodies colliding.

At least we're outside.

Generally speaking, athletes don't rate high on my list of

For all my neuro-spicy homies.

Recycling programs
for this product may
not exist in your area.

ISBN-13: 978-1-335-01002-5

Daniel, Deconstructed

Inkyard Press
22 Adelaide St. West, 41st Floor
Toronto, Ontario M5H 4E3, Canada
www.InkyardPress.com

Printed in U.S.A.

DANIEL, DECONSTRUCTED

JAMES RAMOS

inkyard PRESS

the schools to close. I don't think I'd be able to handle that much change so suddenly.

The tension is palpable. Last year a lot of these people were competing against each other, and now they have to play together. It seems to be harder for some than others, like the football team, although they always appear to be actively trying to maim one another during practice, so maybe that's just business as usual for them.

A guy from Track jogs over (they never just walk) for water. "That's a cool camera," he says to me, nodding toward the one I'm cradling in my hands before dumping the entire cup over his head and letting it run down his shirt.

Gross. But he's right. It is a cool camera. It's a Yashica Electro 35 G rangefinder, released in 1968, of Japanese manufacture. It uses 35 millimeter film, and it's aperture-priority, with a shutter speed of 1/500. It's got a nice weight to it, heavy enough to feel like an actual camera but not so meaty that it feels bulky or clumsy. It was originally designed to use mercury batteries, which is ridiculous because *mercury*, but modern ones work too if you have an adapter, which I obviously do.

I don't say any of this aloud. That would be info-dumping, and I learned a long time ago that most allistic people do not like to be info-dumped on.

What I actually say is: "Thanks."

With a smile. People like it when you smile, for some reason, even if there's no reason.

To which he responds, "It looks old. Like, old-fashioned, I mean."

It is both. My grandfather bought it in the seventies. He worked as a stringer for the *Pioneer Press*. The film still has to be developed by hand, which takes a long time but isn't nearly as complicated as it seems at first.

What I actually say: "It was my grandpa's. He was a photographer."

"That's cool," Track Guy says.

"Are you into photography?" I ask. Because I'm still unsure if there is a purpose to this exchange or if this is simply small talk, which I am notoriously bad at.

"Not really."

Oh. Small talk, it is. I can feel this conversation dying. It is a slow, painful death that I hasten along by dropping my eyes and pretending to mess around with my lens until he jogs away. When he's gone I focus on what's happening on the soccer field.

I'm planning on editing the footage I've shot over the summer into a team highlight reel. They definitely deserve it. Being this close to the action has given me new appreciation for how brutal this sport can be. It's like football, but with less protective gear.

At least I get to be behind a camera. Having the filter of a lens between myself and the rest of the world is comforting. And it's a nice change of pace, filming "in the field," documentary-style, instead of the same static green screen setup we use for the broadcast announcements.

Sports photography is tricky because everyone is constantly moving. You can't stage anything, and you don't get do-overs, so if you miss your moment it's just gone. But all of that is also what makes it a lot of fun.

One of the girls from the opposing practice team—a midfielder, I think, if I'm remembering the careful breakdown Mona has given me of the team positions—snaps the ball past her defender, where it's intercepted by the striker, who launches it with pinpoint precision directly at the net. Mona throws herself sideways with complete disregard for the fact that she's aimed at slick lawn and unforgiving dirt, and manages to connect with the ball and send it back into play right before she connects with the ground.

I wince. That, she'd explained to me once, is called a "ground dive," and it can be as painful as it looks.

But her sacrifice saves her team from being scored on, and when she scrambles to her feet and dusts off her uniform, I breathe a quick sigh of relief. Her face is flushed, but she seems okay. I know better than to worry. Nothing keeps Mona down. I lift my camera, and almost on cue she turns to where I'm standing and flashes me a big toothy grin and a cheesy thumbs-up just as I snap the photo. Then she rushes back to her position on the court.

Seriously, I don't get how she does that.

When practice ends and everyone starts clearing out, I head to the parking lot and post up against the tailgate of my truck. The sky is this warm, rosy magenta shot through with crisp streaks of gold. There's a breeze and a humidity in the air that tells me it might rain. Rain is my favorite when it happens in the morning. I parked in the farthest corner of the lot, under a lone hazy lamp away from the rest of the cars, so I feel like Humphrey Bogart as I try not to think about all the footage in my camera that's just aching to be developed. I know I managed to get decent stuff of the whole team, but there are a few shots Mona will definitely want for her Instagram.

She emerges from the building a couple minutes later with a few of her teammates. They're laughing and smiling about something, and I see her scan the lot until she spots me. She says something quickly to the others, then breaks away and jogs over to me.

"Excuse me, stranger, I'm looking for my best friend Daniel, he's this funny-looking guy who always has a camera with him. Have you seen him?"

I try to keep a straight face, but she's already laughing, and it makes me laugh. "Wow, sorry, I haven't seen anyone like that, but he sounds like a real loser…"

She posts up next to me and rests her chin on my shoulder. "Get anything good?"

"Of you? Nah."

"Fuck you," she laughs, and shoves me with her shoulder. We're about the same height, but she's got sneaker advantage right now. She's got a hoodie on over her uniform and her duffel bag slung over one shoulder, and she smells like body spray and mint gum.

"How's your knee?" I ask.

She lifts the leg of her shorts to examine it, then shrugs indifferently. "Guess I'll know tomorrow. Hey." She pushes off the truck and stretches. Mona can't stay still for more than thirty seconds at a time. It's physically impossible for her. "Some people are going to the beach. You wanna come?"

This being the land-locked Midwest, we don't have what people traditionally think of as "beaches." But being that this is Minnesota, Land of 10,000 Lakes, we do, technically, have 10,000 beaches. But the beach, for us, means Bde Maka Ska, the largest lake in Minneapolis. It's a cool enough place to hang out, with the right people. But that's the catch— I am not "the right people," at least not for Mona's crowd.

"I can't. I've got a session tonight." A LARP session, to be specific. I can't miss that. "And I have to get ready for the festival." All of which is true, and totally not just an excuse, even though it sounds like one. Tomorrow marks the opening day of the summer festival, and I'm supposed to be there getting photos and footage, which we'll use to put together a "what happened while we were away" segment during the first week of school. "And you're supposed to be there too, remember?"

A bunch of the athletes volunteered to run a car wash to raise money for their clubs. Members of the soccer, volleyball, and football teams are all going to be there. It's something of a Jones High tradition.

"That isn't until noon," Mona says. "It's not like I need to be up at the crack of dawn, and spraying cars with hoses is easy."

"Well, my job is not. These clips and photos won't edit themselves." Also true. Besides, this took a lot out of me, and tomorrow will be even more taxing. I need to decompress.

I try to picture it—me with the jocks and the cheer squad

dinking around at the beach at night—and it's just incongruous. I have nothing in common with any of them.

"I don't think your friends like me much," I admit.

Mona frowns. "What makes you say that? Did someone say something to you?"

There's a protective edge to her voice. She already looks like she's ready to fight someone. I know from prior experience that she has absolutely no qualms about confronting anyone who talks shit about me. "No, nothing like that. It's because they always do that thing."

She relaxes a little. "What thing?"

"You know, the thing where people talk about you in a really obvious way because they think you haven't noticed. They're doing it right now." I tip my chin at her other friends, who are standing at their cars chatting and clearly watching our conversation in their peripheries.

"Oh. That? Oh, you poor dingus. They are talking about you…because they think you're cute."

"No way. That can't be right."

"I am right, and why can't it be?"

"Because people do that all the time."

"Because you're cute all the time."

"No one's ever told me." I shrug.

"Well, I'm telling you now. I think you're cute. And they don't know you. Because you don't put yourself out there. You're a cool guy. I know that. Other people should, too."

"I think you might be a little biased."

"And I think you think too much sometimes."

I laugh.

"Fine," she says, "then come over and we can watch a movie or something."

"What about Marcus?"

Mona rocks back on her heels, and something strange happens. Her shoulders sag, and the smile on her lips falters. For a split second, it's like she shrinks by a few inches, and the look on her face is like shattered glass. "Oh. That," she says quickly, almost too quickly. "That's not a thing."

I've seen this expression only a handful of times before, but I know what it means: Mona is upset.

But why?

Marcus is on the basketball team, because of course he is, and he's exactly the kind of guy I'd picture Mona with— six-foot-three, built like, well, a basketball player, and whose personality is at least fifty percent sports.

"I'm sorry. What happened?"

They'd gone on a handful of official dates and hung out a couple times, and it seemed like they were on their way to becoming a serious couple. Well, an official one, at least.

"I dunno," she says. "We weren't really on the same page. About anything. The chemistry just wasn't there."

I find that extremely hard to believe. "I'm sorry."

She shrugs. The broken-glass look is gone. She's right back to her old self. "Eh. It's not like we were together, anyways. I mean, we're cool, just not…you know."

There was a time, not long ago, when I incorrectly believed that people always meant exactly what they said, and said exactly what they meant. But I know better now. Much better. If anything, I know now that people tend to say the opposite of what they actually mean or feel. It's something that still doesn't make sense to me, but I'm at least aware of it.

And it's exactly what Mona is doing right now. Well, I'm ninety percent sure it's what she's doing.

Suddenly I have questions, too many of them, and they all come bubbling up in my mind one after the other. Did he do something wrong? Say something? Why isn't she telling me why she's upset? How long has she been upset? Is she keeping something from me? Why would she do that? Is it somehow because of me?

I have no idea what to say, because this is a situation I haven't remotely prepped for, a situation I wouldn't have even considered as a possibility. People rarely surprise me like this.

I hear someone call Mona's name, and my mind empties. I know she hears it too, but she ignores whoever it was. "You good?" she asks me.

No, I'm not. I don't get it. She's asking *me* if *I'm* good? Am I supposed to ignore the look I just saw?

She pokes my shoulder and grins. "Is this the on button? Do I need to unplug you and plug you back in again?"

This is a bit we do often. Sometimes when my brain goes off on a tangent and I check out for a while, she'll pretend to reboot me. It's a dumb joke, but it's usually enough to nudge me back to reality.

I guess we are ignoring it, then.

"Go have fun," I insist. "You kicked ass tonight. You deserve it."

I try to push her, but she's solid, so she barely budges. "Go celebrate. For real. They're waiting for you."

And they are. Pretending not to be waiting on us while very obviously waiting on us, probably wondering what the holdup is.

"Okay…" she says as she starts backing away from me. But then she raises a stern finger. "But you better text me later."

I cross my heart with my index finger. "I promise."

She smiles, satisfied, and then turns and bounds toward the others. Her enthusiasm is contagious. It almost has me changing my mind about going with her, LARP be damned. Except I realized something a long time ago that Mona, for whatever reason, hasn't yet:

We really shouldn't be friends.

The older we get the less our friendship makes sense. It won't be long before it doesn't make sense at all. Soon she'll realize that I'm holding her back, keeping her down.

And when she does, she'll let me go.

Because nothing keeps Mona down.

CHAPTER 2

I was twelve years old when the Sinclair family moved to Golden Valley and Mona literally became the girl next door. Back then I was taking online classes and regularly seeing a behavioral specialist, and my parents thought it would be a wonderful idea for me to go over and introduce myself, and so they conspired with her parents to set us up on a "playdate."

At twelve years old.

I still remember the first thing I ever said to her. Back then, I was big into cryptozoology, which the dictionary defines as "the study of animals whose existence is disputed or unsubstantiated." That was my special interest. I could literally talk about cryptids for hours. And so it was that when I'd found myself seated in the Sinclairs' study across from a girl I'd yet to say hello to, the very first thing that came out of my mouth was this:

"Did you know that the first recorded encounter with the Loch Ness Monster was with an Irish monk in the year 565?"

Despite that rocky beginning, we actually ended up getting on pretty well. We bonded over movies, of all things.

More specifically, movies we were both too young to like so much, according to our parents. She was into old conspiracy thrillers like *Three Days of the Condor* and *The Manchurian Candidate*, and I liked Westerns like *The Good, the Bad and the Ugly* and *The Magnificent Seven*. Our tastes crossed because of our mutual love of Clint Eastwood.

Eastwood led us to *Dirty Harry*, which was only a hop and a skip away from *Chinatown*. That was my gateway to an intense Jack Nicholson phase, which detoured into a Tim Burton obsession via *Batman*. We both bawled until we were dehydrated watching *Edward Scissorhands*.

Nicholson also led us inevitably to Kubrick, and *2001: A Space Odyssey* put us onto sci-fi classics like *The Day the Earth Stood Still*.

But all things eventually lead to Harrison Ford.

Mona and I both harbor a borderline unhealthy obsession with Harrison Ford. The man does not make bad movies. Of all the films he's been involved in, we both have our favorites. Mine is *Blade Runner*, naturally, because it's one of the greatest cinematic masterworks of all goddamn time, while Mona's is *Raiders of the Lost Ark*, for...the exact same reason, actually.

When her family moved to New Hope, I assumed she'd forget about me. But she didn't. To her I was still the boy next door.

Even if I'm not.

It's only the late afternoon, but the parking lot is already nearly full when we pull in. A promising sign—it means something big is definitely going down tonight.

I carefully edge my truck into a space as far from the cluster of other cars as I can find while Phoebe impatiently drums her knees with her palms. "Dear god, Daniel, you drive like an old person," she grumbles. I ignore her remark. We're both anxious to get started. As soon as I've parked she hops out and swings the bag containing her beat-up old MacBook over one shoulder.

I go around to the back of the truck and drop the tailgate. It's the golden hour. The sun is starting to set on what promises to be a warm August night, with a few weeks of muggy days left before autumn sweeps in again. We haul out our duffel bags and start suiting up.

It's a quick, quiet ritual. Clusters of people are doing the same all around us. Most of us gear up in silence; there's almost a religious feel to the atmosphere. Phoebe's outfit consists of glossy calf-length boots with chunky soles that give her like eight inches of height, and this layered, asymmetrical matte-black parka that makes her look like, in her own words, "a wilting rose made of knives."

Me, I'm in street-style joggers with giant pockets and mid-top steel-toed boots with a tactical poncho in faded camouflage—I call it Street Soldier Chic.

We strap on our wrist comms—made of foam and a couple of 3D-printed components, they're about the length of our forearms, with a housing for our phones. Lastly, I clip my sword—a curved black katana that is one hundred percent fake—onto my belt. We give each other a quick once-over to make sure everything is in place, then head in.

An unsuspecting passerby might think they'd stumbled

upon the set of the next Mad Max movie, or a bunch of bank robbers from the future, but nope. We're only here to LARP. That's Live-Action Role Play for the uninitiated, which is just about everyone, and the few who have at least heard of the term mostly think of the medieval, Renaissance fair variety. But LARP can happen anywhere, and in any setting. Ours tonight happens to be cyberpunk.

You've still got your basic character classes—wizards, warriors, healers, etc.—each with their own inherent strengths and weaknesses and special abilities. Only all of the fantasy elements have been replaced with science fiction. It's the nobility and gallantry of Arthurian legends and medieval tales smashed together with the nihilistic despair and cold, gritty futurism of Philip K. Dick. It shouldn't work, but it totally does.

"How do I look?" I ask, doing a slow twirl for full effect.

Phoebe nods approvingly. "Sharp, as always. Me?"

"Looking lethal, Low-Jack."

She grins appreciatively. Once we're in our gear everything changes. Phoebe isn't Phoebe anymore. She's Low-Jack, the best Hacker around. I'm not Daniel Sanchez anymore, I'm Hunter XX, aspiring Bounty Hunter and Smuggler who'll take any job so long as the pay is good. And this isn't a repurposed steel mill in the Warehouse District on the edge of town next to the old train depot, this is Silo City, a postapocalyptic metropolis where the world has reverted back to a sort of quasi-feudal way, and the few consolidated ultra-corporations vie for power and control of what resources are left with crime syndicates and warlords, with the dregs of humanity scrambling for whatever scraps fall by the wayside.

It's awesome.

Phoebe and I are both under eighteen, which means we're Urchins, wards of the rough-and-tumble streets scrambling for crumbs and credits for food and mods. It also means we both have to wear the bright orange wristbands that designate us as real-world minors so no one serves us alcohol or initiates any "adult" interactions with us. The Facilitators put those on us as we check in. Facilitators are NPCs—non-player characters—or staff who play a specific role in, well, facilitating the game. It's their job to keep things moving without taking anyone out of the experience. They also act as referees when needed, stepping in to reinforce the rules or keep the peace if things start to get out of hand.

"You sure about this?" I grunt as Low-Jack and I stomp through the main thoroughfare. I let her lead the way; she knows where we're going. It's crowded here, and if this were a hallway at school I'd be freaking the hell out. But here it's different. Here I'm different. Crowds may set off Daniel Sanchez's anxiety, but they don't faze Hunter XX.

"Definitely," says Low-Jack.

The sheer size of the place means it's slick and drafty and slightly moist, like the inside of a cave. It smells like paint and hot glue and foam and aerosol. Plywood facades are dressed up to look like they're made of dingy steel and covered in bright graffiti. Strategically placed fog machines pump steady plumes of thick gray cloud that cling to my steel-toed boots as I clomp through it. Cables dangle loose and limp from the rafters high above us, and banners with fake corporate names and brands flutter gently. Neon pink-and-blue lights flicker and blink all around us. An eclectic blend of trap, trip-hop, and industrial instrumental music rumbles from the PA system.

We duck into a cantina. It looks like a postapocalyptic Apple store. Clumps of people are hunkered over computer stations or hovering around old arcade cabinets beneath the hazy neon glow from orb lights woven through the low-slung tarp ceiling. The event is free-form, meaning there's no real obvious overarching narrative. There are side quests and missions, if you know where to look, but there's really no right or wrong way to participate. The only rule is: don't break character.

All of your archetypes are here. You've got your Hackers, your Grifters, your Corrupt Corporate Bigwigs, your Crooked Law Enforcers, your Kingpins and your Petty Thugs, all looking to carve out their own personal chunk of this city and more than willing to do the same to anyone who stands in their way. Everyone's got a character, an archetype, a role to play. Everyone knows where they fit in the grand scheme of things, so the story always unfolds exactly the way it's supposed to. Unlike real life. Real life is messy and confusing and nonsensical. No one seems to know what they're doing or what they should be doing. Most people, at least. Because most people don't pay attention. They aren't observant. I was like that once. Blissfully unaware. Woefully ignorant. Not anymore. Not ever again. That's one lesson I only needed to learn once.

We make our way to the back of the space, where a tall red-haired woman dressed almost exactly like Trinity from *The Matrix*, but with a microchip implant blinking on her right temple, is sitting behind a long workbench lined with all kinds of weapons and gadgets.

"What's your business here?" she grunts.

Her name is Dove, but here she goes by Shrapnel, which is badass as far as monikers go. Her family has been part of the LARP scene since the nineties. She's twenty-four, just like my older brother, Miles. They went to school together, which is how we met. Miles has always been popular and extroverted. He always used to have friends over, and Dove was around as often as Mona is now. But I can't remember the last time they hung out together. It was Dove who introduced me to all this. She was older, cooler, and the fact that she was into this thing, that it carried her seal of approval, made it okay and safe for me to try. For that, I'm indebted to her.

"Chasing crumbs," I say, trying to infuse my voice with equal parts bravado and savvy. "Word is you've got a few."

"Maybe I do," she says, rolling her broad shoulders. "But you know what they say about a free lunch."

We gotta grease her. Of course. We take out our phones and open the app.

If you want to truly immerse yourself in the game you need to download the app. That's how you access The Lore— the overarching narrative that the story follows. It's also what keeps track of your stats, your capabilities, and, most importantly, your funds. Lastly, it's how you gain access to side missions and under-the-table jobs that you just won't be aware of otherwise.

Combined, Low-Jack and I have a total of ten credits. It's hardly anything, and it's our last bit of money. Hopefully it's enough to improve our situation, but given that this is the second-to-last session, I'm not holding my breath.

Shrapnel grumbles something unintelligible and runs the transaction. We are now officially broke.

"Wait here." She pushes off and dips back behind the thick black tarp that partitions this part of the space from another, smaller one.

I scan the crowd while we wait for Shrapnel to return. It's a sea of gas masks and goggles, weathered armor and slick, glowing prosthetics. After what feels like a decade she comes lumbering back out and plops a small red cylinder onto the tabletop. "You didn't get this from me."

It's a flash drive, one with only a gig of capacity at that.

"Thanks for this," I tell her.

"Don't thank me yet. How's the Knucklehead these days?"

Knucklehead is her nickname for Miles. She's the only person who calls him that, just like he's the only person who calls her Dovetail. Both nicknames, as I found out more recently than I care to admit, are half-assed Sonic the Hedgehog references, because both Miles and Dove have always been heavily into retro games and even heavier into being a pair of dorks.

"Still not married." He and his fiancée, Shante, have been

planning their wedding for what feels like an eternity. In reality it's been maybe six months.

Shrapnel pushes off the table as another customer approaches. "Tell him I said hey."

"Do you want his number?"

"I have it," she says breezily.

I'm not sure when this happened, or the exact moment it began, but I have noticed that somehow, at some point, I became this ambassador between the two. I became the person they each went to for updates on the other person. I'm not entirely sure what sparked that shift in their relationship, or why on earth they chose me of all people. But none of that matters right now. Because right now, Hunter and Low-Jack have work to do.

Here's the deal. Something's going down in Silo City. Something big. It makes sense since it's almost the end of the season. Low-Jack managed to score some intel from one of the Facilitators about a special job going down tonight—a job with plenty of credits and maybe even a coveted corporate sponsorship on the table. A sponsorship means access to more intel, which means more lucrative jobs, which means more credits.

Tonight's mission is simple: pick up the package (which we've done) and deliver it to the connect, without being intercepted by any "interested parties," of which there will likely be plenty. Payment is to be received upon delivery. Simple in theory, but there's got to be more to it. It is only a flash drive. We could deliver it, untouched and exactly as is, or—

"We should open it," says Low-Jack, as if she can read my mind.

"What if it's encrypted?"

A couple of Net-Knights glare at us, their hands hovering menacingly over the electro-batons at their waists. The weapons aren't real, of course—just PVC pipe wrapped in foam and PlastiDipped—and neither is the animosity. In this world we Urchins are a constant thorn in the side of the Net-Knights, whose job it is to maintain some semblance of peace and order. In truth, they work for whichever gang or corporation pays the most on any given day. Allegiances are traded like stocks around here.

"What if it's not? Whatever this is, it's valuable."

"Which means it's dangerous. We tamper with that thing, we could end up in a worse way than we are now."

"Or, consider a concept: we could come out of this even better than we're hoping."

She's got a point. Taking risks is part of how you survive in Silo City.

"Fine. Let's do it."

We've got to find someplace secluded to connect this drive to Low-Jack's laptop. We can't do it out in the open; that will draw too much attention. Fortunately, I know these streets well enough to know just the spot.

"Follow me," I say. I make it all of three paces before a tall stranger swings out in front of me so abruptly that I freeze midstep and still nearly collide with them.

"I think I'll be taking that," growls a deep, modulated voice from beneath a sleek, visored helmet.

My hand instinctively reaches for my weapon. Low-Jack's does the same. I don't recognize this newcomer, whoever they are, but they've got such hard-core stage presence that I can't help but stare at them. They've got on a dark letterman-style jacket with the sleeves pushed up to expose glowing pink tattoos that run the length of their wiry forearms. An electro-baton hangs low on their right hip, and they're shouldering the biggest fucking gun I've ever seen like it's nothing. They hoist it easily, and swing the business end in my direction. The helmet is giving Judge Dredd vibes, but the jacket, the low hip holster, and the tall, spiked tactical boots are giving punk rock Han Solo.

My eyes flicker back and forth between the barrel of the incredibly large weapon and the bright orange wristband on its owner's left wrist.

So then, this transfixing stranger can't be any older than I am.

That's when I notice that they're also wearing the sword-and-shield emblem of the Net-Knights. So this is no regular shakedown from a rival Urchin eager to cash in on our hard work.

This is much worse. This is a Junior Net-Knight, here to arrest us, and if I had to wager a guess, I'd say we've just gotten ourselves caught up in a sting.

"Fuck," Phoebe mutters, which confirms she must have just come to the same conclusion as I have. Now we're both weighing our options. We could try to bolt, but even in the unlikely event that we somehow manage to get away there's no way in hell we don't immediately draw the attention of every other Knight in the vicinity. We could fight back, but unless you're packing some major black-market tech and firepower (which we most certainly are not) you'd be hard-pressed to go against a Knight, even a Junior one, armed to the teeth with state-sanctioned, state-of-the-art gear and weapons with the stats to match, and hope to come out in one piece. Or even alive.

Phoebe and I both know all of that, and it's obvious that this Knight knows it too. Just like they know what we must be thinking now. Phoebe sighs, steps forward, and drops the drive into the Net-Knight's waiting hand.

"Smart move," they say, and I can hear the grin I can't see on their face. "You just earned me a promotion. For that, I won't turn you in. Good doing business with you."

The Net-Knight hoists their gun and saunters past us, brushing my shoulder as they go.

No.

This can't go down like this. I won't let it. Hunter won't let it.

This is what I love about LARP. The freedom to be someone else. In a way, it's not so different from the masking I do every day. Except whereas my usual mask is meant to keep me from standing out, here, that's exactly what I want to do. Hunter can be as bold and as brash as I want him to be. That's why it's such a rush to be him, and that's why, instead of quietly accepting defeat and sulking off somewhere, I raise a defiant finger at the Net-Knight and declare, "Give that drive back to us. *Now.*"

The Net-Knight pauses, plants their feet, and squares their shoulders. I can feel them sizing me up even through their visor. "And if I don't?"

I plant myself firmly, rolling my shoulders and standing as straight as my back allows. "Then I'll take it from you."

"What are you doing?" Low-Jack demands.

"I have no idea..." I mutter it more to myself than to her. All I know is that I'm swept up in the thrill of it now, and I can't stop myself.

I signal for a Combat Moderator, and a stocky man with a gray wizard-esque beard and a microchip implant blinking on his right temple comes lumbering over. His name is Greg, but here he's called Cyrus. He's also been part of the LARP scene since the nineties. He was one of the first people Dove introduced me to in the scene. He's a grumpy old head with a heart of gold, which is probably why most of the characters he portrays are, you guessed it, grumpy old heads with hearts of gold.

A small crowd is gathering to witness our showdown. I steady myself, and unsheathe my blade while Cyrus checks my stats. When he announces them, I hear the Net-Knight chuckle. They hoist their BFG...and lay it on the ground. Then, they reach to their hip and unclip the electro-baton dangling there, which they brandish with an effortless twirl.

Shit.

Here in Silo City there are two basic combat systems: weapons, and hand-to-hand. Both are fairly simple and user-friendly, and they follow the same basic principles. If your weapon hits your opponent's body, it counts as points against them. The number of points is based on the strength of the weapon and the kind of armor or enhancements on the body part it hits.

My entire half-baked plan had hinged on their trying to shoot me. With a gun that massive, the recoil would have hopefully given me a window to rush in and take them out with my blade. Assuming, of course, that they missed. But by electing to use their baton, they've just made this a hand-to-hand fight, which is less about stats and more about actual—simulated—fighting.

"This is a bad idea…" Low-Jack groans in a last-ditch attempt to dissuade me from this foolishness.

But I'm too caught up in the impulsiveness of it. These people want a show, and I'm going to give them one if it's the last thing I do (and it just might be). So, with my sword in hand, I look one last time at Low-Jack, and utter the immortal words of Han Solo himself:

"I know."

We square up, like two gunslingers facing off in the Wild West. I'm no pushover, here or in real life. These weapons are boffered, so neither of us are in real danger of being hurt, assuming we both fight fair and don't go for each other's faces or groins. Still, this opponent looks like they know a thing or two about fighting, real and simulated.

And then Cyrus gives the signal, and my head empties. All there is to do now is attack.

I rush forward. Time slows. My blade hums through the air, an arc of deadly steel (read, cardboard and EVA foam).

I slash diagonally, bringing my weapon down on their right shoulder.

This is me against the Establishment. This is the triumph of the human spirit in the face of impossible odds. This… is cyberpunk.

In my mind, the blade slices deep, through armor, flesh, and bone, and I cleave the Net-Knight clear in two…but reality is crueler, colder, and what actually happens is that the Knight, a fraction of a second faster than I'd anticipated, bends just out of harm's way, while bringing their baton to bear in a low, powerful sweep that connects with my left thigh with a hard thwack.

"Hit!" barks Cyrus.

I let out a cry of frustration. Everyone knows what I must do now. Even if I'd been wearing any sort of armor or had any cybernetic enhancements—which I absolutely do not—a direct hit from an electro-baton would still be enough to drop me. So I fall to one knee in dramatic fashion, to the groans and jeers and whoops of the onlooking crowd.

This ain't over yet. I've still got three working limbs, one of which is clutching a sword.

The Net-Knight must sense what I'm thinking, because they suddenly lunge forward, swinging the baton and bringing it down just below my shoulder.

"Hit!" Cyrus roars again, ever so helpfully.

Dutifully, I drop my sword. The Knight towers over me, and a funny feeling swirls inside me as they level their baton and hover its tip just below my chin.

"Do you yield?" they demand in a low tone.

I weigh my options, which doesn't take long, because I don't have any. It's over. We both know that. A part of me wants Hunter to go out in a final blaze of glory, obstinate to the bitter end. A true cyberpunk. But that would mean leaving Low-Jack to fend for herself, and as rash as Hunter is, he can't abandon a friend.

"I yield," I say through gritted teeth.

Instantly the Knight steps back, and offers me a gloved hand. I stare at it for a moment before deciding not to be a sore loser, and they help me back to my feet.

"You fought well. I respect that."

Somehow, the compliment fills my chest. "What's your name?"

The Net-Knight bends to pick up their BFG and hoists it on their shoulder, and god I like watching them do that. "We don't have names," they respond in that raspy, modulated voice. "But my call sign is Zee-Four."

Zee-Four? Interesting. I give a tight nod. "Next time our paths cross, Zee-Four, I'll be the one to put you on the ground."

They cock their head to one side, and I get that feeling that they're sizing me up again. "I'm looking forward to it," they reply, and I'm sure I hear a smile in their robotic voice.

CHAPTER 3

"Tonight's campaign kind of sucked," Phoebe says as we make our way back to my car.

"Oh," is my response. I know well enough that she isn't complaining, only stating her opinion. So I don't feel the need to commiserate, which is great for me because I don't agree. Phoebe usually has much higher expectations about these things than I do.

"What are you doing tomorrow?" she asks. "Are you going to the festival?"

I nod. "Isn't everyone?"

"Not me. That sounds awful."

"It shouldn't be that bad. As long as I prep for it."

I get where she's coming from. Socializing, especially with strangers, can be uncomfortable for me. Phoebe understands that better than most. But we deal with that discomfort differently. Whereas Phoebe's MO is to simply avoid the difficulty altogether, I prefer to at least try to build a tolerance for it. Phoebe doesn't get that, and I don't expect her to. She does her schooling via correspondence, so she doesn't have to worry about things like that. I envy that, sometimes. Other times I feel like it's me that is in the better situation. She gets to be herself at all times, but she also pays the price of missing out on a lot of formative experiences. You only go through high school once. Hopefully. But I both respect her decision and know I can't live in a bubble and keep myself isolated for the rest of my life. That's no way to exist. And I don't want to go through life with qualifiers, like there's some invisible asterisk next to my name. I don't want to be different.

Nothing good ever comes from being different.

"How's the herbo these days?"

It's Phoebe's play on the term *himbo*, which actually fits Mona's personality fairly well, when you think about it.

"She's…herbo-ing. Does it work as a verb?"

"Sure." I suppose she is herbo-ing, but not at her usual intensity. I still think something is bothering her more than she's admitting, and I still hope to find out exactly what that is.

Not that I can really ask Phoebe what she thinks. Phoebe doesn't dislike Mona necessarily. I'd know if she did, because she would have told me as much a long time ago. But she's also never expressed any real opinion about her, beyond what seems like vague indifference, and she doesn't know that much about her.

"What are you doing tomorrow?" I ask, in a sudden urge to change the subject.

"Working. As always."

I'm not surprised. Her parents own the boutique we both work at, a fact she didn't make me aware of until two months after they hired me. It was another two months after that before she casually mentioned to me that she'd been the driving force behind their decision to hire me. *"We needed more neurodivergence in that place,"* as she'd put it, *"and I could smell the autism on you."*

"I'm also putting the finishing touches on this Power-Point presentation I'm working on," she says. "I'm trying to convince my parents to let me start HRT now instead of waiting until I'm eighteen."

"Why do they want you to wait?" I ask with a frown. Phoebe has known she wanted to start hormone replacement therapy since she started transitioning four years ago—well before we met. She's rarely unsure of anything.

Phoebe shrugs. "It's not like they're opposed or anything, they just say it's a big decision and they want me to be sure about it."

"And they think you'll have some deeper insight into what you want to do in a couple months than you do now?"

Phoebe laughs. "That's exactly my point. In fact, that's slide three!"

"Well, if you feel like it, you should come by the festival when you finish," I say. "To celebrate your inevitable victory. You might have fun."

She scoffs. "I could never."

She's probably right. I definitely couldn't imagine her in that crowd. Or at my school.

Not for the first time, I wonder which one of us is happier.

It's after ten when I get home, but I hear voices and music coming from the kitchen when I come in. Mom, Miles, and

Shante are all sitting around our big dining room table—
one of those massive old wooden ones that'll shatter your
kneecap if you run into it, an heirloom passed on to us from
my grandma. We're a family of night owls, or at least that's
what everyone except me says, because aren't all owls night
owls? Does that mean other people are day owls? Is that
even a thing?

Anyways.

Mom's on her phone, speaking mostly Spanish, so she
must be talking to family. Mom's second-generation Cuban
American. She speaks fluent Spanish, but my older sister,
Simone, is the only one to take to it, and Mom never insisted on Miles and I learning to. It was too much work, she
said, and if we wanted to learn we would, like Simone did.
Besides, we weren't ever going to go back to Cuba, because
none of us had ever been there to begin with. I've contem-
plated trying to learn the language, but I have enough trouble figuring out what people mean when they're speaking
my first language. I'm not sure I could manage a second one.
I give her a quick kiss on the forehead as I move past her to
get to the fridge. "Hey, *mijo*," she says. "Say hi to your tía."

She holds up her phone. "Hi, Tía," I say loudly enough
for her to hear me. I don't have to understand Spanish to
know what they're talking about. The wedding. It's essentially the only thing anyone around here has been talking
about for the past six months. Planning guest lists, choosing
the wedding party, scheduling photoshoots, finding ven-
ues and vendors, setting up a gift registry, menu tastings,
rehearsals—it's mind-boggling.

My mother *lives* for this shit. There isn't a single aspect of this chaotic, hectic process she isn't thrilled about, which, from what I'm gathering, is both a blessing and a curse for the soon-to-be newlyweds.

"What's all this?" I ask. The mix of music and conversation is entirely too much noise for my tastes, but no one else seems to be bothered by it, so I pretend for the moment that I'm not, either.

"Trying to settle on a decent playlist for the reception," Miles tells me. "Which, I'd like to remind everyone, is in fact a party, so it doesn't have to be a string of eighty-seven ballads."

Mom pauses her conversation to playfully swat at him. "Yes, a *party*, not a *house* party."

"All I said was I thought we should just play show tunes," he goes on while trying not to laugh. "We can choreograph a routine like a show in Vegas? With feathers and glitter? It'll be great."

"Which part of that will be great, exactly?" Mom asks. "The feathers?"

"The glitter, actually. Obviously."

Mom leans forward and stage-whispers, "Are you sure you want to marry this boy?" to Shante, who laughs and shrugs like she isn't. Shante is a lot like my brother, which explains why they're engaged. They met in college, and they got engaged last year. I have to admit, though, that she's definitely the brains of that outfit. Not that Miles is dumb. She just seems slightly more…mature? Like, if someone told me to go find an adult, and those two were my only options, I'd choose her. Maybe I'm biased because I grew up with him, and I've witnessed some of the horribly dumb things he's done over the years.

Mom shakes her head, and Miles laughs. "How was the game?" he asks me. Miles never got into LARP. It was too close to sports, he always said, and sports was never his thing, much to our father's continuing dismay.

"It was fine. Dove says hey."

"Oh…how is she?" he asks slowly.

"She seems good."

I could be wrong, but it almost sounds like he didn't want to ask. I'm getting the same vibes I get when I accidentally broach an uncomfortable subject. But I must be mistaken. It's just Dove. How could she possibly be an uncomfortable subject?

Maybe all the noise is keeping me from thinking straight. I grab a packet of saltine crackers from the cupboard and slather them with cream cheese and *pasta de guayaba*—guava paste—and retreat to the basement. I pass the study on my way down, where Dad is reading on his tablet while jazz music plays in the background. Thelonious Monk, one of his favorites. That was almost my name. Thelonious. But Mom put her foot down on that one. I'm grateful for that.

"How was the game?" he asks. He doesn't look up from his tablet, and I know it isn't because he isn't interested; he knows how much the games stress me out, just like he knows how much I don't like meaningless small talk or being interrupted on my way to my room.

"It was cool," I say as I hit the stairs.

"Alright." Dad's one of those sophisticated old heads. We have a similar temperament. Neither of us are what you could call outspoken, not like Mom and my brother. Dad's much more zen than I am, though.

The moment I cross the threshold of my basement room and hear the door click closed behind me I feel the tension I've been carrying between my shoulder blades fall away. Most of the walls are covered in foam eggcrate soundproofing panels to block out as much outside noise as possible. LED light strips line the baseboards. I touch the control pad and set them to blue. A soothing color.

It's only once I'm here that I can finally unmask. It's like peeling off a suit of armor. I don't have to worry that my facial expression doesn't match how I'm feeling, or if I'm making too much or too little eye contact. I don't have to be preoccupied with whether my tone is too harsh or too flat, or feel self-conscious about the way I move my hands—all shit that takes up a ridiculous amount of space in my head whenever I'm anywhere else with anyone else. That's the trouble with being on the autism spectrum. You don't perceive or process the world the way everyone else does, so you don't behave the way they do. That means you instantly stand out in ways you don't even realize. At first, anyways. Because the rest of the world is very good at making sure you know exactly how different you are.

Masking is how many autistic people protect ourselves. We develop habits or mannerisms that mimic those of "normal," or "neurotypical" people so that we don't stand out. But masking can be exhausting, both physically and mentally. It's like method acting, only you're in a movie you don't understand playing a character you can't relate to. Oh, and no one lets you read the full script.

First things first: I slip out of my shoes and give them a cursory inspection to make sure there are no rocks or pebbles wedged in the grooves of the soles before sliding my crease protectors back into them, followed by a fabric softener sheet. Then it's to the bathroom so I can remove my contacts and brush my teeth. I'm lucky to have the basement bathroom all to myself; I've seen what the one upstairs looks like, and if I had to use it I would simply not bathe.

Back to my room. There isn't a lot in here. My pillow-top twin bed and memory foam mattress and weighted blanket. The desk that holds my desktop computer. A theatrical poster for *In the Mood for Love*, directed by Wong Kar-Wai with cinematography by Christopher Doyle, who's hands down one of the most innovative cinematographers of all time.

Developing the film from today is too much work to start tonight, but there's stuff on my other camera, some pretty sweet footage of the sky from this morning just after dawn. I connect that camera to my computer and start transferring the photos. That's one of my favorite times to shoot, when the air is fresh and crisp and the light is pure and new. There's a nakedness to everything; it's like I'm capturing the world as it is before anyone's put a mark on it yet. The world without its mask.

I've got thousands of photos saved on this hard drive, some of them years old. I never really delete anything, and it's always better to capture more than you need than not enough. Most of the early stuff is just horrible. Before I started experimenting with light and angles, before I knew what depth of field or white balance was. I should probably delete all that. I'll never do anything with it. But it is cool sometimes to look back and see how much I've improved.

For some reason, the thought occurs to me that I wish I'd gotten photos of Zee-Four. I bet they'd look badass. I bet I wouldn't even have to do much staging or editing. Maybe I'll ask them if they'd want to do that. It would give my portfolio some variety. And the thought of spending more time with them is…exciting?

That's odd.

It's probably—no, *definitely*—silly of me to have a crush on someone whose face I've never even seen, and to be completely fair, I'm not sure what I'm feeling is a crush. But it's certainly something.

Come to think of it, maybe not knowing what they look like is fueling this feeling. For me, faces can be a barrier. Expressions can be mystifying. Body language makes much more sense to me, and something about the way Zee-Four moves lives rent-free in my head.

Leave it to me to catch feelings for a complete and total stranger. Not even *just* a complete and total stranger. A *fictional* one. Whoever's under that armor isn't actually a Net-Knight, just like I'm not actually a Grifter. They've got a real life outside of Silo City. Heck, odds are they're nothing like who they portray here. Which makes this crush, or whatever it is, even sadder.

Oh, well.

While I'm waiting for everything to upload I put on

Radiohead's *Kid A* album and turn it up so that it's just loud enough to resonate throughout my room without being overwhelming or obnoxious. And to drown out these weird, random thoughts about Zee-Four. Radiohead is the perfect band to stim to, and *Kid A* is their most stim-able record if you ask me.

My room is also one of the only places where I can stim without feeling weird about it. Stimming is short for self-regulatory behavior, and what's actually weird is that most people do it in one way or another. From what I've observed people do it most when they're trying to concentrate or focus on something, like when someone taps their foot or twirls a pencil in their fingers while they're taking a test at school—which, for the record, drives me insane—or maybe rocking back and forth in a chair while trying to pay attention to a lecture—also insanity-inducing, BTW—it's all stimming.

For me, stimming is a lot like dance, except there aren't any specific movements. It's just me letting go, letting my body do what it wants and just vibing until the world around me doesn't feel so oppressive and invasive. It's about freedom and release and just existing.

I don't do it just to concentrate. Sometimes I do it to calm myself down, or to distract myself from everything else that's happening, or to block it all out. Sometimes it helps me anchor myself when I start to feel overwhelmed and anxious. Sometimes I do it when I'm happy or excited.

But it doesn't take long to realize that most people will think something is wrong with you if you just randomly start waving your hands around or kicking your legs, even if there's a perfectly logical reason for doing it. Even if it's really no less valid than someone twirling a pencil or tapping their foot to help them focus. So I don't do it. Not in public. Not where people can see and judge.

My phone chimes. It's Mona. She's sent a selfie of herself at the beach with her tongue sticking out, and she's scribbled in big red letters "Wish You Were Here!!" along with an arrow pointing to the empty space next to her.

I can't decide whether to laugh react or heart react, so I send heart eyes and a laughing emoji.

Because she has to be joking. She's at a beach surrounded by her friends. I can't imagine how my presence could enhance that scenario. But it's sweet of her all the same. Mona's the one person who's never judged. Not that she's ever had the chance. I've never shown her this. The real me. Unmasked. Stimming. It's better that way, for both of us.

CHAPTER 4

"I know this is a lot to ask of you, Daniel, but would you please try to relax and actually have fun today?"

To accentuate his request, Bridge hovers a fluffy cloud of pink cotton candy in my face.

Today is day one of the annual Golden Valley Glistens Festival. The city has been putting on this festival for eighty-two years, in celebration of its founding, so it's a pretty big deal around here. They've closed off Broadway Boulevard, and the street is lined with food trucks and vendor tents. The parking lot of the Signal Hills Shopping Center has been converted into a pop-up theme park.

I shake my head. The day is halfway over, and I've still got plenty of small-town, home-grown, Midwestern wholesomeness to commit to film. "Can't have sticky fingers. Now, shut up and smile."

I take a second to adjust the aperture on my camera. Bridge and I have very different opinions about what exactly constitutes having fun. Then again, Bridge and I have very different opinions about just about everything. Like what constitutes a decent nickname, for example. His real name is Landon, which everyone allegedly mishears as London, which somehow evolved into London Bridge before the London part just got dropped altogether.

We met three weeks ago, during the midsummer open house our school hosted to give the incoming students an early chance to visit and familiarize themselves with our campus. He was Sandburg High's "Social Media Wizard, the Eyes, Ears, and Mouth of the Student Body, CNN and TMZ rolled into one delicious being," as he explained to me, and now that he's officially at Jones High he came onboard as one of AV Club's coanchors. He's also my self-described "brand-new bestie."

I'm still not sure what he means by that. What I do know is that in the relatively brief span of time in which we've seen each other at AV Club meetings, we've essentially become the archetypical trope of Loud, Borderline Obnoxious Extrovert with Golden Retriever Personality Adopts the Skittish, Cat-Like Introvert.

He frames his face with the cotton candy in one hand and a corn dog in the other and sticks out his tongue. With his rusty red hair, a face dusted in freckles, and lopsided smile, Bridge knows he's adorable, even if he's a little much sometimes. And he also knows what angles work best for him, so between the two of us, this is going to be a great photo. We're surrounded by the usual carnival fare: rigged games and janky old rides where half the thrill is knowing the thing might kill you, overpriced candy and creepy mascots who are probably people you know beneath the dead eyes and the musty fur suit.

Most people think it's pretty great. I think it's alright. Mostly.

Someone calls Bridge's (fake) name, and we both turn. It's Anita, one of the cheerleaders. She's in her uniform, which means she's probably here to help with our school booth.

"Hey! Smile."

She strikes a quick pose, and I snap a few photos.

"How was that?" she asks.

"See for yourself." I pull up the photos on the monitor and scroll slowly through them. I took four in total, but I'm not looking at them now. There will be time to review everything I shot later. Right now my attention is fixed on Anita, and her reactions to each of the photos.

"Wow, they turned out amazing," she says. "I love the lighting."

This. This is what I love about film and photography. I don't really understand people, and they wouldn't understand me, but they do understand my work. I give them something tangible to interact with, something they can quantify. They appreciate it, and connect with it, and in a way, at least for a little while, it feels like they're connected to me, too. It's only in moments like these where I truly feel like I'm seeing the world the same way everyone else sees it.

"These are great," Anita says. She looks up at me, and I immediately drop my gaze to the camera monitor, the connectedness abruptly severed.

"I'll send them to you," I tell her. "If you'd like."

"That'd be great. Thanks!" She smiles.

"She's nice, right?" Bridge says as she skips away.

"Who, Anita? Sure, she's cool." I'm too busy adjusting my

camera settings to study the twinkle in his eyes and the grin on his face.

"You know she's single, right?"

"I did not, actually."

"Well?"

"Well, what?"

"You know what."

For once, I do. I think. But I also really don't feel like having this conversation again. Bridge labors under the immutable belief that having fun is at least fifty percent flirting. With anyone, or anything. For real. I've seen him flirt with a pair of jeans. Jeans he was wearing. It was both bizarre and weirdly fascinating. Me, on the other hand, when it comes to flirting, I don't. Because I don't know how. And half the articles I've ever read were written by a guy wearing a fedora and strange facial hair who very obviously knows even less about the subject than I do. The other half insist that it's something that comes naturally, that you should trust your instincts and just go with the flow. Useless advice for someone who has no instincts and is neurologically hardwired to not go with the flow. Whatever that even means.

So I don't flirt. And I can almost never tell when someone else is flirting. Having said that, though, there's no reason for me to think that Anita was flirting with me, or has any romantic interest in me. I'm not sure what set Bridge on this particular talk track. Aside from the fact that since the moment he found out that I was single, he's taken it upon himself to be, in his own words, "my own personal Cupid."

I already know more about him than I do most of my other classmates, which is because he talks a lot. Not that

I mind. Hanging out with people who like to talk means I can get away with not talking as much, and that works out great for me, because most of the time I don't have that much to say.

The other great thing about people who just have to talk all the time is that it only takes a slight nudge to spin the conversation in an entirely new direction. It's a neat little trick I learned for keeping away from topics I'd rather not discuss. It works with Bridge at least eighty percent of the time.

"Have you been on the Tilt-A-Whirl yet?" I ask him.

He makes a face. "You know those things make me nauseous."

"Fine, the Ferris wheel, then."

The weather is gorgeous and muggy and it looks like someone put an Instagram filter over everything. The air smells like fresh popcorn and cotton candy, and there's just enough of an errant breeze to offset the humidity.

This particular wheel is one of those slow-moving, slow-rocking monstrosities where everything creaks and clicks and whines. Probably not mechanically sound, but the view is great. From the top we can see the entire festival site, including the farthest corner of the lot, where our school has a booth set up along with the car-washing station. Mona is over there somewhere, along with the other jocks in their swimwear, with their hoses and buckets and sudsy sponges. There's a line of ten cars slowly crawling through, and a couple of the cheer squad and dance team members are twirling big multicolor signs.

"Did you know that February 14th is Ferris Wheel Day?"

"No," Bridge says impatiently, "because February 14th is Valentine's Day."

"It can be both."

"Daniel…" He sighs. "Is it wrong that I want one of my best and most cherished friends to find solace and comfort in the arms of a lover?"

I don't know what criteria Bridge uses to determine his best friends, but I doubt I've met those qualifications in less than a month. I appreciate the sentiment, though. "It is when you say it like that. You sound like my mom." Whom he hasn't met, but would probably get along very well with.

"Yes, and you obviously don't listen to either of us. Look down there. See all those people? There's so many of them. There has to be one for you."

I look down. Golden Valley is a city of about twenty thousand people, and I think every single one of them turned up today. It feels like all the faces around me are at least somewhat familiar. People I might have seen at a grocery store, or a restaurant, or a gas station. Parents and classmates and teachers and all their families.

Oddly enough, what Bridge says makes me think about Mona, not myself, which I've been doing a lot since yesterday. Mona actually is my best friend, and she's stated several times that, for whatever reason, I'm also hers. The gravity of that fact gives me the confidence to believe that my intuition, flawed though it may be, is correct in telling me that she's in a funk over the whole Marcus situation. The real question is, what should I do about it? Should I do anything? Mona did insist that it wasn't a big deal, but she seemed happy—happier—when she and Marcus were hanging out. In fact, I saw her a little less for those few weeks.

Friends are supposed to look out for one another, and best friends are supposed to be, well, the best at doing that. So as Mona's best friend, it's my moral obligation to do what's in her best interests, and the fact of the matter is that she wouldn't be wasting so much of her time and her potential with me if she had someone else. Someone new. A Marcus who she actually *does* have a lot in common with.

"Daniel, did you hear me?"

Bridge's voice only vaguely registers in my head.

That someone else can't be only a friend. Mona's already got plenty of those, and she's demonstrated time and again how willing she is to ditch them to hang out with me. So it can't be just anyone. It has to be the right someone. The question is who? I want her to be happy. I want her to have everything she deserves to have. But how do you give someone what they deserve when they deserve so much?

"Daniel, sweetheart, are you hearing me?"

Mona is bisexual, and I know how much it aggravates her when she dates a guy and people assume she must be straight now, or when she's with a girl and those same people act like she's a lesbian. I understand why it makes her so angry. It's ridiculous.

But that doesn't mean she doesn't have a type.

I do a quick mental review of her most recent dating history. Before Marcus, she'd briefly dated Heidi Xiong from the track squad. They were together for about a month before breaking up, and they're still friends now. She also told me once how cute she thought Juanita Willis from the volleyball team was, and she's shown me some of the flirty texts they used to send each other (although she'd had to explain to me just what made their messages flirty, because to me they read like ordinary conversations between two close friends). She also once made out with Aaron Paulson from the football team at a party, but he was apparently bad at it so it only happened once. Before that, it was—

"Earth. To. Daniel!"

Bridge is practically shouting now. The sudden noise derails my train of thought, and I realize that the Ferris wheel has stopped, and we're back on the ground. Bridge is climbing out of our carriage.

It's time for another scene change.

"Hey," I say, pointing. "We should check out the car show after this!"

I feel like I'm on the set of a Fast & Furious movie. Gleaming grilles and glistening paint and doors that open the wrong way—a lot of them look more like jets or space ships than they do cars. Clean, flowing lines refracting the sunlight. Streaks of neon pinks and purples and blues, shot through with the gold light of the setting sun. I know nothing about cars, except that they are beautiful, and all that shiny chrome and slick paint just begs to be photographed.

I take a deep breath, square my shoulders, and wade into the thick mass of people, clutching my camera like it's a weapon. In a way, I suppose it is. Most people will at least attempt to get out of your way if they see you holding one. Either that, or they'll pose for you.

Car photography is tricky, especially in such a crowded space. All those shiny surfaces are like mirrors, and the reflections of whatever is around can easily end up in the photos. Which means perspective is key. By carefully choosing the right angles to shoot from, you can eliminate a lot of that visual noise.

I snap a shot, then adjust some of my camera's settings. I'm searching for my next subject when my eyes are drawn to this canary yellow Ford Mustang, or more specifically, whoever the gorgeous stranger is who's stepping out of the passenger side.

No, *stepping* isn't the right word. *Sliding* seems more appropriate. It's such a smooth, self-assured motion. Not a hint of self-consciousness. Effortless. A distinct lack of performance. I get the immediate impression that this person wouldn't care if there were five or five hundred people gawking at them. I don't know if this car belongs to them, but if it doesn't, it definitely should.

What is this strange stirring in the pit of my stomach? This bottom-dropping-out-from-under-me sensation that feels like I've just fallen through a trap door?

For a moment I forget there's a camera in my hands. A square jaw and a sharp, almost elvish nose. Brown skin that seems to glitter under the lights. Dark, curly hair half tucked beneath a trucker hat with the NASA logo on the front. A Ziggy Stardust T-shirt beneath a weathered jean jacket. Everything about them seems vintage, lived-in. They aren't looking in my direction, which means I don't have to worry about making accidental eye contact. In the immortal words of Mr. Spock: fascinating.

"Who is that?" I hear myself ask. I'm pointing, which I know is a faux pas, but I'm startled, and for a second my mask slips. "In the checkered pants."

They're surrounded by several other people who look to be around our age whom I don't recognize. But I'm guessing Bridge knows at least one of them. He glances around until he spots who I'm talking about. "Oh. That's Gabe. They're amazing, obviously. We were at Sandburg together."

Which explains why I've never seen them around before. Gabe. A name to go with the person. "You said 'they.'"

Bridge nods. "Gabe's nonbinary. They/them pronouns."

Got it. "What do you know about them?"

"Let's see," he begins, then starts rattling off factoids almost faster than I can process them, counting off with his fingers as he does.

"They're in a band. They play the drums and guitar. They sprained their ankle during sophomore year and spent the first semester on crutches. They were on the debate team. They're really into Dungeons & Dragons. And, last I checked, they are completely and totally single. Why don't I just introduce you two?"

I freeze. Meeting new people is quite literally always a terrifying prospect, even when I do have time to rehearse. For me, meeting new people is like Batman beating Superman in a fight. It can go well, in theory, but only under the right conditions and with loads of prep time and no small amount of luck.

I have none of that right now, which means I would have to improvise. Historically speaking, that never goes well for me.

"It's cool."

"It's no big deal. For real," Bridge insists. "I can make it so low-key, you have no idea. It'll be natural as fuck. I am the most amazing wingman you will ever possibly know."

It isn't like that. I don't think it is. He's got it all wrong. It's not me I want to introduce to Gabe. It's Mona.

But before I can even begin to figure out how to verbalize any of that in a way that Bridge will understand, he's looping his arm in mine and tugging at it until he's almost literally dragging me behind him. I could fight back, but that would only cause more of a scene. So instead I trudge after him as he plows deeper into the crowd and toward this absolutely gorgeous stranger, fully confident that I'm about to make a complete and total ass of myself in front of them.

CHAPTER 5

This is actually happening. Bridge is actually dragging me through this crowd, toward this gorgeous stranger, Gabe, whom I know next to nothing about, so that he can actually introduce us. And I don't know how I feel about it.

Because I want to meet them. I feel the same way now that I did back when Mona and I met for the first time. Charisma. I'm drawn to it, like most of us are. Captivated by it. Because it's something I so distinctly lack.

This feels like…the Vertigo Effect, so-called because it was made popular in Alfred Hitchcock's classic film *Vertigo*. Also called a dolly zoom, it's a filmmaking technique in which you basically pull the camera away from or toward the subject while zooming in or out in the opposite direction. The result can be disorienting and anxiety-inducing, both of which are terms I'd use to describe this very moment.

Bridge walks right up to Gabe like he doesn't have a care in the world, which I suppose he doesn't. He calls their name, and instantly has their attention.

"Bridge! What's up?" Their face lights up the way everyone's does when they see Bridge, and I shift awkwardly to one side as they hug each other. I feel a little voyeuristic watching people hug each other, and I never know what to do in these situations.

"This is Daniel," Bridge announces. "My brand-new bestie."

The way he says my name makes me sound way more noteworthy than I am.

And then Gabe is looking at me, and I can't help but look at them. In the brief second of eye contact we share before I shift mine to my camera, there's what seems like a spark of recognition in their eyes.

"Hi, Daniel."

Something about hearing them say my name makes my insides feel funny, and I steal another glance at them, taking a mental snapshot instead of a literal one. The planes of Gabe's face are aesthetically pleasing. It's like they were etched out of hard clay. I like that they have freckles, because a lot of white people don't think Black people can have those, which is ridiculous, but whatever. Their eyes are the shade of brown where you can't see the pupils, which to me is a little scary, because it means one less indicator as to what they may be thinking. I'm also legitimately jealous of their bone structure. Their jawline is sharper than mine, and their cheekbones are higher, too.

"You're in a band?" I blurt desperately. I sound like a game show contestant who's shouted something they know isn't even remotely the right answer just to beat the buzzer.

Sometimes, especially in a group setting where there are lots of people involved in a conversation, what someone says can get overlooked, or unintentionally ignored. That happens to me all the time, or at least during the rare instances when I try to dip into those metaphorically choppy waters. Either my voice isn't loud enough, or the subject has already changed and what I say isn't even relevant anymore, or I time it wrong and start talking at the same time someone else does.

None of that happens now. Instead, a sudden hush falls over everyone at the precise moment I choose to speak, a two-second lull in the conversation, and my voice rings out loud and clear in that perfect window of silence.

And now everyone, including Gabe, is looking at me. "Yeah..." they say questioningly. "Have you seen us gig?"

"No," I quickly admit, about a second before it occurs to me that maybe saying yes would have kept this from becoming more awkward than it already is.

"Oh. Well, you should fix that. We're playing tonight, in—" they glance at their phone "—half an hour. Check us out."

I feel my cheeks flush. I don't know what I want. I'm torn between my standard desire to be but a silent observer, a fly on the wall, and wishing I had all of Gabe's attention to myself, so that I could pick their brain without interruption.

"I will," I stammer.

Gabe smiles. "Good."

I don't understand these conflicting and contradictory urges. They make no sense, and I very much dislike when things don't make sense.

There is something distinctly James Dean–esque about Gabe. I'm a little envious of the people who can be their unfiltered selves. People who can just exist without constant recalibration and course-correction. People who don't spend hours rehearsing before a conversation and then hours analyzing it after the fact. People who don't second-guess themselves.

People like Mona.

And speaking of.

It's close to dusk when the car wash starts wrapping up and breaking down.

I find it much easier to move through a crowd when I've got a clear destination in mind. Gabe's band is on in fifteen minutes. I need Mona to be there when they go on. If Mona does have a type, I'd bet good money that it's something like Gabe.

When I get to the edge of the sudsy parking lot area, I pause.

In film, a scene will usually start with what's called an establishing shot, which is a shot meant to lay a foundation of where and when the scene takes place, and who's in it. Establishing shots are often also wide shots, which are ones that include both the subject, like the actor or actors, and their surroundings.

The Athletes are messing around while they pack everything up, rolling up hoses and flicking water at each other and chasing one another with buckets. Everyone is laughing and completely oblivious to everything outside of their little bubble. It's a wholesome scene, and everyone is exactly in character. In every teen drama or comedy ever filmed since the beginning of time, the athletes are always super hot and super fit, which tracks, to an extent. The athletes are the most...athletic...kids on campus, so physically, lots of specimens among their number. The difference between film and real life, of course, is that none of the real ones are being portrayed by actors and actresses who are really in their mid-to-late twenties. So it's a little different.

Nevertheless, they are nice to look at.

Despite this idyllic scene, being The Outsider affords me a certain objectivity that allows me to see beyond the surface.

Once the setting is established, a few full shots, in which the subject fills the frame, head to toe. They can include multiple subjects, and are great for capturing things like a character's body language and mannerisms.

Heidi and Juanita, one a confirmed former fling of Mona's and the other a maybe fling, are here. Aaron isn't present, at least at the moment, but Marcus is, goofing off with some of his teammates. It's always easy to find Mona. All you have to do is find the nucleus of the action and she's guaranteed to be there, right in the thick of it. Her hair is still in braids, and she's got a long T-shirt on over her swimsuit. She's walking around, picking up stray sponges and loading them into a bucket. And here's the thing: she's only walking, not bouncing, or skipping, or striding, which are all ways she normally moves around. They are very obviously keeping their distance from each other. In fact, Mona is rigidly keeping her entire body oriented in the opposite direction, which I know can't be accidental because he's running around dodging the spray of hose water.

I approach cautiously, with full awareness that this isn't my scene, but not with any fear. The athletes are gumdrops, himbos and herbos one and all. It isn't bullies you need to worry about here—it's the crippling sense of inadequacy you almost can't help but feel when you're surrounded by people who look like they were sculpted by a master.

Close-up shots are exactly what they sound like. They fill the frame with a particular part of the subject, like their face, for example, which is why they're good for showing emotions, reactions, and specific actions. Mona sometimes gets this look when she's really, really concentrating on something, just pure focus and intent. She's got that look now, but picking up sponges shouldn't take that much focus. Which means she must be thinking about something else.

The way her face lights up when she sees me is as gratifying as it is mystifying. And yet, that light seems just a shade dimmer than normal. I'm sure no one else around her has noticed. But people are their most authentic when they think they aren't being watched.

"Where were you, dude?" she asks loudly as she twirls a bucket in her hand. "I was waiting for you to bring your truck through for a wash."

Up close she smells like sunshine and aloe vera. Also industrial soap. "My truck isn't dirty."

The others acknowledge my arrival with far less enthusiasm, if they do at all. I can feel the bafflement in the air, the question they're all thinking but that no one will ask aloud.

What is he doing here?

"There's someone I think you should meet," I tell her.

She eyes me suspiciously. "Meet? What do you mean?"

And that's when I realize I've made a tactical error.

The meet-cute. You see it all the time in the movies, especially rom-coms. When the two soon-to-be lovers cross paths for the very first time. It's a vital step that sets the tone for the entire relationship. It has to be charming, it has to be memorable, and most of all, it has to be, as the name implies, cute.

And I've already nearly fumbled it.

Side note: I have to say that of all the idioms out there, to fumble something is easily one of my all-time favorites. Way back before my dad and I both realized that my interest in sports was absolutely nonexistent he tried to introduce me to football—American football, that is, which I automatically disliked on principle alone because it's named wrong. He'd explained what fumbling a ball was in real time, as I was witnessing it on the TV screen, and so now saying it conjures just the most visceral mental image. I love it.

Anyway, fortunately I think I can recover.

"What I meant was, there's a band I think you might like. They're playing in a few minutes."

Now, I don't like lying. But this is also, technically, the truth. In service of a greater cause.

My plan is simple. Does Mona need to have a significant other? Nah. But that doesn't mean I can't find her one. A good one. Someone like her. Someone amazing. That will solve everything. That's what's missing, like a single puzzle piece. And just like a missing puzzle piece, sometimes you only find it when you least expect it. At least, that's how it works for me; I'm terrible at puzzles.

We make it to the pavilion just as Gabe's band is setting up on stage. I'm already buzzing with anticipation. It's a standard roster. A vocalist, a bassist, and Gabe, the drummer, straddling a stool behind a matte-black kit, the sticks dangling from their spindly fingers. The vocalist, who's also got an old six-string hanging from their shoulder, fiddling with the mic stand. The bassist is anxiously glancing around the stage, eyes darting between his bandmates and the crowd. Sweat is already beading on his brow. I can taste the nervous energy wafting from both of them.

But not Gabe. There's something aggressively zen about the way they're just there, seemingly immune to the scrutiny of the hundreds of eager eyes laser-focused on the stage.

I've seen this before. That same energy. That same laser-like focus. It's exactly how Mona is during a game.

If I hadn't been sure before, I am now. What Mona needs is someone who's the opposite of me. Someone who gets all the things that go right over my head. Someone who doesn't mind being the center of attention. Someone who can reciprocate her energy. Who better to do that than someone new and exciting?

And then their set begins, and the band ignites. There is nothing but the music, the noise, the sound, pure and loud and frenzied. I can tell from the look on Gabe's face that they could be playing in the middle of a hurricane and it wouldn't take them out of their zone.

I look over at Mona…and she's staring down at her phone.

I don't have time to say anything. Concert photography is a lot like sports photography. Things move fast, and in less than optimal conditions, and you don't get any do-overs. Tech-wise, it means a low aperture and a fast shutter speed.

Perhaps counterintuitively, I do like live performances. I love them, in fact. There's something magical about experiencing so many disparate elements coming together and creating something cohesive and powerful right before my eyes, and something thrilling about knowing that there's no margin for error, that the performers are dancing along that razor's edge between success and total failure with only their skill and ability keeping them from the edge. All that with an entire audience watching and listening and sometimes recording. It's walking an audiovisual tightrope.

I look over at Mona again, searching her expression for a sign that she's detecting any of what I'm getting right now. She's watching the stage, swaying in time with the music. I can't tell if she's watching the entire band or any one member in particular, and her face isn't giving me anything to work with. But she has to be feeling this, right? If I of all people can pick up on a vibe like this, then everyone else already has. I'm always the last to notice these things.

She must be feeling something. Seeing Gabe up there. A kindred spirit, a soul alike; at the very least she has to think Gabe is cute. I do.

As the crowd cheers for the band's last song, I call over the noise, "Come on. I wanna get some photos."

Again, a technical truth. I do want photos.

"If you say so," Mona says with an easy laugh as we push through the crowd toward the side of the stage. Even now I can't help but marvel at her complete lack of nerves. Here I am dragging her to a meeting with a bunch of complete and total strangers, and she isn't even anxious. Meantime I've literally had nightmares about being in her exact situation.

We catch up to Gabe's band as they're packing up their instruments off to the side of the stage. Gabe sees us approaching and does that thing cool people do when they jerk their chin up as a way of acknowledging someone. "Daniel, right?" they ask. "What'd you think?"

Hearing my name come out of Gabe's mouth again catches me off guard. But then, it usually does when people remember my name or recognize me. It's jarring being reminded that I'm being perceived sometimes. I always assume I'm just an NPC in other people's minds.

"You all killed it. This is my friend Mona."

Side note: I'm not sure when or how the term "killing it" came to be a good thing, but it's widely used enough that I've added it to my conversational tool kit.

Gabe glances at Mona. I've already got my camera ready. This is a historic moment, and I'm going to capture it. Their eyes lock. My breath catches in my throat. "Soccer team, right?" Gabe asks. "I hear you're really good."

Mona shrugs. "Come to a game and maybe you'll see for yourself."

Gabe smiles. "I might just do that."

Is this for real? Am I seeing something of a sparkle in their eyes as they talk to each other? Am I really feeling this palpable energy between them?

I glance over at Gabe's bandmate, the guitarist. He's watching the two of them while strumming absently at his guitar strings. Is he seeing the same thing I am? He has to be, right?

They've both got heavy "main character energy." More than that, they look so right together. Their contrasts only make them look more like a couple. Opposites attract, as the saying goes, and aesthetically they couldn't be more so. But this works. The bubbly, extroverted ray of sunshine and the tall, dark, and mysterious moonbeam. It's a trope in itself. If this were a movie, this specific moment would be in slow motion, with a warm, hazy filter and lots of close-ups and push-in shots.

And then—

"It's good to meet you."

"Yeah, I'll see you around."

Wait. What? That's it?

Reality snaps back into focus. Gabe and their bandmates are hauling away their instruments, and Mona is back on her phone like nothing happened. As if this wasn't a monumental shift in the status quo. As if they hadn't just both been introduced to their perfect counterpart.

What the actual heck?

"Hey, did you get the photos you wanted?" Mona asks me. "Wanna get out of here?"

"Um..." I don't know what to say. I'm still very deeply confused. "Sure?"

"Cool. C'mon." She ropes her arm in mine, and we're moving.

★ ★ ★

"What did you think of Gabe?" I ask as we make our way back through the festival.

It's much more of a vague question than I'd usually ask, but I'm casting a wider net than I ordinarily would. Call it me trying to be subtle.

"Gabe seems really cool," she replies thoughtfully. She seems to have perked up a lot, or at least she's doing a good job of pretending.

I nod. I can't flat-out ask her if she wants to date Gabe. It's probably too early to know, given that we've all only just met. What I'm looking for is the potential for her to feel that way later on. Could something develop between them? Does she think so? Does she hope so?

They look like the leads in a big-budget romantic comedy, a light, feel-good summer flick coming to a theater near you. They have power couple potential. Heck, I wouldn't be surprised if they ended up dating before school even starts.

I'm fairly certain that Gabe is exactly who Mona needs. The question is, is Gabe who she wants?

Probably not just yet. Meet-cutes sometimes work that way. When the couple first encounter one another, they don't always realize that they're meant to be together. That comes later, with character and plot development. Little do either of them know that they've got someone looking out for them. Someone with their best interests at heart, who doesn't mind quietly working behind the scenes to ensure they both get their happily-ever-after. I'll be their own personal fairy godmother. And then, when my job is done, I'll ride off into the sunset, alone, but complete in the knowledge that the people I leave behind are all the better for it.

CHAPTER 6

In film, transitions are how one scene switches to another. There are lots of ways to handle them, and each one conveys that change a little bit differently. The standard, or hard, cut is the most common and the simplest, because it's just starting one scene right after the other.

Sometimes it takes me longer than most people to fully transition from one scene to another in real life, especially if the previous one was heavy.

Today was definitely heavy. It takes me all the way to dinnertime to decompress from today. Even that doesn't feel like quite enough.

It's just my parents and me this evening. If I had to choose one thing I dislike about my siblings moving out, it's that there's no one here to field my parents' attention at the table. It used to be that I could slip through an entire meal with minimal engagement when I really didn't want to be bothered, because there were two other people present to keep the conversation going, and I didn't have to feel rude or antisocial. But with that buffer gone, it's almost impossible to get away without telling them how my day went. Which is a question I especially hate. How can you categorize an entire day like that? Sometimes I don't mind talking; it gives me an opportunity to vent when I need to. But other times, like now, I'm still processing and would rather do so internally.

Tonight Mom has made something called *carne con papas*, which is essentially Cuban beef stew, served with rice. It's delicious, but my mind is too far removed to enjoy it the way I might otherwise.

"How was the festival?" she asks as we eat.

I stall by popping another forkful of food into my mouth. "It was…a lot."

"I'm proud of you for going," Dad says. "You know what they say: 'life begins at the end of your comfort zone.'"

"Yes, but you don't want to overexert yourself, either," Mom says pointedly.

This has been a, let's say, point of contention between my parents. On the one hand there's Dad, who thinks experience is the best teacher, and the only way I'm going to learn is to get out there and figuratively get my hands dirty, which he had to explain meant learn from my mistakes and grow from them. Mom, alternatively, thinks I should be cautious, take my time, and make sure the choices I make are the right ones. She doesn't want to see me get hurt, which I truly appreciate.

My philosophy lies somewhere in the middle of their ideological tug-of-war. I can exist in an allistic society, and maybe even thrive, just as long as I keep doing what I'm supposed to. Just as long as I keep playing my role. And luckily, I'm very good at that.

I just shrug and think I've managed to avoid their questioning once I escape to my room after dinner. I download the photos from my camera and start prepping for tomorrow. But ten minutes in, there's a soft knock on the door, and Dad peeks his head in. "How'd it go today?" he asks. "Really."

I shrug. "It was cool."

"Nice."

He lingers, posted up in the doorway, and I know he can sense that I've got something on my mind. "Can I ask you something?"

"Shoot."

"Did you date when you were my age? I know that was a really, really long time ago, so it's cool if you don't remember."

"Oh, you got jokes."

I do, because I'm hilarious, but I don't mean anything by it. My parents aren't that old, as far as parents go.

He enters the room and perches on the edge of the bed. "I dated, yes, but it wasn't anything serious. Not until your mom."

"Were you always in love with the people you dated?"

He whistles thoughtfully. That's the thing about my dad. He doesn't say anything without thinking about it. "Puppy love, maybe," he says at last. "But I was a knucklehead at your age, so I didn't know what being in love really was until much later."

I nod.

"Can I offer you some advice?" he asks. "Don't sweat this stuff. There will be plenty of time to do that later, I can promise you that. You're only a senior in high school once; try to enjoy the ride and have fun."

Have fun. Sure. Everybody says that like it's easy.

"But really," Dad continues, "no two relationships are exactly the same, and neither are the feelings two people can have for one another. All I can tell you is that when it happens, you'll feel it, and you'll definitely know."

I definitely felt something meeting Gabe. Hopefully the same is true for Mona.

And Gabe.

"Thanks, again," I tell him.

Dad smiles as he stands up and stretches. "Hey, don't worry about it. That's a figure of speech, by the way."

"I know. I…figured."

Dad laughs and wags a finger. "Good one. I knew I liked you for a reason."

Dad, like me, is also on the spectrum. So he understands the way I see things better than anyone else in my family, even Mom. But unlike me, he's had years and years to learn how to live with it. He says I'll get there, eventually. It's a little easier to believe coming from him.

In film, preproduction is the period of time when everyone is getting ready to make the movie. Locations are scouted, the cast and crew is assembled, storyboards are drawn—everything that needs to be done before the cameras start rolling is done during preproduction. To Aisha

Howard, our Student Council president, summertime is pre-production for the upcoming year, and especially this year.

Aisha is all about the community. Homecoming to me mostly just means the dance. But for Aisha, it's more than that. Heck, it's more than an event. It's a chance to do some good, to effect positive change. For the community, of course.

I like Aisha. She's direct and analytical. I don't often have to play detective to figure out what she means, because she usually says exactly that. Her mom is the superintendent for the district, so she could probably get away with being whatever kind of student she wanted to, but she chooses to put her heart into everything and actually try to make a difference and be a force for good.

This is far from the first meeting like this we've had. The moment Aisha found out about The Merger she called everyone together to start prepping for it. She probably knew from her mom way before any of us did. But she didn't say a word about it until it was announced.

Today we're talking about Homecoming. This year the dance is just the culmination of a month's worth of events, from the festival, to the parade, to Spirit Week, to the election of the Homecoming Court and the actual game. The whole thing was already kind of a big deal around here, but Aisha's got the whole town involved this year.

Everyone is here. AV Club, Student Council, the Spirit Committee (they're in charge of—wait for it—school spirit!), Marching Band (for some reason), and all of the fall sports teams.

Will Gabe be here? I think I'd like to see them again, even if Mona isn't here.

I purposefully get here later than everyone else in the hopes that my arrival will go as unnoticed as possible, but of course Bridge spots me as soon as I enter and excitedly flags me down. I reluctantly join him on the bleachers, where he's lounging next to Solo, our senior tech specialist. Solo's real name is Solomon and why yes, he was named after the Biblical king. He's also the thirstiest person I've ever met in my entire life. Solo isn't a romantic like Bridge, he's literally just thirsty. Like, chronic dehydration levels of thirsty. The kind of thirsty that permeates a person's entire personality to the point that it's a trait in and of itself. Aside from that he's a cool guy, though.

I give the rest of the bleachers a scan and conclude: no Gabe.

"So, what do you think?" Bridge asks me the second I sit down. He's positively beaming at me, which only adds to my confusion.

"What do I think, about what?"

He scoffs and waves a hand. "You know. Gabe."

Okay, but why is *he* thinking about Gabe? Did he bring them up because *I'm* thinking about Gabe? How would he know that? Am I being obvious somehow? And if he wanted to know what I think about them, why didn't he just say that from the jump? "Gabe seems really great."

Once I've had more time to process everything that happened with them, I'll probably be able to articulate my actual feelings much better. But as it stands right now, that's the best I can come up with.

Apparently my answer isn't enough for Bridge, who is now gawking at me. "Really great? What does that even mean?"

"I don't know."

He clicks his tongue. "You don't know?"

"That's what I said." I feel like the sting of annoyance in my tone is justified. Because I know there's a point he's getting at, but for some dumb reason people often won't just say what they mean. So even when I *do* say what I mean, they keep digging.

Bridge holds his hands up. "My bad! Don't get mad! I thought maybe you were into them, that's all."

Before I can even react to that, Destiny shoulders her way into our row with an enormous grin. She's short with big wavy hair, like Gretchen from *Mean Girls*, except she gives secrets away instead of keeping them. "What's up, Third?" she asks me. She's our coanchor, along with Bridge. I've known her much longer. That's her new nickname for me. Third. The first time she called me that I thought it was some weird *Ender's Game* reference I didn't understand, but now I know it's because I'm the perpetual third wheel. I flip her off, and she just laughs. "Speaking of, I hear you're having—" she checks to make sure no one is listening and then drops her voice anyways "—difficulty finding a date to the dance."

Not this. It's too early in the morning. "Did Bridge say something about it to you?"

"I have my sources," she says, ambivalent. That means he definitely did.

I glare at him, and he drapes an arm over my shoulder. "I care about my bestie. Is that a crime?"

Destiny waves him away. "As I was saying, if you need assistance I can put in a good word for you. Spy out the land. Facilitate, if you catch my drift."

I do. "I'm good, Destiny, but thank you. What about you? Who are you going with?"

Redirection, a useful tactic for changing a subject to something less anxiety-inducing.

"TBD. I'm currently fielding applicants," she says with an air of disinterest.

"What's the holdup?" Solo asks.

"Sweetheart, I am Mjolnir, okay? Not just anyone is worthy of or able to handle this, feel me? Besides, this is senior year. Senior year is all about making memories, and I do not want to look back on this and see some fuckboy on my arm. Oh, no."

"Good for you," Bridge says emphatically.

Lucky for me, that's when Aisha calls everyone to attention. She's tall, with a mocha complexion and big warm brown eyes. She dresses like she just came back from vacationing in Paris—lots of oversized blazers, turtlenecks, and sometimes an actual beret. She's definitely an art house hipster, but she's so sweet and down-to-earth that the look works for her. People love her, and they listen to her. A hush falls over the gymnasium as she starts speaking.

"Homecoming is a time-honored tradition," she begins,

"but this year it has special meaning. This year, in addition to our incoming freshmen, we have many more students who will now call this campus their home, and for those of us who already called it that, this is an opportunity to welcome our new family with open arms. This year, Homecoming is about celebrating all of us, both new and old, and about making sure each and every one of us truly feels at home."

It's a rousing speech, and it gives me an idea. Hopefully, it's a good one. All of Aisha's speeches are rousing. That's because she always knows what she wants, and she always has a plan for accomplishing it. And those plans always work out.

I need to be more like Aisha.

CHAPTER 7

Practice today is grueling. Well, it looks that way, at least. The first game of the season is at the end of the week, and I can tell that everyone is eager to play for real.

The team takes a break, and Charmaine, one of Mona's teammates, comes jogging to the water cooler. We nod in acknowledgment of one another. Ordinarily in this situation that would be the end of our interaction, but after she's through with her water she lingers, and I get the sense that she wants to talk.

So I look up. "Having fun?"

It's a genuinely stupid question. But I barely know Charmaine, and I honestly feel like most conversation starters are stupid.

But it does the trick. "Yeah, I guess," she says with a shrug. "Hey, so…what's up with you and Ramona?"

"I'm not sure what you mean."

"Right, as if you don't know what I'm talking about. You know, neither of you are subtle about it."

And now, I'm worried, because I honestly don't know what the heck she's talking about.

Lucky for me, there are a few context clues. It's something she felt she needed to ask me about privately, so it has to be something potentially embarrassing or sensitive to either myself or Mona, or possibly both of us, which is the most likely case given she's asking about something between the two of us.

Something involving Mona and myself, that's potentially embarrassing to both of us, yet something that can't definitively be confirmed without directly asking.

I need more data.

"What do you think is up between us?" I ask.

This is a neat little trick called deflection. I've seen my parents do this to each other all the time. If I'm doing this right, she'll think I'm just being coy, and hopefully give me just a little bit more information or context from which I can extrapolate.

Charmaine shrugs. "I dunno. Something."

Interesting. And annoying. Mostly annoying. Another instance of someone not saying what they actually mean. She doesn't give me anything else before rejoining the team.

Practice ends, and Mona comes jogging over to where I'm waiting with my camera. We're quickly joined by her teammates, who congregate around the cooler.

She's all smiles, as usual. "Ready to go?" she asks.

We're supposed to be going to see a movie today. Before I can answer, Charmaine calls her name over the noise.

"We're gonna grab ice cream. You coming?"

Mona doesn't skip a beat. "Not this time. I'll see y'all around, though."

She says it like it's nothing, but her friends look disappointed. She has to sense that, right? It's glaringly obvious, even to me.

"Oh," Charmaine says pointedly. "Just the two of you?" She arches a brow, and her eyes dart back and forth between us.

And then, with everyone watching, Mona wraps an arm around my shoulder and presses her head against mine. "Are you kidding?" she says. "We're like Frodo and Sam."

Now, my knowledge of Tolkien lore isn't nearly as comprehensive as Mona's, but it strikes me that if anything, she's more like Gandalf, the magical one with all this enormous power and charm, and I'm Bilbo, the grumpy hobbit who'd rather be left to his own devices.

"I call dibs on the elf," one of her teammates says.

"Being the elf or doing the elf?" Mona asks.

"Yes."

And just like that, the entire group is laughing and arguing over which member of the Fellowship they are, and I'm able to relax knowing the likelihood of my being dragged into this conversation is low. While they're throwing around words like *hobbits*, *rangers*, and *dwarves*, I'm absorbing it all as if I were filming it. Mona's friends are fun. More fun than I am, that's for sure. And they all have a lot more in common with her than I do. This is a happy little moment, with a bunch of happy people, and Mona is at the center of it, laughing and joking around with the rest of them. I didn't need to be here for this to happen. In fact, it's because of me that it ends, when Mona pokes my arm.

"You ready?" she asks cheerfully.

I mean, I am. But, "You sure you don't want to go with them? I really wouldn't mind."

"Nope," she says with total conviction. "You and I made plans. You don't get off the hook that easily. Let's go."

The Riverside is this old-school theater that was originally built in the 1930s, but then it burned down in the late fifties and sat there, charred and abandoned and by all accounts super haunted, until the current owners bought it when I was a kid. They rebuilt it to look exactly the way it had originally, in the same Art Moderne style that's vaguely nautical, complete with the mauve-colored facade and the neon marquee with big block letters in chase lighting, framed by shimmering purple Vitrolite glass columns.

It's one of the city's best-kept secrets. It's tucked away behind a winding maze of cul-de-sacs and dead-end streets and alleys. Not a place you find by accident. It's a discount theater that plays new movies a couple weeks after they're released, so if you're on the fence about something that's coming out and aren't sure if you want to shell out for a full-price ticket you can just wait a while and see it for much cheaper. But the real draw is that they also screen old and indie films, stuff you can't see at your local Cineplex. From art house to foreign films to local festival fare, the Riverside is off the beaten path. Mona and I are just about the only teenagers who go here, so there's a zero percent chance of our running into any of our classmates. The crowd is made up of cinephiles and film students and hipsters who don't watch "mainstream flicks" and middle-aged couples who want to relive dates long past.

They're showing *Metropolis* tonight, a German silent film from 1927, directed by Fritz Lang and starring Brigitte Helm. It's a pioneer of the science fiction genre, and I'm pretty sure Mona and I have both seen it before. Not that it matters; we're both big rewatchers, just one of the many reasons why Mona is one of the only people I can stand watching movies with. In addition to our similar tastes, we both agree that people who talk during movies are the absolute worst kind of people in the entire world. Okay, not the worst, but they are definitely horrible, and horrible people to have to sit through a movie with. I say "sit through" instead of "watch," because talking makes paying attention to anything happening on the screen physically, mentally, and spiritually impossible.

I don't usually eat during movies. Even the sound of my own eating is too distracting for me. But Mona buys a large popcorn, same as she always does. It never bothers me when she eats during movies, even silent ones.

The interior here is just as vintage as the outside. The auditoriums are decked out in heavy red curtains and have narrow, carpeted aisles. The seats have velvet cushions and cast-iron sides. They're stiff and they don't recline, and there are weird stains on some of them, but they're solid. Besides, a little discomfort is good for the viewing experience; it keeps you alert and paying attention.

We settle into our seats—the same ones as always, way in the back, almost directly underneath the projector—and I move to put my arm on the armrest, but quickly draw back when I see that hers is already there.

"My bad," I say.

She looks down at the armrest, then back up at me, grinning. "Oh. Did you want this? I'll arm wrestle you for it."

I roll my eyes. "I'm not going to arm wrestle you for anything."

She sits up and leans closer to me. "Come on. Why not?"

"Because you would destroy me. I've seen your biceps."

A smile spreads across her lips. "Come on," she pleads, poking my shoulder. "I'll go easy on you."

"No thanks."

"Fine. How about we share?"

"There's no room. Unless you're trying to hold hands the whole time."

"Okay."

I steal a quick glance at her, and she's looking at me, but she isn't grinning in the way that lets me know she's teasing me. She almost looks like she's for real?

"You're serious?"

"Nah," she says, withdrawing her hand and leaning back in her seat. "I just like messing with you. Unless you actually want to?"

I drop my hands onto my lap and smooth them out on my jeans. "I'm good."

Neither of us end up using the armrest, and my mind wanders through the entire runtime of the movie. Because this is one of those moments that doesn't make sense to me. I'm sure if her family hadn't moved in all those years ago, we wouldn't be friends now. We don't really have that much in common. Even small things, like animals. She loves dogs. She's got two; an enormous husky named Indy (naturally) and a boxer named Radagast, after a Lord of the Rings character. Meanwhile, I'm saddled with a moderate dander allergy that makes sustained contact with any creature with fur…sniffly. For me, not the animal.

Food is another area in which we don't see eye to eye. Mona loves anything and everything spicy, and she'll try anything at least once, and most likely love it. Then there's me, who would cycle through the same few meals for months at a time if Mom would allow it.

Lastly, don't even get me started on our hobbies. Aside from the few things we do together, like this, we might as well exist in different dimensions. Whereas I have to have routine, structure, and order, Mona thrives on chaos and adventure. She told me once that she doesn't figure out what she's going to wear on any given day until it's time to get dressed, and I simply could not function like that. I don't understand how anyone can, really. But that's just me.

Which is precisely the problem.

After the movie we usually go for smoothies. There's this little mom-and-pop nook a block away, and after that we typically end up at a small park nearby.

It's this old park, nothing special, just a playground and a swing set next to an enclosed dog park and a little pond, but it's set in a clearing behind an apartment complex, surrounded by trees, and there aren't any streetlamps or houses in the way, so at night you can see the stars and the moon. It's just isolated enough to make it feel like we're the only two people in the whole wide world. We just hang out on the swing set and drink our smoothies and talk about nothing in particular while we look up at the stars.

"Tell me something," she whispers.

"There's a theory that the Loch Ness Monster is an elephant."

I feel her laugh on the side of my neck. "No way."

I nod. "Yeah. In the thirties there was a circus that traveled around the area and they would stop by the loch and let the elephants swim in it. And allegedly since the locals weren't used to seeing that, they thought it was some kind of monster."

She laughs. "That's ridiculous."

"To be fair, when you compare images of a swimming elephant with alleged monster sightings or descriptions of Nessie, there is a lot of similarity."

"Maybe. That's a stretch, though."

"It is."

"Tell me something else."

"Okay. Did you know that in the original comics Superman couldn't fly? Yeah, he was only able to 'leap tall buildings in a single jump.' It wasn't until around the forties that he was officially given the ability to fly. Until that he kind of jumped everywhere."

"That makes sense."

"Right?"

She doesn't ask for another fact, and the squeaking of the swings is the only sound to be heard.

Sometimes I apologize for things that are in no way my fault. I know it's not necessarily an autism thing, but that definitely contributes to why I do it so often, and it's also why I still do it even though I've heard from multiple people that it's annoying. Which is me explaining why I do it now:

"Sorry for keeping you from having ice cream with your friends."

I'm staring up at the sky when I say this, but I can feel what I know is Mona's disapproving and annoyed look.

"You aren't 'keeping me' from anything," she insists. "Besides, I'm probably not missing anything. Lately everyone seems to be wrapped up in their boyfriends and/or girlfriends. Not that I have anything against any of that, obviously, but when you're the only one in a group who's not kissing someone else, things get…awkward."

"It sounds like you need to find someone to kiss."

She chuckles. "Is that what it sounds like?"

"Sure. I mean, would you like that? Is that…what you want?"

"What, someone to kiss?" She sighs. "Yeah, who wouldn't?"

She looks down at the sand beneath her, and there's something that almost sounds like sadness in her voice. But then she shakes her hair and nudges my arm. "Besides, sometimes you're easier to be around than they are."

That can't be true. "How so?" I ask.

"You don't expect anything from me."

That broken glass look flashes across her face again, but she turns her head in the opposite direction so that I can't see it anymore. I don't expect anything from her. Meaning they do. What kinds of expectations could they possibly have of her that she can't live up to?

"I don't want to talk about it anymore," she says suddenly, just before I'm about to ask the dozen or so questions that are queued up in my head.

I nod. "Okay."

We go back to looking up at the sky. These warm summer nights are my favorite. The air is sweet and the breeze is cool enough to keep the humidity from pressing down on us. I'm glad we're together, even though I feel guilty about keeping her to myself despite what she said. Even though I think there's something she isn't telling me. I can worry about all of that later. Right now, there's nothing else but the two of us.

CHAPTER 8

"My presentation went well," Phoebe says as we pull into the Warehouse District. "My parents and I are gonna start looking for a doctor who's at least partly covered under their insurance. I don't know how any of that works, but I'm excited."

"That's incredible," I say. "Congratulations."

I appreciate that Phoebe knows I mean it without my going out of my way to act like I do. I am truly excited for her. But I'm also anxious to get to this week's LARP session, and for more than the usual reasons. A fact Phoebe picks up on before we even get there.

"You're still in your feelings over that Net-Knight, aren't you?" she asks me as we turn into the lot.

Zee-Four. I carefully reverse into a spot. Not because I have to, but just so I know I can still do it. "A little."

I really like the term "in your feelings," because it can be hard to be sure what I'm feeling sometimes, even though I know I'm feeling *something*, and the term really captures that.

"Well, you should let it go. We need to focus tonight."

Phoebe's right. Tonight is the last session of the season. I really don't want to end things as broke and miserable as I was when it started. But if we expect to come out anywhere close to the top, we're going to have to pull off something drastic.

Neither of us have a game plan for tonight. Unless…

"I have an idea," I begin as we gear up.

Phoebe glances up from tying her boot to look at me. "Your tone seems to indicate that it'll be an idea I won't like."

"We might still be able to deliver that flash drive, or at least get our hands on it. If…"

"I'm already not fond of the sound of that *if*."

"—If we can convince the Net-Knight who confiscated it to give it back."

Phoebe swings her bag over her shoulder and looks at me like I've lost my mind. Maybe I have. "Do I need to list all of the reasons that's a stupid idea, or is that fact implied in my tone sufficiently enough?"

"Yes, it's a bad idea, but do you have one that isn't?"

She doesn't, based on how she silently straps her phone into her wrist comm. We head to the entrance and get our wristbands, and as we funnel into Silo City, we pass by a group of Corporate Bigwigs, and I gasp. "Oh, shit."

The blood in my veins runs cold as I catch sight of someone in a trim purple suit and big dumb glowing sunglasses that I'd recognize anywhere.

Phoebe freezes. "Oh, shit, what?"

"It's *Him*."

I don't have to say his name. She knows exactly who I'm talking about.

"Oh, shit."

She grabs my arm and steers me through the crowd. I have no idea where we're going. I'm too busy trying to shrink myself as much as possible so he doesn't notice me.

My breath hitches. So close...

"Daniel? Hey!"

My legs lock. Low-Jack tosses me a look, urging me to continue, but I slowly pivot to see him muscling his way toward us.

"Sorry, I meant Hunter. That's your name here, right?" he says with a smile, as if I have any reason to be happy to see him. "What's up?"

And just like that, Hunter is gone, and I'm Daniel again. It's one of those uncomfortable instances of real life interfering with the game. It feels exactly like someone throwing a bucket of ice-cold water on my face just as I'm finally starting to doze off. Although, in all honesty, I'd prefer that over this.

"Hello, *William*," says Phoebe. This time the icy tone in her voice is genuine and intentional. It's something I've come to appreciate about Phoebe—her unflinching loyalty to her friends. She doesn't know him personally, but she knows about us and our history. She knows that Will is the boy who broke my heart and my head in equal measure. And that's enough for her.

"I didn't think you came to these things anymore," I croak. I've been counting on that, actually. Will was my best friend, back before I met Mona. Or at least I'd thought he was at the time. That, of course, was before I found out about all the shitty things he was saying about me to everyone else when I wasn't around.

It didn't help that he was also my first crush.

He was never as into LARP as I am, and I was relieved when his infrequent appearances withered altogether. I'd assumed he'd found another, less niche hobby to occupy himself with. It wouldn't be the first time.

He starts to reply, but Phoebe cuts him off.

"We're doing a thing," she says, a little more forcefully than absolutely necessary. "A time-sensitive thing."

Before he has a chance to respond she's latched onto my shoulder and is steering me away.

"You good?" she asks me.

I shake my head. "No."

"You wanna leave?"

Another tight shake of my head. "No."

"Good. We have a mission to complete. Now, this plan of yours. This terrible plan."

Right. I grin. Hunter XX doesn't run. I'm not about to let Will—whatever his in-game name is—ruin this. I shake myself and refocus. "Yes, the plan. I really think we've got a shot at getting that drive back."

"They're a Net-Knight," Phoebe reminds me. Unnecessarily.

Net-Knights are a lot like Paladins in that they've dedicated themselves to a higher purpose, sworn to defend the cause of righteousness. To protect the weak, oppose the corrupt, blah, blah, blah. Historically, Urchins like us, we don't exactly get along with the Net-Knights, who are so busy trying to uphold this idealized version of the law that doesn't even exist that they're blind to the reality of life on the streets, what it's really like for people out here, and what it actually takes to survive. They try to impose a black-and-white morality on a morally gray world, and it's people like us that feel the brunt of their wrath when the world doesn't fit their ideals. So, yes, I agree with Phoebe that my plan is a bad one.

And I also can't deny that the prospect of hunting down Zee-Four is helping me overlook that fact.

"A *Junior* Net-Knight," I counter. "Who may not be completely indoctrinated yet. Who could potentially be bought."

"With what money? We're broke, remember? Thanks to the very same person we're talking about."

"Well, there are other ways a person can be persuaded."

"What the hell are you talking about?"

I know she isn't being coy. She really has no idea what I'm talking about, and if I'm honest, neither do I.

"They're a Net-Knight," Phoebe says again.

"Junior Net-Knight," I remind her.

"You know that doesn't make a difference."

"I think it's worth a shot."

"Do you? Really? Or does Daniel?"

I hate to admit it, but she's right. It's one of the most fundamental, important tenants of LARPing—don't confuse characters with the people portraying them. The actions we take, the decisions we make, and the relationships we have here have no bearing on who we are IRL. To be someone else, someone different than who we really are, is kind of the whole point.

Everything I know about Zee-Four is tied to the game, meaning I know nothing at all about them. So whatever relationship we have or had or will have is limited to the game. And any "spark" or "connection" Phoebe thinks she saw was between our respective characters, not us. We're only playing our roles. That was between Hunter and Zee-Four.

"Fine," Phoebe says with an exasperated sigh. "Let's find them. Speaking of, is our Net-Knight a guy or a girl, do you think?"

Huh. I actually never thought about that. All I know is that they were tall, square-shouldered, with perfect posture and a long, confident stride, and that the way they hefted their BFG did things to me that I doubt were intentional. None of that had anything to do with gender. But then, how many things actually do?

"I honestly can't say."

Phoebe shrugs. "Not that it matters anyway. Let's move."

The thing about Net-Knights is that they tend to just prowl around, looking for trouble so they can dispense justice and "fix" things. Which usually means roughing people up and/or confiscating their belongings in the name of "keeping the peace." You can tell the ones who are on a specific Bigwig's payroll because they tend to lurk in little packs. Then there are others who wander solo.

I'm hoping our friend Zee-Four turns out to be the latter.

"You sure about this?" Phoebe asks for the last time. "We can't trust a Net-Knight. You know that."

"Yes." The memory of that big-ass gun pointed at my center mass sends a rush of frustration through my mind and a shiver across my body. Hunter did feel something, and I have to admit that Daniel did, too. So I can admit that Hunter would totally be okay with being folded like a pretzel by Zee-Four.

I don't know what my deal is. Hunter is brazen, but for the first time, Daniel is, too. All of a sudden I'm wanting to do things I'd never dream of doing before. Reckless things. Dangerous things.

I'm just playing the role, I remind myself. The role of a poor, desperate, street-smart Urchin determined to make it in this messed-up world. People like us can't afford to have a sense of morality. Literally. We cannot actually afford it.

A siren wails, and I wince at the piercing sound. Phoebe sidesteps a procession of people who are suddenly barreling down the aisle straight at us; she grabs my elbow and tugs me aside with her.

"Thanks," I mutter as I gather my bearings. Loud noises are worse for me than they are for most people. It's a sensitivity many autistic people share.

"Don't mention it," Phoebe says. She's studying the group that's approaching. It's a group of Net-Knights, a dozen of them at least, marching in a tight, angry cluster, their boots clopping in unison. "Out of the way!" the head Knight shouts. "This is The Duchess we're escorting. Out of the way!"

The Duchess? Phoebe and I exchange incredulous looks at each other. According to The Lore, The Duchess is Silo City's biggest, baddest, and most ruthless crime lord. Every criminal enterprise comes and goes through her. The bounty on The Duchess is astronomical, but I always assumed it was impossible to earn. She's too well-connected, too powerful. Untouchable.

Apparently I was wrong about that.

I strain to see through the gawking crowd for a glimpse of the woman who essentially runs this entire city, and when I do, I gasp. At the center of their cluster is none other than Shrapnel, a smirk on her glossy red lips and her wrists in enormous cuffs.

"Hold up... Shrapnel was The Duchess this entire time?"

"Seems that way," Phoebe states, and if she's at all surprised about it, she isn't showing it. "But we've got bigger problems."

I follow her gaze to see Zee-Four, marching at the back of the procession, bringing up the rear with their BFG in their hands. My heart leaps in my chest.

We wait for them to pass us by. People scurry out of their way, and heads turn and follow them as they pass. Zee-Four's head swivels as they move, and I instinctively drop my gaze when their head swings in our direction, even though I can't tell what they're actually looking at with their helmet and visor on.

"Come on." Phoebe starts after them, and I follow.

The Knights escort The Duchess to an off-limits part of the warehouse. Zee-Four doesn't stick around for very long. They break off from the others, and we tail them for a while, as they meander through the crowded aisles. Most people give them a wide berth, which is understandable seeing as most people are either looking for trouble or already up to it. I can't help but admire how they walk around as if they own the place. I suppose that's the kind of confidence power gives you. That, and an enormous gun.

Finally Zee-Four turns down a back alley. I nod at Phoebe, who draws her weapon. This is it. I suck in a deep breath, and step forward.

"Hey. You."

Not my best work. But it gets their attention. Zee-Four stops. I can't sense any fear in their stance as they slowly pivot to face us.

"Well, well, well," quips their gravelly, modulated voice. "I figured it'd only be a matter of time before you lot tried to settle the score. I'm glad you did."

"We're not here for revenge. We're here with a proposition."

"Oh?" Zee-Four crosses their arms instead of reaching for their weapon. A good sign.

Hunter is smart. Resourceful. He knows that he's got to appeal to convictions. That's how you win people over, especially idealistic people.

"What's your story, huh?" I ask.

"I'm an Urchin, like you. But unlike you, I decided to try and make the world a better place instead of a worse one."

"Oh, yeah? How's that working for you?" Phoebe adds. I shoot her a cautionary look. We cannot blow this.

We Urchins are junior members of whatever class we want to be part of. Essentially it means there are certain experiences we aren't allowed to participate in.

Hackers like Phoebe are sort of like wizards, in that they can tap into the power of software to rewrite the rules of reality. With enough access, they can do just about anything.

Splicers are the healers of this world, the ones who can install your cyber-upgrades and make you stronger, faster, and smarter by fusing human with machine. Their services don't come cheap, but if you can afford it you're dumb not to utilize them. Having a Splicer in your pocket can mean the difference between life and death on the streets.

The Bigwigs who run the hypercorporations and the Kingpins who rule the underworld, those are the Nobility class, even if there's nothing truly noble about them. They have the money, and that makes them untouchable. They control the way the world works, and the only way to make it is to get in good with them or become one of them, neither of which is an easy task. They may not be literal royalty, but you can bet they act like they are. They've got the hottest, flashiest augmentations and cybernetics, the hottest tech, and the most cutting-edge weapons, and they make sure everyone else knows it.

And then, you've got your Nomadic classes like Bounty Hunters, Assassins-for-Hire, and Smugglers. People who will do anything and everything for the right price.

That's me. A jack-of-all-trades, if you will. But even that isn't enough to make it. Sometimes you have to take the unconventional path to come out on top, and an alliance between a Net-Knight, a Hacker, and a Grifter is about as unconventional as it gets.

"What if you aren't making the world a better place?" I ask. "What if you're only helping the true criminals get away with their crimes?"

"So says the Grifters?"

"We're all Urchins. The world doesn't care about us. All we can do is look out for each other."

"I'm still not hearing a proposition."

"We need that flash drive back," I say with all the confidence I can summon. "It's worth more than you can imagine. Enough for a fresh start for all of us. There's no way either of us can get to it. But you? I have a feeling you can go where we can't. So, basically, what I'm proposing is that you help us get the drive back, then we deliver it to the people that can pay us—all of us. We all do what we do best. It's simple."

"So, that's it," Zee-Four states. They don't sound impressed or convinced. "You expect me to betray everything I've worked for, all my ideals, principles, and morals, to help two broke Grifters who may or may not betray me the first chance they get?"

"Yeah, basically."

They un-cross their arms and shift their weight. "Alright. I'm in."

I do a double take. Did I hear that correctly?

Phoebe shakes her head. "I don't understand. Why would you help us?"

Zee-Four chuckles. "Oh, right. Let's just say..." They reach for their helmet, undo the latch, and lift it off their head. "We've met before."

I gasp. Standing there with a great big grin on their face is none other than Gabe.

CHAPTER 9

What. The. Shit?

That cold water feeling hits me again, only this time, I like it?

"Uhh…hi? Did you know who I was," I sputter, "at the festival?"

Gabe shakes their curly hair and smiles. It's dazzling. A Mona-esque smile. "Of course. You're hard to forget."

What the heck does that mean? Did I do or say something super awkward or embarrassing? I don't recall anything like that happening, and I definitely would.

"Why didn't you say something sooner?" I demand.

Zee-Four—Gabe—shrugs. "When would I have had the chance? Besides, I assumed you'd already put two and two together. Why else would you have come to me of all people for help?"

My face flushes with a sudden rush of embarrassment, because if I'm totally honest, I just wanted a reason to interact with them again. And the reason for that, well…

"Yeah, I totally knew it was you. Definitely."

Lying makes me feel like a crumbling cookie inside, but fortunately Gabe doesn't buy it.

"No, you didn't, did you?" they ask with a chuckle.

"I had no idea."

That's when I notice Phoebe glancing back and forth between the two of us, waiting for someone to clue her in. "Yeah, Phoebe, this is Gabe," I explain quickly. "We go to the same school. Or, we're about to."

Phoebe nods in understanding. "Ah. Cool. So, why are you agreeing to help us?"

Gabe shrugs and hoists their weapon. "I dunno. Some people are worth breaking the rules for, I guess."

Gabe is looking at me, not Phoebe, as they say that. Which is odd, seeing as Phoebe was the one with the question.

"Alright, then," they say. "Let's get this show on the road."

"Yes," Phoebe says, tossing me an apprehensive look, "let's."

Gabe—aka Junior Net-Knight, aka Zee-Four—leads us through the maze of a city until we come to a brightly lit room with clean white walls. We follow them inside and immediately freeze.

This is the hub. The hive. All of the people Phoebe and I actively avoid gathered ever so inconveniently in a single place. Corporate heels in their slick suits and sleek, minimalist augmentation patches. Knights and their electro-staffs and BFGs. It's much more form over function here. Things look less cobbled together than anywhere else.

I don't like it.

Gabe looks right at home here. Of course. This is their world.

"Wait here." They keep on going without even bothering to make sure we're obeying their order. Not that we wouldn't. This is the absolute last place either of us would want to cause a scene in.

"Have I mentioned how horrible of an idea this is?" Phoebe mutters under her breath as we watch Gabe disappear behind a guarded partition. "And did you seriously not recognize them?"

"I swear I didn't," I insist. I'm still trying to process all of this. I don't like being messed with like that. It's not that I can't take a joke, or even being the butt of a joke. What I can't stand is being made fun of, or teased, or messed with, without knowing. If you're gonna make a joke at my expense, let me in on it. Otherwise it's being cruel and a bully. I don't believe that's what Gabe has been doing. Or maybe it's that I don't want to believe it. But I don't know enough about them to even have a gut instinct about it.

But then Gabe reappears with a triumphant grin on their face, and I put a pin in that train of thought. For now. Phoebe and I follow them back outside, and I breathe a sigh of relief when they casually toss the drive to me. "See? Cakewalk."

We stare at the flash drive in my palm. It occurs to me that this could still very much be a trap, but at this point I'm beyond caring.

"Low-Jack? You're up."

Phoebe boots up her laptop and crouches. I hand her the drive, and she inspects it carefully before plugging it in.

Gabe and I peer over her shoulders as she opens the file folder to reveal a QR code. There are codes like this scattered all over the city, but hackers like Low-Jack are the only ones who are able to decipher them—as in, they're the ones who have admin access codes. That's why it's so critical to have a hacker on your roster if you expect to get anywhere. We glance at each other. She nods and unclips her phone and scans the code.

The code unlocks a passcode, which she enters into her laptop. Her mouth falls open as she scans the drive's contents. "Oh, wow…"

It's a collection of photos, JPEG files. Phoebe opens one of them titled *CorporateTiesOne*. The photo is of Shrapnel—no, The Duchess—shaking hands with some random guy, another NPC, I'm assuming, but someone with connections, judging by the slick suit they're wearing. The next one, titled, *CorporateTiesTwo*, is the same thing, only it's another random person she's shaking hands with.

"I've seen some of these guys around," Phoebe says. "This is evidence. Proof that The Duchess has been making deals with…the Governor…all the CEOs of these businesses… the head of the Net-Knights…"

"It makes sense why this drive is worth so much," I say. "If this evidence gets into the wrong hands, they'll have enough dirt on The Duchess to force her to do whatever they want."

"They'd become the most powerful person in Silo City," Phoebe concurs.

"That would've been the case," says Gabe, "up until about twenty minutes ago, when the Knights arrested her. Now this thing is worthless."

"Not necessarily," Phoebe says. "This last file shows The Duchess with the Grand Judge, which means—"

"She's got the law in her pocket. Whatever she's charged with won't stick."

"Unless we get this drive to the right people," Gabe asserts.

"Yeah? And who might that be?" Phoebe says with a scoff. "This is obviously a trap. Why would she have given us the drive knowing it has all this damning evidence on it?"

"Maybe she didn't know," I counter. "She's an information broker, but that doesn't mean she screens everything she deals with."

"There's only one way to find out," Phoebe concedes with a deflated sigh. I understand how she feels. This seems hopeless.

"Who were you two gonna deliver it to?" Gabe asks when neither Phoebe nor I say anything else.

"We don't know who they were," I admit. "All we had was a name: Mr. Nimble."

Gabe snorts. "Mr. Nimble? Seriously?"

I shrug by way of response. Gabe shakes their head, and slips their helmet back over their head. "Well, let's go find this guy."

Mr. Nimble turns out to be Greg Junior, Grumpy Greg's

son. I've met him a few times outside of the sessions. He's in his late thirties, and is the exact opposite of his father—quick, slick, and charismatic. At least, those are the kinds of characters he plays. Wheelers and dealers, particularly the sleazy kind. He loves playing sleazy characters, and Mr. Nimble is no different. He seems to be a Corporate Bigwig who probably owns some communications conglomerate. Think Bill Gates crossed with Eldon Tyrell.

"Do you have the merchandise?" he drawls in what I'm sure is an intentional Jack Nicholson voice.

Phoebe nods, and offers up the drive. He accepts it with a sly grin, and slips it into his breast pocket. "Sit tight."

Mr. Nimble isn't nearly as quick as his name would suggest. One minute turns into four. My nerves start to trickle like ants on a wire. Thirty more seconds, and I'm starting to notice people breathing.

"Something isn't right," Gabe mutters, drumming the holster at their hip with their fingers.

"Maybe we should bail," Phoebe suggests tersely.

"Not without that drive," I insist. "Or our money."

It happens so fast I barely have time to process it. One moment the three of us are waiting in relative silence for Mr. Nimble, and the next, we're being rushed by a gang of what looks like Bounty Hunters, all heavily armored and brandishing swords, guns, and knives. Phoebe and I toss terrified glances at each other.

Gabe.

Did they know about this? Were we set up? Who the hell are these guys?

I look Gabe's way, and am least a little surprised that they seem just as shocked as we are. And then, as if in answer to all the questions racing through my mind, Mr. Nimble himself appears, sauntering toward us with a sly grin on his face.

"To be completely honest," he says, dangling the drive from his fingers, "this was always how it would go down. You could've given this thing to anyone in the city, and it would have landed you right back here. But I should thank you, because when I deliver this to The Duchess, she's gonna make me filthy stinking rich." He pockets the drive and nods to the men who are surrounding us. "Boys, get rid of this scum."

And that, folks, is how the three of us end up spending the last half hour of the last session of the season in the Pin, a room that is both a prison and a place you get sent to when your character dies.

It's not that bad. They have air hockey and table tennis set up in here, plus the Wi-Fi signal is stronger than it is in a lot of other places for some reason.

We eavesdrop on everyone else in the Pin and piece together what went down over the season. A shadowy group made up of Net-Knights, Corporate Bigwigs, and Crime Bosses have been secretly working to erode The Duchess's stranglehold on the city. They were the ones who compiled the evidence on the flash drive, and who orchestrated its delivery to the authorities. But of course, The Duchess has eyes everywhere, and was wise to the plot. She seized the opportunity to sniff out her would-be betrayers, and solidify her power once and for all. While we rot (not really; they do have air hockey, after all) in prison as unwitting pawns, a series of targeted assassinations sweeps through the city streets, and in the aftermath of her bloody revenge, The Duchess stands as the absolute power in Silo City.

Because in cyberpunk, the bad guys almost always come out on top.

Ordinarily when you die in-game you have to spend a set amount of time in the Pin before you can reenter the game with your starter stats reset. But since it's the last night anyway, I end up watching Gabe and Phoebe play air hockey until the session is over. It's time that I use to reflect, mostly on what I know about Gabe.

I know that they're in a band, and that they play drums. I know that they're nonbinary and use they/them pronouns. I know now that they also LARP.

"Do you make your own gear or do you buy it?" I hear Phoebe ask as they play.

"Most of it I build myself," is Gabe's response. "I've had a few pieces commissioned over the years, but I like to make my own stuff when I can."

Interesting. "How long have you been into LARP?" Phoebe asks next.

I like this. Being an observer, a fly on the wall. I don't have as much to be self-conscious about when no one's paying any attention to me. I can just listen, and learn.

"Since I was a junior," Gabe answers. "My ex-girlfriend introduced me to it, but I was already into cosplay, so it wasn't much of a jump, you know?"

Cosplay. And girlfriend? *Ex*-girlfriend. Noted.

"What about you?" Gabe asks.

"I started my sophomore year. A friend got me into it."

"Nice." Gabe nods, and then turns to me. "And you?"

I'm too stunned to respond. I forgot they could still see me. It's jarring to be so suddenly engaged.

"Oh. Um, since I was twelve," I say, stumbling over my words. "Well, I didn't start making stuff and getting really into it until later, but that's the first time I came."

"He was the friend I was talking about," Phoebe adds. "We were dating at the time."

Gabe's eyebrows shoot to their hairline. It's the same expression people usually get when Phoebe or I mention the brief moment in time when we thought dating each other was a good idea because it "made sense."

"We only dated for three weeks," Phoebe adds. "So it isn't awkward or anything. And we're still friends, obviously."

She isn't downplaying that, either. We actually did only date for three weeks, which was exactly the amount of time it took for us both to realize we were incompatible romantically. I've heard it said that no breakup is truly mutual, but I suspect that only applies to allistic ones, because—in the rare instance I do think back to our brief attempt at a relationship—what comes to mind is a lackluster *Yeah, that was a thing once.* And I know Phoebe doesn't think about it much, either, because if she did I would hear about it more. Phoebe doesn't have much of a filter.

"So, we're all single then…" Gabe says, nodding absently. "Nice."

Yes, I think to myself. *Very nice indeed…*

★ ★ ★

After the last session of the season there's always a big wrap party to celebrate the game. I never stay for that. To me, seeing everyone shed their characters and costumes underneath the bright warehouse lights, with the fog machines and the neon strobe lights switched off, kills the magic and totally ruins the vibe. It's a glaring reminder that this is all pretend.

And yet, when Gabe asks if I'm going to stick around for it, I'm severely tempted to say yes. It's only the fact that I have to drop off Phoebe tonight—who might actually hate parties more than I do—that keeps me from agreeing.

"Bummer," Gabe says with a whistle. They've got their jacket hanging off one shoulder and their helmet tucked under the other arm, resting against their hip. "Anyway. You two should come to my workshop sometime."

Phoebe lights up. "You have a workshop?"

Gabe nods.

"Let's go!" Phoebe exclaims. It's the most enthusiastic I've ever seen her.

"Yeah?" Gabe looks at her, and then they both turn expectantly to me.

This is a lot at once.

"Sure," I manage. "I'd be down to hang out sometime."

Gabe smiles. "Got a phone?" I nod. "Good. You should put my number in it."

"What happened to not trusting a Net-Knight?" I ask Phoebe as we head back to my car. I've got Gabe's number programmed into my phone, a fact I'm still struggling to wrap my head around. It feels like it's burning a hole in my pocket.

"Okay, so firstly, your Gabe is a *Junior* Net-Knight—"

"A technicality—"

"—who incidentally really came through tonight. Secondly, that was before I knew said Junior Net-Knight had a workshop."

"So what? A workshop is really not that big of a deal."

"Come on, Daniel! I want to at least see it! You saw the gear they had on. That could only come out of a top-tier workshop."

She does have a point. I wouldn't mind seeing it either, honestly. But for once I'm being much more cautious than Phoebe is, and I'm more than a little hesitant to visit some stranger's home.

Even if said stranger is alarmingly charismatic. Even if said stranger isn't really that much of a stranger at all.

"If you really want to see it, you should. You don't need me to go along."

"Yes, I do. Because, in case you didn't notice, you're the one they really want to have over. I'm the plus-one."

I hadn't noticed that, actually.

"By the way," Phoebe adds, "I think your Net-Knight friend has a crush on you."

"What makes you say that?" I ask.

"Everything," she says simply, as if that is at all a satisfactory explanation.

"That doesn't really tell me anything," I point out.

"I'm sure you'll figure it out. You're smart. Besides,"

Phoebe adds, "I could be wrong. I mean, I'm not. But I could be. So if you want to know for certain, we both know who you should ask."

"Yeah, that'll happen."

"Oh, good!"

"That was sarcasm."

"Ah. Nicely done."

"Thank you."

The very thought of someone like Gabe having anything approaching romantic feelings for me makes me literally laugh out loud. There's no way in heck that's even remotely possible.

Not when they've already met Mona.

CHAPTER 10

I love texting. It's so much simpler a means of communicating than talking. There's no body language or tone to decipher, just words. The trouble with text conversations for me is that I have no idea how to initiate them. Which is why, for the entire week leading up to the first day of school, Gabe's number sits unused in my phone.

Not that I don't think about it. Every. Single. Day. Because I do. A lot. Several times a day, in fact. From Monday to Sunday night this big, tangled knot of discombobulated thoughts and feelings just sits in my head, shoved into its own corner where I can ignore it, but not completely forget that it's there. But I can't figure out what I would text that doesn't sound ridiculous, or like I'm trying too hard. Or like I'm not trying hard enough. I don't even know what it is I actually want to say in the first place. Every time I think about Gabe my thoughts derail and become so jumbled that I can't even start to untangle them. How much of Gabe is Zee-Four? How much of Zee-Four is in the real Gabe? How could I not have realized they were the same freaking person? And now that I know they are, what about those feelings I thought I had for Zee-Four?

With the beginning of school looming, I have an entirely new set of problems to worry about.

The night before, I stop by my sister's shop.

My sister was named after Nina Simone, the iconic singer and civil rights activist who both of my parents absolutely adore. She opened her shop about a year ago. She's always had a strong passion for hair; if she were autistic I'd call it her special interest. She's good at it, too. Always has been. And after working her ass off to save up the money, putting herself through 1,550 hours of cosmetology training, getting her license, and apprenticing at other shops, she was finally able to open up one of her own.

I couldn't be more proud of her. But our mom, on the other hand, well, let's just say she measures the success of her children by a different standard. It's why Simone doesn't come around as often as Miles. No matter how well her business is doing, no matter how much her client base is growing, Mom will always find a way to steer the conversation to her love life, or lack thereof.

Simone has been cutting my hair since before she went to school for it. She's the only one I trust with it, even when I was her guinea pig. I usually come by every two weeks, three during the summer. Today I'm only here for a lineup.

"How's the wedding planning going?" she asks as I settle into a chair. "I bet you're sick of it by now, huh?"

"I almost wish they'd just elope already."

She chuckles. Simone didn't do what she was supposed to

do, or, what my folks expected her to do, and they've never outright said that they're disappointed, even though I know that they are. Especially Mom. I can tell because she likes to tell me not to end up like my sister. And if her opinion wasn't clear before, it was beyond obvious by how much praise and attention she heaps on my brother now that he's getting married.

"The usual?" she asks, draping the long plastic cape across me.

"Yes, please."

I've been getting the same haircut since I started growing it out: the curly fade, a tried-and-true classic.

"Your hair's getting long. You should think about putting twists in it."

"You mean I should think about asking you to put twists in it?"

"I mean, unless you find someone else who's better."

"Yeah, right."

She goes to work. Simone has a gentle hand, which I appreciate because as a general rule I don't like people being this close to me for extended amounts of time. But aside from the buzzing of the clippers I can almost pretend she isn't even there.

"How can you tell if someone has a crush on you?" I ask.

The buzzing stops. The question has been weighing on my mind ever since Phoebe suggested that Gabe might have one on me. I still think it's a ridiculous notion, but I want to base that conclusion on more than just how I feel about it.

"As someone who's been the object of many a crush, I

can tell you confidently that there's no one way to know," Simone says from behind me.

Damn.

"However," she goes on, "there are usually signs."

Reverse damn. "What are they?"

Simone clicks her tongue. "Someone who has a crush on you is gonna want to spend time with you," she explains. "They might ask you personal questions to get to know you."

"Don't people who want to be friends do that, too?" I'm not sure Gabe and I are friends, but that would at least be easier to accept.

"Maybe," Simone says. "But the difference is the intent. A crush might come up with reasons to touch you, like tapping your shoulder, or brushing your hand. They'll probably flirt with you, too."

"How do I know when someone's flirting with me?"

"That's a tough one to answer. Everyone does it differently. Some people don't do it at all. You could do what I do and assume everyone's flirting with me. I'm usually right."

The clippers turn back on, and she works in silence as I mull over what she's just said.

"Couldn't I also assume no one's flirting with me?"

The clippers cut off, and Simone comes around to face me. "I mean, sure. That's a sadder, boring option, but you do you."

Do me. Historically, that hasn't worked out so well for me. I guess what I do is a *version* of me. Simone wouldn't understand that. She's aggressively herself at all times, which is probably why she and Mom don't get along so great.

"How is Ramona, by the way?" Simone asks abruptly.

That makes me frown. "She's fine, I think. Wait, what's that got to do with anything?"

Usually when a subject changes this quickly, it means I missed some sort of connecting context.

"You know, this conversation would be a lot easier if we both stop pretending that's not who you're talking about."

"I'm not talking about Mona. Why would I be talking about her right now?"

"Why wouldn't you? Oh, that was a serious question. Okay. I'll play your weird little game. Let's examine the situation for a bit, shall we? You two are together all the time—"

"That's not true. She isn't here now."

"—and when you aren't together you're always texting."

"That isn't true, either."

"Who's the last person you texted today?"

"You, when I asked if I could come by."

"Excluding family?"

"Okay, that *was* Mona," I admit. "But we were talking about school."

"Is she the only person you ride to school with?"

"We're carpooling."

"You surely see how that doesn't help your case, don't you?"

"Friends carpool."

"Yeah, and how many of her other friends does she *regularly* carpool with? And I've seen the way she looks at you."

"Wait, what?"

Simone waves the clippers. "Hey, I'm just the messenger.

But I know what I see, and I see it a lot. Make of that what you will. The real question is, how do you feel about Mona?"

"What do you mean?"

Simone sighs dramatically. "I mean this with love, but for someone so smart you can be so…not smart, sometimes."

Oddly enough, that is far from the first time someone has told me that. But Mona *cannot* have a crush on me. There's just no way. But if Simone thinks so, then maybe the idea isn't as ridiculous as it sounds. And that could be bad. I'm the last person she needs to have a crush on. I need to get to the bottom of this, and fast.

The other thing she said barely registers. How I feel about Mona is immaterial. Especially if she's hinting at my feelings being anything approaching romantic in nature. That isn't possible. I'd definitely have noticed that by now.

At least, I think so…

I can't afford to let what Simone said bother me, at least not tonight. I'm going to need as much rest as I can get, so it's bedtime at a firm 9:30 p.m., which to my family is basically 6:00 p.m.

Somehow, it still doesn't feel like enough.

The first day of school is almost always the same. My routine hasn't changed since the ninth grade. Sunrise is at 6:43 this morning, meaning it's still dark out when I wake up at five sharp.

Mornings are like swimming pools. I'm not the type to just dive right in. I need to acclimate, dip a toe in, ease into the water at a nice, controlled pace that allows me to adapt to the changes in my immediate surroundings. Which I almost never get to do, because there's always someone who insists on belly-flopping into the water RIGHT NEXT TO ME and dowsing me in ice-cold chlorine. And then there's always someone else who is all, *It's much better to just jump in all at once! You get used to it quicker!*

That's why I don't like pools, but at least I can avoid those. The same can't be said for mornings, at least not most of them.

Having my own bathroom is a fact for which I am eternally grateful. It means I can proceed through my routine undisturbed and unbothered.

The weather report gives a high of seventy-eight and a low of sixty-one. About what I expected, so I've already planned to dress accordingly.

Toeing the line between fashionable and practical takes a considerable amount of work, especially given that I don't inherently give a solitary damn about fashion, mostly because it seems completely arbitrary. Back-to-school shopping is a chore I don't look forward to, a necessary evil. Fortunately, Mona and I typically spend the day at the mall, and having her with me makes the whole process bearable at least. I definitely owe my drip to Mona, which she never misses an opportunity to remind me. If I had a choice I would wear the same four outfits every day, one per season. But that is a noticeable oddity, and so I've learned to compromise with variations on the same themes.

I do have a few rules. Any article of clothing that makes direct contact with my bare flesh—shirts, boxers—must be tagless. I'm very particular about textures. Flannel, the unofficial uniform of the Minnesotan during the fall and the winter, is a texture that feels exactly like a cheese grater against my skin. I hate the scratchiness, the stiffness, of it. Wearing flannel feels like fighting with my clothes all day long. I'm less particular about colors, although as a general rule I prefer solids. Minimal patterns and maximum pockets. Layers are key, because I need to be able to add and remove as the temperature and humidity change throughout the day.

Breakfast for me consists almost always of two scrambled eggs and a glass of orange juice. Which absolutely irks my mom, who is of the opinion that this is not nearly a heavy or healthy enough breakfast to sustain a growing young man, despite the fact that my last growth spurt was during sophomore summer and according to my pediatrician puberty has essentially wrapped up for me.

The backpack I have now is the same one I've had since freshman year. I hate the way new canvas feels and the sound it makes when it rubs other fabrics. If it were up to me I'd still have the same backpack from middle school, but Mom made me get rid of it after she saw that I had taped up the bottom to keep it together. After I eat, I grab it from where I placed it next to my bedroom door, slip into my shoes, and head out to face the day.

It's a fifteen-minute drive from my house to school, twenty on the days I pick Mona up first. Which is most days.

The Tri-City School District encompasses, you guessed it, three cities: Golden Valley, New Hope, and Crystal, all of which are technically considered suburbs of Greater Minneapolis, which is the forty-sixth most populous city in the United States. I believe the term is conurbation—a region comprising a number of urban areas that have merged to form one continuous urban area. Suburban sprawl, if you will. I don't have to drive through too much of it to get to Mona. The Sinclairs only live a few miles away.

Mona, as always, is already wide awake when I pull up to her place. Whereas I prefer to slowly ease myself into the day, Mona just dives right in. She told me once that she sometimes takes cold showers. I tried that exactly once. Somehow it made my morning even worse.

"What's up, bestie?" she sings as she hops into the passenger seat. "You look chipper, as always."

She's made this joke before, or some variation on it. I've been told I have resting bitch face, but Mona once posited that it wasn't as simple as that. She says I always have this look on my face like I'm trying to do a really complicated trigonometry calculation in my head, or like I'm studying really hard for an exam literally all the time. In a way she's totally right. I am constantly studying, constantly focusing, constantly calculating, to make sure my mask is on, because if I'm not careful it'll slip and fall right off. And I can't let that happen.

Mona, on the other hand, is somehow already wide awake and in a good mood. I suspect that might have something to do with the fact that she is literally the most hydrated person I have ever met. Today, like every day, she has a gallon of water with her. She also dresses like she's either just about

to film or just finished filming a commercial for Nike—
yoga pants, sneakers, an Apple Watch, and a baseball cap.
Depending on the time of year she'll top that with a varsity
jacket or a sweatshirt, or just a T-shirt. All in our official
school colors, of course.

"Very funny," I tell her. Nothing about how Mona's acting or what she's saying gives me any indication at all that
she might have a crush on me. Is it that I'm just not seeing
the signs, or could there not be any signs to begin with?

Frederick Jones High School is nestled among the maple
trees on a hilly campus just south of the Golden Valley/New
Hope border. In theory it's the perfect setting for budding
intellectuals to culture themselves while discovering their
own potential. At least, the website says as much. But theory doesn't always apply to the real world, and such is the
case here.

The building itself wouldn't be out of place in an old horror movie, all stone arches and spires and stained glass windows. Collegiate Gothic, as they describe it in their glossy
fliers. Most of the old school buildings in the state are designed in the same style.

Today we both have to be here early. The soccer team
meets to run drills or practice or whatever it is they do in
the mornings during the season. And I have to prepare for
the double storm that is Broadcast Day and the First Day of
School. I'm anxious. Because today, I have a goal. An objective. A somewhat loose plan. My least favorite type of plan,
incidentally, but it's better than not having one.

Everything that's happened in the last several weeks has

been swirling around in my head. Mona and her strangeness with her most recent breakup. Gabe and their LARPing. The Homecoming dance and The Merger. Bridge and his insistence on finding me a date for some reason. AV Club and the weekly broadcast. In film, the difference between a bunch of random scenes tossed together and an actual story is the plot. The goal. The objective. The "Ultimate Boon," according to Joseph Campbell's Hero's Journey model. I finally know what that is. I finally know how to make sense of everything that's been happening around me, and what my place in it all is. I'm the director. The one behind the scenes *and* the camera. I may not be the protagonist, but this is my story.

Today, I start telling it.

Mona and I part ways once we're inside the building, and I head straight for the newsroom.

It's twenty minutes to broadcast, and it's an absolute circus in here.

The room is divided in two segments: the broadcast studio, with the green screen and the three newscaster desks, and the control room, where the TriCaster and recording equipment are.

AV Club is divided into two groups: production and tech/equipment. Production is mostly Destiny and Bridge, our anchors who also write their own scripts (pending teacher approval, of course). They're both already seated behind the center desk. Bridge is spinning circles in his chair—he told me it's his preshow ritual—while Destiny is live-streaming for her sizable social media following. She runs the school's podcast, too. She loves to talk, and people love to listen to her.

Then we've got our graphics folks, audio Techs, TriCaster and teleprompter techs, and the film crew, headed by yours truly. It's our job to take the storyboards, sketches, and whatever ideas and concepts the other departments come up with, and figure out how to actually capture the footage. Sometimes that means hours of filming followed by hours of editing just for a three-minute segment; other times it's just following someone around with a camera and hoping for the best.

That's when I notice that Aisha is pacing tightly in front of the green screen with her nose buried in her script. I hurry over to her. I can sense when vibes are off, and her vibes are way off.

"Hey, what's up? Talk to me, lady." That's something I've heard Dad say to Mom sometimes when something's bothering her and he doesn't know what. For some reason it always gets her to answer, even when she's in a bad mood.

"I'm good," she insists. "Really, I just…didn't get a lot of sleep last night."

I feel like there's more to it. Her eyes keep darting over my shoulder. I glance behind me to see Omar, our sports correspondent, chopping it up with a couple of our varsity football players he'll be interviewing this morning. His eyes flicker in our direction, and when he realizes I'm watching him he drops to one knee and starts tying his shoe. His shoe that wasn't untied to begin with. That's when I understand what's really going on.

Omar is Aisha's ex. I think. I never know quite where those two stand with each other. They both will always insist that they're friends no matter what, but sometimes it seems like they still have feelings for one another. Whatever the case, there's clearly something between them that neither one wants to deal with, and watching them try to dance around whatever that is anytime they're around each other is just awkward.

I turn back to Aisha, who is aggressively chugging her coffee. "Hey, you got this," I assure her. "You're amazing."

"You're sweet."

"Just being honest."

And I am. If I didn't think she was amazing I definitely wouldn't tell her so. That would be lying, and I don't lie very well.

Solo is perched like an enormous bird behind the Tri-Caster at the playback station when I join him.

"You're staring," I point out.

He barely notices. "She's so fine, bro. God knew exactly what he was doing when he made that one."

Apparently he's got the hots for Aisha this week.

"You think she's single?" he asks me, only sort of whispering. Solo isn't great at modulating his voice.

"Your guess is as good as mine," I reply. I've already lost interest in this topic. I've seen it happen. Everybody has. Two friends who decided to risk it all for love, except things don't work out the way they'd hoped, but now they can't go back. They're both trapped in this weird relationship purgatory where they can't go back to the way they were before, but what they tried to become just can't exist, either.

It's awkward for everyone.

I couldn't risk that with Mona. Even if I wanted to.

It isn't until I'm behind the camera doing my thing that I'm able to relax for the first time. This is what I love. When this broadcast plays later today, everything people see will be what I want them to. What I've chosen to show them. Everyone watching will be seeing through my lens. Through my eyes. Nothing is vague, or ambiguous, or confusing. Everything is clear-cut, simple, and easily understood, processed, and defined.

Real life hasn't always been the same. But it will be. I can make it all make sense. Behind the camera, I can do anything. Because I can see everything. And what I see now is the making of the most epic love story this school—maybe even this town—has ever witnessed. Mona and Gabe. Both have main character energy. Both are currently single. But I can change that, and Homecoming is the perfect backdrop. I will give Mona the happily-ever-after she deserves, and at long last she'll be free to be everything she's meant to be.

And me? I can finally ride off into the metaphorical sunset, a spectator, behind the lens where I belong.

CHAPTER 11

When it comes to composition, there are only two questions that matter, two questions you absolutely have to know the answers to in order for anything else to work: What is it you're trying to say, and how are you going to say it? I try to apply that principle to everything. What am I trying to say? That I'm just like everyone else. That I'm totally normal, totally allistic, with absolutely nothing to hide.

By the time broadcast wraps up people are starting to arrive on campus. The energy is completely changed from the time I arrived, when hardly anyone was here. First period begins at the ungodly time of 8:20 a.m.

Mona's already sent me a text:

How did AV go?

I smile and reply that it went great, and ask her about practice. She's probably on her way to class, or busy talking to someone, so I don't wait around for an immediate response. Instead I pocket my phone, take a deep breath, and push out into the crowded hallway. The classics are all here—the Athletes, the Introverts, the Populars, the Underclassmen, so on and so forth. I don't know exactly where Gabe will fit into this colorful cast of characters, but I know they will fit.

Campus is a strange mix of old and new. Here you may find, for example, a modern computer lab with state-of-the-art laptops, tablets, and docking bays, nestled in a room that looks like something out of *The Tudors*. There are lots of high, arched windows to let in natural light, and plenty of nooks around. Low benches in front of tall bay windows and sturdy wooden chairs arranged in front of stately mantels. When weather permits, it's not uncommon for classes to be held out on one of the terraces or in the courtyard.

It's all wildly uncomfortable. I hate the noise fluorescent lights make. That buzz-hum that never goes away. Even when the bulbs are brand-new. It's like when a fly just won't leave your face alone for some reason, except it's worse because I'm the only one who seems to notice it. And that's on top of everything else. This whole place is an echo chamber. People have to be loud to be heard, which means other people have to be even louder to be heard, and the cycle repeats until everyone is practically screaming. Everything seems to have been built using the loudest and most abrasive material available, like the lockers—why are they so loud? even when people don't slam them, and everybody slams them—and even the floors. The screeching of sneakers against laminate could probably be used as a form of torture.

It's different when I'm outside, where there's enough open space for all that noise. Inside, it's too much. It's like all of these sounds and noises are condensed and packed down and funneled directly into my brain. I've tried noise-canceling headphones, but for some reason whenever I wear them I suddenly feel like I'm making way more noise than I should be, so wearing them ends up having the opposite of their intended effect.

Mona and I don't have any classes together this quarter—we've already compared notes and confirmed as much in the student portal—but I wonder if either of us will have any with Gabe.

I'm not exactly disappointed. Walking next to Mona presents its own set of challenges. Namely, stares. The poor, unsuspecting students are mulling around, minding their own business, going about their days, and then suddenly there she is, swaggering down the hall with her head high and a gallon of water swinging from one hand.

Have you ever noticed how some people walk like they're the only person around? Like they just know other people will move out of their way? That's Mona. None of that awkward shimmying and shuffling, or trying to predict where the other person is moving so you can sidestep. Nah. People see her coming and either move the hell out of her way or match her pace because they want to talk to her.

Or look at her. She causes a lot of rubbernecking. Like a traffic accident, only…not morbid?

Not my best analogy.

Navigating this place alone isn't easy, either. Fortunately, I've come up with a system. There are a few rules I've come up with for surviving here. Rule Number One: Smile. I hate smiling. No, I hate smiling when I don't have any reason to. But people do it all the time, which means I have to do it, too. Smiling keeps you safe. Smiling lets everyone around you know you aren't a threat, and when you're a young Black man, there are already people who perceive you as a threat just because of what you are.

I do not understand why people feel the need to touch each other so often. I get the handshake, or the hug, but everything in excess of that? So unnecessary! Sometimes people even touch other people for no reason at all, or because they're bored. Like, what in the hell? That's not even evolutionary.

Side note: it isn't that I don't like being touched. I'm just particular about how I'm touched, and I'm so not a fan of unanticipated or unexpected touching.

But in a place like this, it's unavoidable.

Which is a great segue into Rule Number Two: Press the Flesh. It's important to mingle. Never being seen interacting with anyone is a great way to stand out in the wrong way. And I may not understand the need to touch other people, but I do know it's an important part of mingling. So I've learned to...tolerate it.

As I make my way to my first class, I keep my eyes and ears open for any sign of Gabe. I feel like Hunter XX, on a reconnaissance mission. It's strange feeling like this here, in school, when I'm in ordinary clothes and surrounded by my ordinary peers. But I don't hate it. It's actually somewhat empowering, in a weird and slightly disorienting way.

I know this place like the back of my hand, or like someone who's spent upwards of forty hours a week for nine

months a year for three years here. There are always subtle
changes; maybe they repaint the lockers or renovate a room.
There are always a few dozen new faces, but the bones of
the place are always the same. Almost.

It feels different, more so than it usually does on the first
day of school. The energy is new, and that has everything
to do with the influx of brand-new students. Over a single
summer our numbers have increased by at least thirty percent, meaning at minimum one in three of the faces around
me belong to people I really don't know. It reminds me quite
a bit of freshman year, when I didn't know anything about
anything, only it's louder and with more people.

"Hey, Daniel," calls a girl with bouncy hair as she emerges
from the steady stream of people that are passing by. Lilly is
her name. She sat across from me in AP Algebra II last year.

"Hello," I reply. My body instinctively tenses, and I become suddenly preoccupied with the worry that I'm making too much noise.

Lilly is a perfectly normal, perfectly neurotypical girl.
Like Mona, she has lots of friends. She has no trouble telling
jokes, or maintaining eye contact, or understanding what
people really mean when they say things.

"How are you?" she asks with a smile that I can see from
the corner of my eye.

I think about it. Anxious about the beginning of the school
year, and how I'm going to set Mona and Gabe up. Relieved
that I have something of a plan to do it. And nervous because
a pretty girl is standing less than two feet away from me.

"I'm okay," I tell her, because that's what you're supposed

to say in response to a question like that, as opposed to going into the actual details about how you really feel—a formality that I still don't quite understand. Why ask a question if you don't expect a thoughtful response?

I also know that the socially acceptable thing to do next is to ask the question in return. So, I do.

"How are you?"

"Pretty good, thanks," says Lilly, who is still smiling. I can feel her looking at me, and I know that we should be making eye contact. I force my eyes in her direction, but all I can manage is a second's glance. It isn't that Lilly is ugly. Far from it. I actually find her to be quite attractive. The problem, as usual, is me.

Which is why I have Rule Number Three: Make Eye Contact. You can't just pay attention. You have to also *look like* you're paying attention, which means eye contact, which is a problem for me. Looking people in the eyes is...uncomfortable. With hours and hours—and hours—of practice I can manage it now for short little snapshot bursts, but even then, it's almost physically painful. So being expected to meet a person's gaze and process what they're saying is a lot like being expected to pay attention to someone while they're actively stabbing you.

In the real world several seconds have passed, enough for me to know that by now, Lilly must be catching on to the fact that something is amiss. Miraculously, though, she stays with me. *I can salvage this. I just have to say something normal.*

"I like your notebook." Somehow, I don't feel like that was a normal thing to say at all.

But Lilly laughs. "Are you a fan of Mead or something?"

"Not really."

Her laughter subsides, and I realize that she may have been joking.

And then it happens. The first uncomfortable silence. The death knell of our conversation, if this could be called a conversation. In my experience three of these silences will effectively kill any interaction, and I know that I'm well on my way to having driven away yet another person.

Lilly sighs, and I brace myself for her awkward departure, which will only be awkward because I will inevitably make it that way.

"Do you have any plans for the dance?" I ask. It's low-hanging fruit, but it's something.

"Kind of," she says, smiling suddenly. "I'm trying to figure out who to go with."

"Oh."

We ride another uncomfortable silence. The second. Strange. I feel like somehow, there's something I'm missing, and experience has taught me that when I feel like I'm missing something, I most definitely am. The problem is I have no idea what it is I'm missing.

The warning bell rings, which means that we have five minutes to get to class. I close my locker and sling my backpack over my shoulder. For some reason, Lilly doesn't move.

"I hope you find somebody to go to the dance with," I say.

"Thanks," she says, and it occurs to me that there is something wrong with how she says it. There was less enthusiasm in her voice. It sounded like she was disappointed about something. But what?

Most social situations feel like funerals to me. Which I can confidently say, having been to all four of my grandparents' funerals. The feeling is remarkably similar. What are we all supposed to look at? Do you acknowledge the person next to you or no? Should I laugh at that joke/personal anecdote, or would that be rude? Am I smiling enough? Too much? Is my face doing the right thing? How's my blinking rate? Am I on the same emotional wavelength as the people around me?

That was not my best work, but I can't worry about that now. Not when I have a mission to complete.

I don't see Gabe until the class right before lunch.

I'm already exhausted when I get there. The doorway is at the front of the room, so not only does everyone already here look up when I enter, but they also watch me make my way across the room and all the way to the back next to the window, where I try to make as little noise as possible as I settle into the desk there. There are fifteen people here already, and only a couple more come in before the bell rings.

Mrs. Watts begins roll call, and when she comes to my name I squeak out a "here." You would think I'd be used to this part by now, but unfortunately, you'd be wrong.

Gabe's entrance causes a stir that is the total antithesis of mine. People's faces light up, and they remind me of sunflowers, turning so that their heads are facing Gabe as Gabe makes their way through the room.

And directly toward me.

"'Sup, stranger?" they say as they straddle the chair next

to mine. "I was wondering when I was gonna run into you. You're a hard person to find."

Everyone who was looking at Gabe is now looking at us, and I immediately recognize this feeling, because it's the exact same thing that happens whenever Mona and I are together. This doesn't make sense. *We* don't make sense. And just like Mona, Gabe doesn't seem to sense that.

I swallow. "Were you looking for me?"

"Well, sure. Is it weird that I think it's weird that you aren't in your gear?"

Not at all, because I'm still trying to wrap my head around the fact that you are somehow both a badass and apparently very well-liked drummer and a LARPer who for some reason seems glad to be talking to me of all people…is what I think. What I actually say is, "No, not weird at all."

Mrs. Watts continues. "Alright. How about Gabrielle?"

Gabe sighs and raises their hand. "It's Gabe, and my pronouns are they/them."

"Oh! I'm so sorry. Gabe. I'm sorry."

Gabe shrugs. "It's cool."

Cool. An interesting word choice. Everything about Gabe is cool, from the almost lazy way they're leaning in their chair to the pair of drumsticks dangling from their back pocket. Mona wouldn't have to choose between hanging out with them or her friends. I could see Gabe fitting in with her crowd just fine.

Unlike me.

It's a cliché, for sure, but I prefer eating alone during lunch. I'm not a huge fan of watching or seeing or hearing other people eat, and I'd rather not do it in front of other people when I can help it, especially people I don't know well or at all. Which is about eighty percent of the cafeteria population. Which is why usually I book it there as quickly as I can, grab my lunch and inhale it as fast as humanly possible, and then dip out to the courtyard or one of the media centers.

But when class lets out, Gabe easily keeps pace with me, and we're shoulder to shoulder as we step into the hallway.

"So," Gabe says, "are you going to show me around?"

I fight the urge to reach for my camera to calm this sudden spike in nerves. "Do you need me to?"

Gabe shrugs. "I dunno. I figure you know everyone."

In a way, they aren't wrong, but in another way they totally are. Because I know a lot of things about a lot of people, but I don't really know a lot of people.

You know who does?

"I have lunch now, actually, but I can see if Mona—"

"Oh! Same here!"

Well. Crap.

CHAPTER 12

Everything about the cafeteria grosses me out. There's the aforementioned chewing, of course, and then it's also bright, loud, and crowded. Somehow you're supposed to both eat and socialize at the same time? Hard pass. At least it would be, if it were socially acceptable to skip it every single day. But it isn't. That would raise questions, which would lead to more questions, until the delicate little facade I've carefully propped up and constantly hold in place crumbled away like a sandcastle against the lapping tides.

It helps slightly that Gabe is with me. They feel like a buffer, absorbing and deflecting the worst of it all.

Until we get to the table they pick.

It's an eclectic mix. I have no talk tracks ready for this crowd. I do a quick head count. Mona's teammates Juanita Willis and Charmaine Gibson are both here, sitting next to Heidi Xiong. Sandy Lewis is on dance squad and plays basketball in the winter. Victor Nunez and Tony Vang both play football. I recognize one of the guys from Gabe's band, also, and there are a few other people I don't know, who I assume came from Sandburg.

Conversation comes easily and naturally for everyone here, with myself being the glaring exception. I eat my food carefully, with purpose, so at the very least it seems like maybe I'm preoccupied or tired.

But that doesn't work, because a few minutes in Juanita looks at me and says, "Wait, how do you two know each other?"

Her fingers wag between me and Gabe, who's sitting to my right.

Panic seizes my chest. I hate open-ended questions like this. Where do I start? How much of the story is enough to answer the question without it being too much? And is that really what she wants to know, or is there some deeper, subtextual question I'm not picking up on? I have no clues; in the three years we've gone to the same school I've had maybe as many conversations with her—far too few to have established any sort of baseline. I knew sitting here was a mistake.

Gabe drapes a heavy arm over my shoulder and says, "Daniel and I are thick as thieves."

My back stiffens. The uninvited physical contact is un- comfortable, and yet...not nearly as uncomfortable as if it had been someone other than Mona.

I don't know what to do or how long they're going to leave their arm on me, so I sit there, frozen, and it feels like everyone else is staring at me and starting to realize how weird I'm being and I know I have to do something to get over this awkward hump and then suddenly something else occurs to me.

Thick as thieves?

I find the expression odd, mostly because it doesn't seem like one someone my age would use, especially so casually and in a normal conversation. Also—and I'm most likely doing that thing where I read way too far into something that absolutely is not that deep, but—as I recall, the term "thick as thieves" means that the involved parties have a very close, intimate relationship of some kind, and are coconspirators of some sort. Neither of which describes my relationship with Gabe at all. And yet, I don't get that feeling that I'm being made fun of somehow. Gabe may not have meant what they said literally, but I don't think they said it to make me the butt of a joke.

Just when I've begun to accept this as my miserable fate, Aisha appears out of nowhere, all smiles as usual, and with none other than Mona herself!

This might just be the proof I need to believe there's a higher power.

Mona takes the seat to my left, with Aisha across from her. She leans over and boops my shoulder with her head, and I'm instantly at ease. This is almost literally a dream come true. This is absolutely perfect. Now that they're together I can quietly fade into the background and let nature run its course.

The tide of the conversation shifts as Aisha continues saying whatever she'd been telling Mona before they joined us.

"Spirit Week is at the end of the month," she explains to

everyone, "so we've put together a bunch of themes. To-morrow everyone gets to vote on the five they want. I re-ally want this year's themes to be ones you don't usually see instead of, like, 'pajama day' or 'school colors.'"

"We had both of those last year," says Gabe.

Aisha throws up her hands. "See what I mean? Boooring."

"Last year we had 'hat day' where you had to wear every hat you own at the same time," says Gabe, "and then we gave out prizes to the people in each grade who could get the most on their head."

"That's a good idea," says Mona.

"To be fair though, wearing pajamas to school is really cool," Gabe adds.

"True," Mona says with a nod.

I suppress the urge to stim from excitement. Is this bond-ing I'm seeing right now? It feels like bonding.

"What if you sleep in the nude?" I ask. As soon as the question leaves my lips I regret ever having opened my mouth, because suddenly everyone is looking at me. Which is precisely the opposite of what I wanted.

"I guess that means you gotta show up naked," Mona says with a laugh. And then everyone is laughing, and I'm not sure if it's because of what I said or what she said.

"Hold up," Gabe interjects, twirling a drumstick in their hand, "are you saying you sleep naked, Daniel?"

My face flushes, but before I can answer Mona leans for-ward and says, "Nah, he doesn't. Trust me."

A hush falls over the table, and I quickly glance around to see that everyone pretty much has the same wide-eyed ex-

pression. And then Charmaine slowly raises a hand. "So…
how exactly do you know that, Mona?" she asks pointedly.
Almost accusingly.

To which Mona only grins, shrugs, and takes a bite out
of her apple.

I don't have a single, solitary inkling about what the hell
I'm supposed to do in this situation, but as I look around, I
can take a very small comfort in the fact that I don't seem
to be the only one.

"On that strange note, I gotta run," blurts Aisha. "Oh,
and don't forget to fill out the Homecoming Court nominee submission forms on the school website."

It's the second time I've heard her say that in person, and
the fourth if you count the two times I also heard it during
the broadcast this morning.

Mona heads out right after Aisha does. Those two are always moving, always busy. I made the joke to both of them
separately that they needed to hire a secretary, and they
both responded by jokingly (I think) asking if I was apply-
ing for the job. I used to think they'd make a great couple,
but sadly Aisha isn't into girls.

"Can I ask you a personal question?" says Gabe as we leave
the cafeteria together. "What's up with you and Mona?"

Not this again.

"What do you mean?"

"You two seem close. Like, really close. I was just wondering if you two were, like, a thing."

"I mean, we are friends. Best friends, I suppose."

"Yeah, but see, is that code for something else?"

"Something like what?"

Like dating? Or having romantic feelings for each other? Or Mona having that crush on me that Simone insists is real?

"I dunno, anything."

"No, it isn't code. I don't really know how to speak in code."

Unfortunately.

Gabe smiles at me. "I've kind of picked up on that. I like that about you. It's refreshing."

"Thanks." And since we're on the subject, "I have a question for you."

"Ask me anything."

"What do you think about Mona?"

I glance at Gabe's face. It's blank for a moment, or at least to me it is. "She's cool. She's funny. And she's cute."

I breathe a sigh of relief. I imagine thinking someone is cool, funny, and cute is a great foundation for a relationship. Or an epic love story. But a foundation means nothing if you don't build on it.

"I'm bummed you never got to see my workshop," Gabe says. "I've been dinking around with some cool stuff lately."

Damn. I forgot all about that! "Sorry," I stammer. "I got…"

"Busy? No worries. What are you up to after school?"

Aside from spending a very long time decompressing from the stress that is the first day of school, mentally preparing myself for tomorrow, and planning the perfect way to turn you and Mona into the perfect power couple? "Nothing."

Gabe nods. "Dope. You should come over then."

Come over then? Gabe really does make everything seem so effortless. I wouldn't dream of inviting someone over without allowing for prep time, both for myself and whatever space at home we planned on occupying.

"Okay," I hear myself say, because how could I say no to Gabe? Why would I even want to? But... "Is it cool if I bring Phoebe?"

Gabe shrugs. "That's cool with me. I guess it's a date then."

Yes. Technically, it is. But only technically. So why on earth are there butterflies in my stomach?

"I can't go," Phoebe says when I call to tell her about Gabe's invite. I would have texted, but I was too excited and in too much of a hurry. Our school has a no phones policy during the day, so I'm holed up in a restroom stall and trying desperately to ignore the fact that I can practically see the bacteria surrounding me.

It's not at all what I expected her to say. It's the exact opposite, actually. "What do you mean you can't go?"

"It means precisely what it sounds like. I can't go. I have to work, and I can't call out because obviously I'm the backbone of the place."

"Obviously," I grumble.

"Doesn't this mean you get to hang out with Gabe alone? That doesn't sound bad to me."

Me either, if I'm being honest. But I'm not at all prepped for this. I've got no scripts, nothing rehearsed, and I'm coming off one of the most stressful days of the year. Masking under these conditions is already hard enough; doing it during a one-on-one interaction sounds all but impossible.

"I have to go," Phoebe says, "but I want to hear about this workshop later!"

"Sure," I groan. "I'll take pictures."

I can't decide if I said that sarcastically or not, but she's already hung up the phone.

The creak of the bathroom door being thrown open alerts me to the arrival of someone else in my smelly makeshift sanctuary. Time to leave.

I can do this. I can totally do this. I repeat the mantra in my head a few more times, take a deep breath, and step out of the stall to see Tony Vang at the urinal.

"Aye, bro!" he calls as I attempt to slink past him. I've nearly survived my first day back at school, but socially I'm running on E. I was hoping to skid through the rest of the day without having any more conversations, but it seems someone has other plans.

"What's up?" I ask reluctantly. I don't understand how some people are completely cool with having a conversation with someone else while their dick is out, but whatever.

"Can I ask you something? Does Mona have a date to the dance?"

Ah, of course. I figured this would be a Mona-related interaction. Guys like Tony don't socially interact with guys like me otherwise.

"Why don't you just ask Mona yourself?"

"I planned to. I just figured I'd make sure I wasn't stepping on anyone's toes, or ruffling any feathers. You know, in case you were…" He trails off.

"In case I was what?" I press. This is probably the longest conversation I've had with someone who was actively peeing, but my curiosity overrides my revulsion for a few more moments.

"You know, in case you were—" he drops his voice as if we're talking about something secret "—planning on asking her to the dance yourself."

"Why would you think I might be planning on doing that?"

He tries to laugh away my question, but it comes off just a little too forced.

And now I'm worried. Does Mona expect me to ask her? Am I supposed to? Did I inadvertently say or do something to signal that I wanted to? And if so, what might happen if I don't? Is this what Simone was talking about? I don't think Tony is nearly as smart as my sister, but he does see me and Mona together more than she does. Two different perspectives, but the same conclusion.

I'm not sure how I feel about this.

I always get weird about being in other people's homes, even under the best of circumstances. It takes me a while to read the terrain and figure out what I can and can't touch, what's off-limits versus what I can interact with. I hate asking people where their bathrooms or trash cans are. I never know where I'm supposed to sit, or if I'm supposed to take my shoes off at the door. And it's so much worse when people say "just make yourself at home" because I literally can't do that because I don't live there and it literally is not my home. Not that I don't appreciate the sentiment.

The address Gabe gives me is in North Minneapolis, about half an hour from where I live. I don't know what to expect when I get to Gabe's house, but I can hear Prince's "I Would Die 4 U" playing from inside before they open the door. "Welcome to Casa De Mendes," they say as they usher me inside.

It's a regular living room. Matching black leather couches, hardwood floors, a nice rug, a TV mounted to the wall, and a couple of bookshelves.

"Are your parents home?" I ask.

"Nah, they're on a date."

Just like us. The thought almost leaps out of my mouth, but luckily I catch it right at the tip of my tongue. I don't even know if it's true.

My social battery is nearly depleted. I cannot stay here long.

I follow Gabe as they lead the way through the house and out through the back door, which leads to a tidy backyard with a giant maple tree in the middle. A tire swing hangs from one of the thickest branches, and above that sits a bright red tree house.

"Please tell me that's your workshop."

Gabe laughs as they cross the lawn toward the detached garage. "As cool as that would be, I'm afraid not."

Once I reach the doorway they turn and put their hands on my shoulders and give me a deep, solemn look. "Are you prepared, mind, body, and soul, to enter this most sacred ground?"

I swallow. "I was until you said that. Now I'm not so sure."

Gabe laughs. "You're fun. Come on."

They unlock the door, and I cautiously step over the threshold…and into an absolute paradise. Gabe's workshop is truly magnificent. It looks like someplace you'd find on the starship *Enterprise*. Big shiny tool cabinets and industrial shop desks with power tools and electronic components all over the place. On one wall hangs an assortment of weapons. Some people have daggers, some have swords, some even have bo staffs or sai, because in cyberpunk, you gotta go with what looks dope, even if it's impractical as hell. Gabe has a little of all of that, along with different armor pieces in various stages of completion. Almost every LARP gun is some modified or reconstructed NERF gun. On the other wall there are more weapons, only these are more medieval in nature, like axes, broadswords, and a morning star. In the corner is a gleaming black drum kit.

"Your parents let you use all this space?" I ask in awe.

Gabe plops down on a stool and plucks an LED light from the desk. "Pretty much. Both my moms are engineers, and I got the instinct to take things apart and figure them out from them. They originally cleared this place out so I could practice my drums out here, but over time it just became where I stashed all the shit I was into, so they just let me use it. What do you think?"

What do I think? "I could literally live here for the rest of my life."

"I like that," Gabe says, looking at me with a smile that catches me off guard. I have to look away. My eyes fall on a book I recognize all too well, because Mona has the exact same one at her place.

"You play Dungeons & Dragons?" I ask, staring at the *Player's Handbook.*

Gabe glances at it. "Oh, yeah. A little. I used to play more, but these days I haven't had as much time."

That same feeling of fascination I had the first time I encountered Gabe comes rushing back. Just when I thought I was getting a fuller picture of who they were, something like this happens that makes me reevaluate everything.

"You seem surprised," Gabe says, and I realize they're watching me.

Surprised. That's putting it...mildly. "It's just, in my experience people either like science fiction or fantasy, but it looks like you're into both?"

"Well, yeah. I don't think they're all that much different. I mean, sure, each genre has its own tropes and rules, but I think the stories are the same—it's only a matter of how you dress them up. What you explain as magic in a high fantasy can be technology in a space opera. It's a blurry line, if you ask me. Take Star Wars. Fantasy themes, in a sci-fi setting."

That thought makes me oddly uncomfortable. Why have genres at all if you're going to muddy them and make one feel like the other? But at the same time, it makes sense. I see what they mean.

"So," Gabe says, "what's your alignment?"

There are nine alignments, on the axes of Law versus Chaos, and Good versus Evil. Alignments can tell you an awful lot about a person. They're useful tools for coming up with characters because they provide the moral lens through which a person sees the world and behaves in it.

"Lawful Good."

Those who align as Lawful Good believe that in order for the most good to be done for the most people, law and order must be upheld. When everyone follows the rules, everyone benefits. To me it's such a simple concept that I sometimes can't understand how there are even other alignments. Even if the rules sometimes hurt some people, ultimately they still serve the greater good, and as Mr. Spock himself said, "the needs of the many outweigh the needs of the few."

"What's yours?" I ask.

"That's easy," Gabe says. "Neutral Good."

Interesting. Most interesting. Neutral Good characters believe that rules are only important in service to the greater good. Whether a Neutral Good character obeys the rules or breaks them depends only on if those rules serve the interest of good.

Oh, but this is great. I only talk alignments with a handful of people, one of whom happens to be Mona. I've known hers for a long time: Chaotic Good. It's obvious in everything she does. She's big on following her heart, sticking by her convictions, and doing what she feels is the right thing regardless of what anyone else thinks, says, or does. In fact, she seems to enjoy bucking other people's expectations.

I wonder if that's why she hangs out with me.

Certain alignments are naturally at odds with others, just like certain alignments complement others.

Being that she is Chaotic while I am Lawful, it stands to

reason that Mona and I would have opposing approaches to almost everything. But a Neutral and a Chaotic, like Gabe and Mona? They would see eye to eye on more than they would disagree on.

"I have one question," I start. "And this is very, very important. What are your thoughts on Harrison Ford?"

Gabe clicks their tongue. "You mean *The Ford?* Absolute legend." Yes, this is going to work out magnificently.

CHAPTER 13

"Homecoming, huh?" Mona says absently on the drive to school the next morning. I know I've been quiet, more so even than usual, but I'm still a little worn out from yesterday. First days always take a hefty toll, but yesterday was even more draining than usual. If it weren't only day two, and if I didn't have several things that needed doing, I'd seriously consider taking a mental health day. It's not that I'm in a bad mood, either. Last night with Gabe was incredible, and not only because of their awesome workshop. But good stress is still stress, and I'm feeling it now.

"I'll be glad when it's over," I say, gripping the wheel tightly. "It's all everyone seems to be able to talk about. What about you?"

Mona is staring out the window. She seems to have something on her mind. "I dunno. I kinda get it. Like, it's the last time we'll get to do this, why not go all out, right?"

"I guess so. I never thought about it like that. So, do you have an acceptance speech written yet?"

She glances at me. "Come again?"

"Oh, come on. You know you're going to be nominated for Homecoming Queen. And if you get nominated you're pretty much guaranteed to win."

"I really don't. It would be cool, I guess."

"You think so?" It's a genuine question. Because it would be an absolute nightmare to me.

"Yeah. Like, it would be a nice way to kick off senior year. And it'd be something neat to look back on and tell our kids."

Sophomore year we agreed that once we were both ready to settle down we'd buy a house together and adopt a few kids and a bunch of pets. I made the mistake of talking about our plan with my mom once, and she insisted that it meant we were getting married, even though that was expressly not part of the arrangement. It also prompted my parents to sit me down and give me "the sex talk," despite the fact that Mona and I were clearly planning on adopting children, not creating our own together. And not to mention that Mona and I weren't having sex, had never had sex, and weren't planning on having sex with each other.

"Tony was asking about you, by the way," I mention.

Mona raises a brow. "Really?"

I nod. "He's probably going to ask you to the dance."

I'm watching her expression as I say this. Her reaction is...indifferent?

"Would you go with him?" I ask. "If he actually asks you, I mean."

She shakes her head. "Nah. Tony's cool, but he's kinda basic, you know?"

"No, I don't."

"He reminds me of Emmett from *Twilight*. A little too himbo for me."

"Do you know who you want to go with?" I ask carefully.

Mona glances at me with this sly grin. "Let's just say, I'm weighing my options."

So there's this nod I've practiced for countless hours upon hours. It's one people sometimes do when they are acknowledging that there is more to what is being said, and that they've picked up on and recognize that fact, as well as the coded message, so to speak, behind it. But I don't get it. I never do. And even though I do one of those nods, I definitely don't right now. Heck, I don't even know if there was some coded message in what Mona said.

But coded messages are the currency of allistic communication, and I've been practicing. "What if, hypothetically," I begin, "I knew of someone who I think would make the perfect date to the dance?"

Mona looks at me and squints. My eyes are on the road, so I'm not looking directly at her, but I know that expression well enough to recognize it from my peripheral. "If that were the case, hypothetically speaking, I'd want to know what makes this person so great."

I think back to everything I've learned about Gabe so far. How fascinating they are. Their confidence. The fact that they're gorgeous doesn't hurt, either. Even if Mona somehow wants me to ask her to go to the dance, I'm sure she wouldn't be too upset if Gabe asked her first. There's really no comparison between the two of us.

Which is good, because Homecoming would be the perfect setting for my plan to come together.

"I think you'll find out soon enough."

Mona lifts her chin, and I worry that she's going to press me for a name, and if she does, I might not be able to resist telling her flat out who I'm talking about. Because that's what I'd prefer to do. All this hinting around and not just saying exactly what I mean is exhausting, but I've realized that this is how it works. Setting Mona and Gabe up will require a subtle hand, a nudge here or there. People love the buildup. The slow burn. If either of them knows I'm actively working to bring them together, it might not work. I can't risk that.

"We'll see," Mona says with a grin, and it almost sounds like a threat.

Yes, I think to myself. *Yes, we will.*

Of course I nominate Mona for Homecoming Queen. I would have done that even if we weren't best friends, just like I'm sure a lot of other people do. It does make me worry a little, because I'm not entirely sure how her nomination and inevitable crowning will impact her and Gabe. I don't think Mona can get any more popular than she already is, and it's not like being Homecoming Queen would go to her head. But Gabe might not know that. In fact, as of right now I don't think Gabe knows much of anything about Mona. It's up to me to change that.

But I'll need some advice. Lucky for me, I know a guy. You might say he's my own personal Cupid.

And he's all too willing to oblige.

"Oh. *Oooh*. You're finally out to woo someone?" he says when I find him. Bridge wiggles his eyebrows and rubs his hands together, and I'm already sort of regretting opening this can of worms. Which, side note, is another idiom I really enjoy. Apparently it came from fishers, back in the days when live bait was sold in actual cans. Opening them could result in a writhing, wriggling mess on your hands as the worms tried to escape in every direction. The imagery is gross, but it works, and I love it.

"Question," says Bridge, "who's the lucky guy or girl, and is it one of my leads?"

By leads, he means the text messages he's been sending me periodically since the festival, four in total, with nine names apiece. Each one was allegedly a person who would "date the hell out of" me.

"No. Not one of them." To date, I haven't done more than skim any of the messages except for the first, but only because I thought he was sending me some sort of cryptic riddle. Once he explained that he was "doing the leg work for me," I just started ignoring them.

Bridge squeals gleefully. "Either way, you came to the right guy. Think of it like this: people may have evolved from apes, but when it comes to matters of the heart, we're more like birds. In certain species, when a bird is trying to attract a mate it'll groom itself and make itself as beautiful as possible. Some sing, some dance, but the point is, they put their best foot forward. That's how they get noticed."

Analogies can be tricky for me, when other people make

them. But I think this one makes sense. "You're saying you have to show off to get someone's attention?"

Bridge hisses through his teeth. "'Show off' doesn't quite hit the right note. You've got to show that special someone that you're special too, is all. That you're worth it. The easiest, quickest way to do that is to let them see you at your best. You gotta sell yourself a little bit, put the goods on display, as it were."

Hm. That sounds simple. And it makes sense. If Bridge is right—and I have no reason to doubt that he is—then my job couldn't be easier. All I need to do is help Gabe see with their own eyes how great Mona is, and if they aren't already falling in love with her, they certainly will. It won't even take that long; Mona tends to be great all the time.

Come to think of it, I actually know exactly where to start.

It's all I can do to wait for Gabe to sit down when they show up to Statistics. I've rehearsed this a couple of times. I don't want to pop the question as soon as they sit. That would seem too eager, and this needs to come off as naturally as possible, or else it will feel too much like a setup and it won't work. So I wait. For Gabe to sit down. And check their phone. And unload their bag. And check their phone again.

I can't take this any longer.

I get up and go sharpen my pencil. Something I have historically done a grand total of three times my entire school career. I take my time returning to my desk, and rather than sitting down right away, I perch on the edge of it.

Here goes.

"Hey. Do you like soccer?"

The season started in late August and goes through early or mid-October, depending on how well the team does. They meet for practice twice a week, and there are roughly two games per week, meaning Mona will be as busy as she'll ever be during the first quarter of the school year. The Homecoming dance happens on the last Saturday of September, approximately two weeks from now.

I have to work fast. Lucky for me, tonight is game night.

Gabe looks up at me. "Sure," they say as they tap the desktop with their fingers. "Why?"

"Because I'm going to watch the women's JV team play, and I'd like you to come with me."

I'm not making eye contact with them when I say any of this, because I'm nervous to be doing it, even more so than I feel like I should be. Instead, I'm looking at the ground, kicking at an imaginary pebble with the toe of my sneaker. But I know I can't do that for too long, or else it'll be weird. So, I steel myself and glance up.

Gabe is smiling. Only I can't tell why or what it means. "Has anyone ever told you you're kind of adorable?" they ask.

Sure. My mom. And Mona. But I don't think now is the time to mention that. "I've heard it a few times."

There. That's vague enough to not warrant anything further. Hopefully.

Gabe chuckles. "Yeah, I'm down."

"Really?" I almost feel like maybe they didn't hear what

I'd actually said, and that I should verify that they know what they just agreed to. But I worry that may come off as condescending, so I resist the urge.

A shrug. "Sure."

I wish I could be that cavalier about agreeing to things.

I prefer home games, like tonight's against St. Croix Academy. I don't have to be in a place I'm not familiar with to watch. And from what Mona's mentioned to me, St. Croix is a solid team with strong players, so if Frederick Jones is going to win, they'll have to fight for it. Which means more spectacle, which is great for what I hope to happen tonight.

There's a sizable turnout. The bleachers on both sides of the field are full of spectators from both schools. Gabe and I settle into a pair of spots close to the action, where we've both got a clear line of sight. We're a little early, and players are on the field warming up while the announcer tells us what to expect and how the season is progressing. Mona spots me from across the field, where she's huddled with several other girls, and waves.

"Do you come to all of her games?" Gabe asks.

"Mostly. She calls me her unofficial cheerleader."

Gabe lifts their chin. "Right…"

From a practical standpoint this is most likely a terrible idea. I am not great company during games, but I don't usually have to be, because I'm usually here to work, and my work is the kind I can do alone, without talking to or interacting with anyone else. In fact, working the games is one of the few situations where being rude could be excused. I am busy, after all. Etiquette dictates that you don't bother the camera operator. I wasn't planning on taking any photos tonight, but I've still got my camera dangling from its strap on my shoulder, more as a buffer should the need arise than anything else.

So this experience will be, in a word, painful. For me, anyways. Because from a tactical standpoint, this is the move. Bridge did say the best way to make a match is to get them to see each other at their best, and there's no doubt that when it comes to soccer, Mona is *the* best. I'm not even into sports, and I'm consistently in awe of what she does.

But when I look over to see if Gabe may be starting to feel the same way, I see that they're instead looking down at their phone. The pang of frustration is familiar. It reminds me of Mona's reaction when we watched Gabe's band play.

It's cool, I remind myself. *It'll get better once the game starts.*

It takes a while for things to heat up, so to speak. It feels like St. Croix is playing cautiously, poking around, trying to get a feel for what kind of opponent they'll find in our squad. But Mona and the others seem eager to prove that this new roster isn't here to mess around, and it isn't long before the action begins in earnest.

Mona's playing the central midfielder position, which means, as the title implies, that she'll be keeping mostly to the center of the field, helping advance the ball when the team is on the offense, as well as helping defensively when the other team is trying to score. It's a lot of fancy footwork, almost like a dance, in a way.

"That was called La Croqueta," I explain after Mona sidesteps a defender with the ball, "which is basically shifting the ball from one side of your body to the other using the inside of your feet. It looks easy, but it's not. She's good, isn't she?"

"Yeah," Gabe says. "She's great."

Somehow they don't seem as enthusiastic about that as they should be. That's alright. This is a lot to take in all at once.

"You want popcorn?" Gabe asks.

"No," I reply without thinking. I never eat at these games. They're only eighty minutes long, with a ten-minute break halfway through.

"Okay. Be right back."

Gabe gets up and shuffles out of the row and heads toward the concessions stand. What gives? They don't seem nearly as into this as I'd hoped they'd be. Could it be something to do with Mona? No, it couldn't be that. She's kicking ass just like she always does. Am I doing this wrong?

Gabe slides back in with a buttery container of popcorn just as another scuffle breaks out on the field. "See that?" I ask. "That was a Scoop Turn. A fake-out to make the other person think you're going one way, but then you go another."

"I didn't realize you were so into soccer," Gabe says as they toss popcorn into their mouth.

"Oh, I'm not. This is all stuff Mona has explained to me."

"You guys really are close."

"We are," I say, but then it occurs to me that maybe I shouldn't have said that. "I mean, we're friends."

"What's Mona's favorite color?"

Oh, that's easy. "Teal."

"Favorite animal?"

Again, simple. "Panda bears."

Gabe nods. This is great. We're finally on the subject we should be on.

"When was she born?"

"December eleventh," I answer without thinking about it. "Two weeks before Christmas. She hates it."

Actually, she only hates it now. She's historically vacillated between loving that her birthday's proximity to the holiday meant she got double the presents, and hating it because she feels like everyone is so focused on Jesus's birthday that hers gets swept under the figurative rug, something she (probably sacrilegiously) referred to as being "cock-blocked by Christ" on more than one occasion.

"She's a Sagittarius. Figures," says Gabe.

"When were you born?"

"October ninth. Scorpio season, baby!"

"No way, I'm a Scorpio, too."

Gabe frowns skeptically. "Wait, really?"

"Yeah, my birthday is November seventeenth."

"Ha! I'm older than you."

"By a negligible margin."

Gabe tuts. "So says the youth."

That makes me laugh. I laugh a lot around Gabe. "Can I ask you a personal question?" I'm immediately stung by the irony of my using one of Bridge's signature statements, but I do actually want to ask something a casual acquaintance probably wouldn't.

"Go for it," Gabe says, completely nonplussed about it.

"Are you…attracted to girls?"

Gabe's brows arch in what I think is surprise.

"I did say it was a personal question," I remind them.

They nod. "Fair. Well, the short answer is yes, sure, I am attracted to girls."

I breathe a sigh of relief.

"But," they continue, "I'm not *only* attracted to girls."

I take a moment to process this information. "Okay. So you're bisexual?"

They shake their head. "More like pansexual."

Pansexual. I've heard the term, but I'm unfamiliar with its exact definition, which must somehow manifest in my expression, because Gabe elaborates without my asking them to.

"So, you know how bisexual means being sexually attracted to two or more genders? Well, for me, gender isn't a determining factor at all when it comes to who I find attractive. I know what I like, but it's got nothing to do with gender."

"That's what pansexual means?"

Gabe nods. "Yeah, basically."

Interesting. "Then, I'm pretty sure I'm pansexual, too."

I've never given much thought to who I like, or what I like. Because for the longest time I've been so sure that relationships—those kind of relationships—weren't for me.

Until now.

When the game ends, Gabe and I wait around on the bleachers while the crowd disburses. There's a slight, warm breeze in the air, and the clouds in the evening sky look like cotton candy. Something about tonight just feels good, and I can't place why exactly that is.

I point my camera at Gabe. "Say cheese?"

They throw up a quick peace sign just as I snap the photo. I don't know if it was ironic or not, because no one does that in pictures anymore, probably because no one looks cool doing it. Except Gabe, of course.

"What got you into photography?" they ask me.

I whistle. "That is a big question."

Gabe leans toward me. "It's not like I'm going anywhere."

They sound so reassuring that I suddenly want to tell my entire life's story. In my head, I say, *being behind the camera is the only time I feel like I'm on the same wavelength as the people around me, because sometimes—most of the time—it feels like what I see, hear, smell, and taste is different from what everyone else is experiencing, but when I'm the one controlling what it is people see, when it's up to me to engineer an experience, I feel like I can finally feel what everyone else feels, because they're feeling what I feel.*

What I actually say is, "I like to tell stories. It gives me a voice."

"But aren't you always telling someone else's story?"

The question shakes me. No. Of course not. The stories I tell are mine, because I'm who's telling them. Right?

Before I can formulate a reply, Mona is jogging toward us, in sweatpants and a hoodie, and a big, bright smile.

"You killed it tonight, as usual," I tell her as she throws an arm around me. She's warm and smells like grass. "I brought a friend with me. You remember Gabe, right?"

Mona fawns. "Aw, you came to watch me play?" she sings, batting her eyes and grinning.

"You saw me perform," says Gabe as they run a hand through their curly hair, "it's only right to return the favor."

Damn, I wish I knew whether this was flirting or not. It has to be, right? Either way, the hairs on my arms are standing up. Something just happened, even if I don't know what.

"Gabe makes their own LARP props," I say to Mona. "And they have this badass workshop. It's like the Bat Cave or something."

I'm pretty sure I sound like my mom when she brags to her coworkers or friends about me and I'm standing right there. Which is probably not a good look.

Enough people have left so that we're almost the only ones on the bleachers. I can hear the hum of the stadium lights and the low chirping of crickets in the night.

No one's saying anything.

"Is anyone hungry?" I blurt out desperately. "We could get pizza? Pizza sounds good, right?"

"It's late," Mona says after mulling it over.

"I should probably be going, too," Gabe says. They're looking up at the night sky as if that's how they tell the time, and for all I know, it just might be.

The bitter irony of their only agreeing about wanting to leave is not lost on me.

But I'm not ready for this to be over. Something's got to happen. The seconds are dwindling away. Something's got to give. We are reaching critical mass.

And then, it hits me, with the force of a truck, or what

I'd imagine the force of a truck to be, since I have never, in fact, been hit by one. "Hey, so, I just had a random thought!" I announce. Which is one of the most honest things I've ever said.

They both turn to look at me, and I instantly break out in a cold sweat—at least it feels like I do—and my heart starts thundering in my chest, and I can't believe what I'm about to say, but by god I'm fucking saying it.

"We should all go to the dance. Together. The three of us."

The.

Three.

Of.

Us.

Each word echoes like thunder in my head. In the world of film, there's something called the Dutch angle. It's when you film a scene with the camera at a slight tilt. It creates an off-center effect that's jarring and disorienting, and creates in the viewer the sense that something is not the way it's supposed to be. That's how it feels like I'm perceiving the world around me now. At a steep, unnatural angle, because what's happening just doesn't feel like it should be. This isn't me. This is more like Hunter. Brash. Impulsive. Bold.

Mona glances at Gabe, who's looking at me, and my eyes flicker to Mona, who then turns back to me. A thousand years pass in the few seconds of silence it takes for Gabe speak.

"The three of us?" they ask.

I nod. My throat is almost too dry to speak. "Unless you want to invite someone else."

Gabe shrugs. "Cool. I'm down if you all are."

We both look at Mona, who also shrugs. "That actually sounds cool. I mean, I don't have a date yet, anyways, so..."

She looks at me again, and I see what I think is a question in her eyes. Mona knows me better than most people, so it stands to reason that she knows better than anyone how out of character this is for me. But I had to do it. This is the only way I could make sure that the two of them are together when they need to be. So what if that means I get to be the perpetual third wheel? The Third, as Destiny says. If that's what needs to happen, so be it. Odds are it's exactly what I'd end up as either way.

CHAPTER 14

Surviving the first week of school is always both a hurdle and an accomplishment. This year has been no exception. In a lot of ways, it's been more intense than ever.

It helps to remind myself of the camera. How important it is to focus on what you're trying to capture. All the tiny adjustments that have to be made in order to get what you want to get. What you need to get.

There's a palpable excitement in the newsroom when I arrive on Friday. I know it's because of the nomination results. Who gets crowned hasn't really factored into my plans, but it could add a wrinkle to them. But Mona and Gabe have already agreed to go to the dance together...with me. Right. I keep forgetting that I'm a part of that equation, too.

Because we don't do live broadcasts, everyone who works in AV gets to know things like who got nominated before the rest of the student body. Naturally, we're all sworn to professional secrecy (on pain of death, so say the legends), which Aisha makes sure to mention to us almost a dozen times this morning. We have to keep our secrets, because as Aisha says, "If we don't bring people the scoop, what are we even doing? Where's the theater in that?"

"What if we hate theater?" Bridge challenges.

Aisha doesn't miss a beat in her response. "You don't hate theater, Bridge."

He gasps. "Oh, because I'm gay?"

"No, because you're you."

That makes Bridge crack up.

It is odd knowing that I'm privy to information everyone else wants but doesn't have yet. But I don't let any of that interfere with my work. It's easy to flip that switch and distance myself from my subject, which is an essential skill for anyone hoping to work behind a camera.

There are ten nominees in total. Bridge and Destiny read through the results with all the pomp and circumstance of award show hosts. I'm not at all surprised with the results. Homecoming nominations are essentially a popularity contest, but that isn't necessarily a bad thing. Because unlike how it often plays out in the movies, the popular kids are well-liked because they're decent people. Being a jerk, as I have observed, is not the way to make your peers like you. Who would have thought?

Mona is the second to be announced. Of course she is. I can picture the look on her face when she finds out. She'll be pleased.

Bridge insists on reading his own nomination because, like Aisha said, he's him.

And then, the last nominee to be announced.

Gabe.

For Homecoming Queen.

Just like that, my heart drops to my stomach.

"I am going to die," Bridge moans after we finish shooting. "What am I supposed to do? How am I supposed to survive with this burden of secret knowledge?"

"I'm sure you can last a few hours," I tell him. I'm barely paying attention to him. My thoughts are consumed by Gabe, and how they're going to react when they find out about their nomination.

"You don't understand," Bridge insists, which is correct. "My job is telling people things. Now there's this thing everyone wants to know, and I can't tell them?"

"Technically you have. It just hasn't aired yet," I point out absently.

Bridge scoffs. "You and your logic. Thanks, Mr. Spock."

It is nowhere near the first time I've been compared to Commander Spock. And much like a Vulcan, I can't count the ability to comfort or console people as one of my strengths.

Despite Bridge's complaining, the couple hours before the broadcast fly by. The show plays from wall-mounted screens scattered throughout the main thoroughfares twice a day: once in the midmorning, and again during the last hour of classes. Which means I get to watch just like everyone else.

While everyone else is still clapping I send Mona a three-word text.

Told you so.

Her reply comes almost immediately.

Screw you. 😀

I can imagine that wherever in the building she is now, she's surrounded by people, being swept up in a wave of congratulations. But I can't picture Gabe right now, how they're feeling, or what they're doing. I can't imagine they're happy about the *queen* part. But how unhappy? Pissed? Sad? Insulted? A combination of all three? I want to text Phoebe for her perspective, but I don't know if she'll be able to help any more than I can. All I know is that I want nothing more than to be there with Gabe.

So when it's finally time for Statistics, I nearly run to class. Not that I have the slightest idea of how to handle this. I've been so preoccupied wondering how they're doing that I haven't come up with anything to say when we actually see each other. I have no firsthand experience with anything like this, but I remember how hard it was for Phoebe when she came out as trans. She got misgendered a lot, sometimes accidentally, but sometimes by people who refused to respect something so basic as her gender and pronouns. It makes me wonder if Gabe's nomination was on the part of people who genuinely made a mistake, or if it was because they didn't want to accept that Gabe is nonbinary.

Either way, by the time I get to my desk, I realize that I'm angry, frustrated, and worried. But if Gabe is feeling any of those things, I certainly can't tell as they saunter into the room and settle into the seat next to mine. "Hey," I say, as neutrally as possible.

Gabe smiles quickly. "What's up?"

Yeah, I can't do this. "Are you okay? I saw the nomination, and... I was worried."

Gabe glances at me, and I quickly look down. "You were worried?"

I nod, still looking down at my desk. "I still am."

Gabe reaches over and touches my hand. The feeling of their palm sends a shiver of electricity through my arm. "That's sweet. But it's all good. I just declined the nomination."

There's something about how they say "it's all good" that gives me the sense that it definitely isn't all good.

"Are you alright?" It's times like these when I wish I was more intuitive. That I could read people the way allistic people can.

Gabe moves their hand and runs it through their hair. "Honestly, I would've turned down the nomination anyways. I'm not really big on being the center of attention."

"Me, either."

Gabe chuckles. "I know. That's why we get along so well."

Wait, Gabe thinks we get along well? I mean, I agree. Generally speaking, I try to get along with everyone. Which isn't always easy. But it is with Gabe. More than that, though, I actually like being around them. I can't understand how anyone wouldn't. Which makes the fact that they and Mona haven't quite connected the way I assumed they would by now all the more baffling. But I do understand why they would decline the nomination. I can't imagine anyone who wouldn't, if they were in Gabe's position.

Mona, Gabe, and I all sit together at lunch, along with a selection of both Mona's and Gabe's friends, but I'm worried about my plan. Gabe said they don't like being the center of attention. But Mona kind of is the center of attention. Is that a deal-breaker for either of them? At the very least it's a red flag, isn't it?

I wonder how many people already know that the three of us are going to the dance together. I assume Bridge does, because he's Bridge, although I'm counting on his being too wrapped up in his nomination to remember or care. I try to take comfort in the fact that I don't really know who's going with who, either, but it isn't that comforting a thought, considering I care less about the dance than most people here. Even when people do find out, I can't see how it could matter. I'm the Third, after all. No one here could possibly think I was an equal part in this. All anyone should be seeing when they look at the three of us is two main characters and a third, secondary one, who if anything is playing the role of sidekick to both of them.

"You don't eat the crust of your pizza?" Gabe asks suddenly, eyeballing my tray.

"No. Do you?"

"Yes, because I'm not a child. Gimme." They reach over and pluck the bare crust off my plate and start munching on it.

Another thought that's been rumbling around in my head is the fact that when I asked Gabe if they were alright, they never did technically answer the question. I'm not sure if that was intentional or if it wasn't, but they do seem to be acting the way they always do. It's reassuring, although I'm still concerned. How can someone be so calm, cool, and collected *all the time*?

Sometimes, when I'm at school, I find myself thinking about Silo City, with its seedy back alleys and garbage-strewn gutters, where it's always dark and the air is heavy with smog. The difference is night and day, and not just literally. But there are similarities. For example, much like in the world of LARP, there are five basic stats I believe everyone has in some capacity. They are as follows:

Charisma. The ability to make other people like you. It can take many forms and look like many things.

Looks. This one is fairly self-explanatory.

Intelligence. Same.

Empathy. The ability to relate to other people. Similar to charisma, but different enough to merit its own category simply because I've seen plenty of charismatic people who are also self-absorbed or totally incapable of putting themselves in someone else's shoes.

Luck. This is the category for things beyond a person's control, like their socioeconomic situation.

I measure each on a ten-point scale for simplicity.

For example, I rate high in empathy. Sometimes I have almost a sixth sense for other people's emotional states. I can tell when the vibes are off. The problem with that, though, is that I rate low in charisma, so I have no idea what to do with all that information, and I'm terrible at translating it into anything useful. It isn't true intuition.

People like Gabe, and Mona, and Aisha, they rate high for charisma, looks, and intelligence, but I think Aisha might rate slightly higher when it comes to empathy. She seems to have a finger on the pulse of what we as a collective student body are feeling at any given time, and more than that, she cares about what's going on around her, much more than most people. Which is why, when she comes rushing toward our table, I assume she has important news, even though she definitely seems to be the opposite of calm, cool, and collected.

"You good?" I ask.

She slides into the seat next to Mona and groans. "It's nothing. The original vendor we're supposed to be renting the dance hall from just fell through. Yeah, apparently they double-booked that night, even though I double- and triple-checked their availability."

"That doesn't sound like nothing."

Aisha waves a hand. "It's cool. For real. I have a Plan B. And a Plan C. It'll work out. Anyways, firstly, Mona, huge congrats on your nomination!"

"Thanks," Mona says brightly.

"And on that subject," Aisha says, leaning forward and looking squarely at Gabe. "I've been talking with the administration and the faculty and everyone on Homecoming Committee, and everyone is in agreement that we should alter the verbiage for nominees. We were thinking about going with Homecoming Monarchs, or giving people the option to choose whether they wanted to be King or Queen. Honestly, I think it's well overdue."

"I appreciate that," Gabe says, "but I really do want to decline the nomination. I don't really see myself being part of the whole spectacle, you know?"

Aisha blinks, her expression blank, as if Gabe just said something in a language she's never heard before. "Oh. So…

even if we change the verbiage, you wouldn't want to accept the nomination?"

Gabe shakes their head. "Changing the verbiage won't change the fact that I was nominated for Queen. That just doesn't sit well with me. I appreciate what you're doing, but it's still a no."

I can see Aisha trying to process this new information. She doesn't argue, even though it looks like she wants to. "That's fair. I respect that. And it's important to me that you know that I respect you, as does Student Council, the faculty and staff here, and all of your fellow students here."

She gets up, pats Gabe on the shoulder, and is off, to do more President things, I assume.

"That was intense," Mona says with a whistle.

I have to agree. "Aisha can be like that."

"I'm sure she means well," Gabe says.

"She definitely does."

Mona leans around me to talk to Gabe. "You're still coming with us to the dance, right?"

That turns heads. I see Tony's head whip toward us with an eyebrow raised and a mouth still full of burger. "Y'all are going to the dance together?" he demands. "All three of you?"

"You should try chewing and swallowing your food before you talk," Mona responds, barely acknowledging him, or the looks some of the others are exchanging. That seems to squelch any other questions or comments anyone else might have had.

A spark of hope. Does Mona sound worried at the idea of Gabe not going? I think she does.

Gabe laughs. "I can't stand up two dates. That's double fucked-up."

Mona breathes a sigh of relief. "Oh, thank god. My heart just wouldn't be able to bear it."

I know she's joking. But I also know that most jokes contain a grain of truth. Or so I've been told.

Could it be that Mona and Gabe are into each other after all?

CHAPTER 15

Compared to the previous week, the one leading up to the dance is busier, but better, because so much is going on that I almost don't have time to be stressed about any of it.

Almost.

It's Spirit Week, which is ordinarily a special kind of hell for me. All of the sensory issues I already have with clothes are exacerbated by all the weird and whimsical costumes they come up with and expect us to wear. Adding to the already limited wardrobe I can tolerate never works out well for me. But participation isn't required, and I can at least rely on my trusty camera as an easy out. When it comes time to vote for Homecoming Monarchs, I cast mine for Mona and Bridge without thinking twice about it.

Before I know it, it's Saturday. Mona, Gabe, and I decide to meet at the venue instead of doing the whole predance, meet-the-parents, take-pictures bit that none of us really want to do. My parents are, to put it mildly, disappointed.

"Make sure you take lots of pictures! I can't wait to see

how cute you all look together!" Mom demands as I make my way out.

I hold up my camera. "Getting pictures is my job, remember?"

"With you in them," she clarifies.

That I can't guarantee.

"Just have fun tonight, okay, kid?" Dad says.

I can't guarantee that, either. "I'll try," is my tepid response.

I'm nervous, but my nerves have nothing to do with me, which feels strange. Usually my anxiety is focused inward, and centered on how I'm going to act, move, and think, and what I'm going to say. Tonight, I'm stressed for Mona and Gabe. Things haven't been progressing between them, and I have this gut feeling that something is missing.

I walk through the front doors and am immediately welcomed by the blaring, synth-heavy chorus of Simple Minds's "Don't You (Forget About Me)," and it only gets more disconcerting from there. The music hits me with a force akin to what a hydrogen molecule might experience inside the Large Hadron Collider. Not that I don't like classic eighties jams; I just prefer not to taste them on a molecular level.

This is Aisha's Plan B location: Skate N' Place, a Minneapolis staple since the eighties. The place started out as only a roller rink, but over the years it expanded to include this dance hall, and became more of a party venue where families host birthday parties or quinceañeras. This was actually even one of the places Miles briefly considered for his bachelor party.

The dance hall is in the shape of a hexagon, with the stage and the DJ setup at one end, and the catering station on the opposite. The dance floor makes up half the space, with the rest reserved for seating. Each of the dozen tables boasts a fiber-optic centerpiece and a tiny model of the solar system.

The theme this year is "Neutron Star Collision." Neon fluorescent galaxies and nebulae and supernovas splash brightly against the walls. Constellations and planets dance around the ceiling. String lights twinkle like stars. Aesthetically it's astounding. The stark geometry bathed in harsh, inescapable red reminds me of the end of *2001: A Space Odyssey.*

I've never dropped acid or had a fever dream, but this is what I'd imagine either might be like.

The first thing I notice is that there is little to no rules-based dancing at a Homecoming dance. No one wants to do that for real, contrary to how these things go so often on TV. Which is extremely unfortunate for me, because rules-based dancing is the only kind of dancing I know how to do. Ballroom, square dances, the Cha-Cha Slide—I know them all. I know the steps.

But plenty of people are just hanging out and having fun. It also helps that I'm taking photos. As usual.

Mona said she'd be "fashionably late," which is a concept I'm convinced I'll never understand, but whatever. I check my phone for any messages, and then start making the rounds with my camera. I feel like a paparazzo, darting in and out, snapping photos of all these pretty, happy people, but it's what I like to do, and it helps put me at ease. I know what I'm doing, and how best to do it. The conversation involved is quick and superficial, which is the easiest kind.

It feels like everyone I know is here. Aisha and Omar in matching mauve, Destiny and a guy I don't recognize but who looks like he could model for some European luxury brand, and Bridge and his boyfriend, Erik-with-a-K. It's nice and a little surprising to see that they came tonight with Solo as their "plus-plus-one," as Bridge explains it, but it's sweet that he's not, well, solo.

"Where's your plus-one and plus-two?" Bridge asks me as he sips delicately at the drink Erik-with-a-K just handed him. They're a cute couple, and they don't seem to be capable of keeping their hands off one another. Not that they're trying.

"En route on both counts. I think."

I hope.

My plan for tonight is fairly simple: get them together and get the heck out of the way. I wonder what kind of couple they'll be. The kind that acts like they're inhabiting the same body, like Bridge and Erik-with-a-K, or the kind that hardly broadcasts that they're together, like whatever it is Aisha and Omar have going on. I wonder, but of course it doesn't matter, and it won't be any of my business or concern after tonight. If all goes according to plan. And it will. It has to. I've put in entirely far too much work for it not to.

My phone vibrates in my pocket. It's Mona.

I'm parking 😊

Finally. I was seconds away from texting her myself. I guess today fashionably late means twenty minutes after the event begins.

Still nothing from Gabe, though. Which, honestly, is on-brand for them. Aside from telling me they'd meet me here, they didn't give anything by way of an ETA. I'd assumed they'd just materialize at random, because Gabe is far too cool to abide by anyone else's schedule or timetable. I kind of really like that about them. I wish I could be so casual about, well, anything.

I hear Mona's arrival before I see it. As I push toward the entrance of the venue, I feel like we've all become paparazzi. When I finally see her, my mouth falls open. She's in a deep blue sequined V-neck sheath dress with an asymmetrical skirt, which I only know because she told me about it when she bought it. What is immediately apparent is that she is completely and undeniably stunning. Despite the sudden crowd, I'm happy for her. Proud, even. That's my friend. She deserves the attention. I'm perfectly content to be just another spectator in this moment. This is her moment, not ours.

Until she spots me and excitedly waves, and it's like she forgets everyone else exists. She cuts straight through the crowd and pulls me into a tight hug that warms my entire body.

"You look…" I don't have the words. I don't think the words exist. "Perfect?"

She grins. "Are you asking me?"

Her question sends me into a panic. "No!" I blurt. "I think

you do look perfect, I just—is that the right word? There should be a better one, because that sounds so clichéd, but everything else sounds clichéd, too, but you don't, you look amazing, and I—"

"Daniel." She squeezes my arm. "Relax. I was giving you shit. Thank you."

"I—oh." I suck in a huge calming breath. "I knew that. No, I didn't."

"No, you didn't." Mona smiles at me, and it warms my insides. "You look dashing, by the way."

"Thank you." Hearing her say it more than makes up for the fact that I'm about as comfortable in this as I would be in a gimp suit. "Shall we?"

The last-minute change in venue did seem to result in this almost feeling like two completely separate events being smashed together, which is cosmically on-theme. The semi-formality of the dance versus the carefree fluidity of the roller rink give this whole thing the feeling of a top-500 pop song—what's happening doesn't make much sense, but it's catchy and fun enough that it doesn't matter. Sometimes this crazy, chaotic universe does us a solid.

"Have you heard anything from our date?" Mona asks.

"I was actually going to ask you the same question," I answer.

We get stopped again by a group of people who want a photo with Mona, and I automatically slide aside and offer to take it for them. I take one with their phone, and another with my own camera.

I hear more fanfare coming from the entrance, and my heart stutters. Gabe causes a different, though just as powerful, reaction as Mona. People flock to Mona, press in close and want to touch her. But with Gabe, people admire from a distance, in more of a stunned awe. Almost like they're a little scared. Which makes sense. But Gabe strolls in with such casual confidence that I wonder if they even notice.

We are wearing almost the same black suit, except their jacket is undone, their shirt is untucked, and their tie is loose at their collar. They've also paired their suit with a pair of Converses. All told, they look entirely too cool for this world. How is one person this attractive in so many different ways? It doesn't matter if they're in street clothes, or dressed as a Net-Knight, or in a plain black suit, Gabe is just...a smoke-show?

That's a term I learned from Simone that means an extremely attractive—or, hot—individual, and I quite like how it sounds, even though I don't use it nearly as much as she does. I haven't had much reason to, until now.

"You look nice," I manage to say.

It isn't exactly poetry, or much of a conversation starter, or even enough to encompass what I'm actually thinking, but Gabe smiles. "Yeah?"

"Of course."

"Because I was actually going for handsome. Although dashing would've been acceptable, too. Or suave. Or maybe dapper."

I bite my lip, but I can't help grinning. "Okay, fine. You're the most handsome, dashing, suave, and dapper person here. Better?"

"It'll do. You look pretty dapper yourself."

My insides dance. Does Mona feel like this when Gabe talks to her? Does Gabe even say things like this to Mona? Somehow, I doubt it.

Aisha takes to the stage with the mic. "Alright, nominees, it's time!"

Mona turns and smiles. "Good luck!" I tell her.

She kisses my cheek. "Thanks!"

"Good luck up there," Gabe says with a wink. I don't know how Mona's knees don't buckle. Mine definitely would have if Gabe had winked at me like that. The nominees line up on the stage.

Aisha begins her speech, followed by a brief introduction of all the nominees. Everyone looks so great from here. I'm glad I put a new SD card in my camera. At this rate I'll fill it before anyone gets crowned.

"And now," Aisha says theatrically, "the moment I'm sure we've all been waiting for…"

She carefully tears open the first envelope she's holding. It's for show, but it's working. I'm stone-still. The entire room is devoid of sound. I'd wager that every single one of us is holding our breath. The seconds pass in excruciating slow motion.

"Our first new… Homecoming… Monarch…is…"

Oh, she's enjoying this.

"Landon 'Bridge' McDouglas!"

He's crying before she even finishes his name. Everyone else claps and screams. It feels like I've been caught in the middle of a minefield, but I grit my teeth and close my eyes and wait for the fanfare to die down.

"And now," Aisha begins again once it's relatively quiet, "please join me in welcoming our second Homecoming Monarch…"

She tears open the envelope and pretends to read the name as if she didn't already know who it was.

"… Ramona Sinclair!"

The room erupts in applause, somehow louder this time. I don't mind this time. In fact, I hardly notice.

CHAPTER 16

After the crowning ceremony everything becomes a flurry of pure chaos. Suddenly everything is moving at light-speed and I'm struggling to keep up.

"Come on," I tell Gabe, weaving my arm in theirs as I move toward the stage. And the crowd. Something I wouldn't have dreamed of doing even two minutes ago. But I'm excited, and I have to work fast. Strike while the iron is hot, so to speak. Another metaphor that makes total sense to me. What better moment for someone to make a slow-burn confession of love than right after watching the object of their affection be crowned as Homecoming Queen? It's positively poetic.

The newly crowned Monarchs are being paraded around like trophies. Everyone is clamoring and cheering, and Bridge is still crying for some reason.

As we inch closer, I take more photos. Everything about this moment will be documented. Hell, I may even make a scrapbook out of it, maybe give it to Gabe and Mona as an anniversary gift a year from now. If they haven't forgotten me completely, that is.

Isn't that the point?

The thought instantly sours my mood. But then Mona's cleaving through the people standing between us, and she emerges, in her brand-new gleaming crown, to pull me into a tight hug.

"Can you believe this?" she says impishly. "They make anybody royalty these days."

"Long may you reign," I tell her. And then I step aside to give Gabe, who's slightly behind me, the floor.

"Congratulations," they say, stepping forward. "Seriously. You deserve it."

Mona beams. "Thank you."

This is it. The moment destiny arrives. They're looking at each other with stars dancing in their eyes and smiles on their faces. I can see how it's going to play out. They'll hug each other, but it'll turn into one of those lingering hugs because neither person wants to break away. They'll try, but they won't want to let go of one another, and somehow their hands are together, and what's this? Mona is leaning in, because of course it will be Mona who initiates this moment that will change them both forever, and Gabe will follow her lead, and then, before either of them can fully rationalize or talk themselves down, they'll be kissing! And it's one of those romantic, real kisses where the camera swoops around in a full three-sixty to capture every angle of what true love looks like, and the music will swell and the crowd will cheer...

And then Gabe crosses their arms. "So, what will your first official act as Queen be?"

Mona laughs. "Getting the fuck out of this dress! Oh, sorry, I mean, getting the 'heck' out of this dress. Cursing isn't becoming of a queen."

"All the more reason to do it," Gabe says.

"Fuck yeah." They both laugh, but it isn't one of those "oh my god I love you so much" laughs. It's a regular old run-of-the-mill laugh between two friends.

What the hell?

None of what's supposed to happen is happening. And now I'm being jostled by all these people surrounding me, alone and somehow separated from Gabe, drowning in it all, holding my camera over my head like it's some sort of life preserver keeping me afloat.

I really hate how this industrial carpet feels beneath my shoes, even if it is decorated with confetti and cute little balloons and fireworks. It smells exactly like the gymnasium at school, except there's an added note of old grease.

And noise. Pulse-pounding, signal-jamming noise. It's like when you're trying to read or recite a sequence of numbers, and someone starts blurting out random ones to throw you off. Only it's everyone. And they're screaming. And I know no one here is doing this on purpose, but it feels like a personal, concerted attack on my senses, and my first, instinctual reaction is anger. Acidic neons and psychedelic strobe lights—it's sensory overload. I can't hear myself think. It's like the noise overrides my higher brain function and I can't tell what my body is doing. It reminds me of *Escape from New York*, only slightly less bleak.

And then, it starts to happen.

I'm standing here, camera in hand, and I just…go completely numb.

I tried explaining to my family once what it feels like to disassociate. It feels almost like an out-of-body experience. Or like being suddenly yanked into another dimension. Everything happening around me becomes distant background noise. I compare it to what can sometimes happen to a computer. If the CPU gets overwhelmed with too many requests or commands, sometimes the whole system freezes. Sometimes it has to reboot completely.

I can't move. I can't think. Someone could come and tap me on the shoulder and I doubt it would even—

"Hey."

It's like glass shattering. A brief second of free-fall and I'm back in my body, and the world around me comes rushing back, and Gabe is standing beside me, their eyes searching mine with what I think might be concern.

"Hey," I say, blinking rapidly.

Gabe smiles warmly. "So…you wanna skate?"

No. "Of course."

"Cool. C'mon, Mona's waiting for us."

We head toward the counter together. Having Gabe next to me makes the ordeal of navigating through the thick bands of loud people easier.

"You ready to get our skate on?" Mona asks excitedly. She's changed out of her dress and into what's more or less her usual uniform—yoga pants, sneakers, and a Frederick Jones T-shirt—but she's still rocking the giant, gleaming crown.

"Not really," I shout, but she's already steering me toward the counter and it's noisy enough in here that I could believe that she didn't hear me.

"What size?"

I stare in horror at the wall of well-worn skates stuffed in cubbies and I would rather saw off both my feet than put them inside a single pair of them.

"He's a ten," Mona says.

I look at her and frown. "How do you know my shoe size?"

"I dunno, I guess I just do." She shrugs casually, or in a way that feels like it's meant to be casual, but something feels off. The shoe guy plops a faded pair of skates on the counter, and Mona snatches them up. "Thanks! Come on."

She hooks her arm in mine and pulls me along. Gabe trails behind us, sliding effortlessly between all the people. I'm still trying to figure out this shoe thing. I can't recall us ever having a conversation about my shoe size. I can't imagine Mona asking someone else. Or maybe it did come up at some point. Why would she retain that information? She couldn't have a vested interest in my shoes. It doesn't make sense.

Of course, I know that she wears a women's size nine. She told me once when we were at Famous Footwear and she was ranting about how hard it is for her to find her size. But it's not weird that I know that. I'm the neurodivergent one.

I wonder what other trivial facts about me she knows.

"Do you know how tall I am?"

"Five foot nine," she says instantly before adding, "I'm half an inch taller than you, remember?"

I do. "How much do I weigh?"

She barks out a laugh. "Dude!"

"That's not an answer. Do you know Gabe's shoe size?"

"No, because I've known Gabe for, like, a month, and I've known you since forever."

Damn. I suppose I can't argue with that.

"I'm five foot eight," Gabe adds. "And I wear a men's eight, since we're exchanging that kind of information with each other."

Mona laughs, but doesn't say anything else.

We make our way to the rink. Stylized planets and stars dance on the ground. There's an honest-to-goodness disco ball. People are wobbling and shuffling around the rink with necklaces and bracelets made of glowsticks while "Separate Ways (Worlds Apart)" by Journey blares from the overhead speakers. They remind me of old-school zombies, but on wheels.

In its defense, roller-skating isn't as bad as dancing, but I don't understand how any of this is supposed to be fun. Especially when I spend most of the time trying to wriggle out from between Mona and Gabe. It's hard to be subtle on roller skates. Every time I try to slow down so they can keep going without me, they wait for me to catch up. When I "accidentally" loop around to be on one side or another, one of them just glides right back around to put me in the middle again. I even try pretending one of my skates comes untied, and they both stop for me.

Eventually I just give up, and it doesn't take long for the whole thing to become a little bit boring. We're all just rolling around in one great big oblong circle over and over again.

I can feel people's eyes on us as we skate. I wish I had something to do with my hands to distract myself from it, but my arms are immobilized. It almost feels like I'm in the stocks, my shame on full display in the public square. Luckily no one is throwing rotten vegetables at me.

Yet.

I don't get it! This was the moment when the sparks were supposed to fly. They were supposed to finally realize what they've been ignoring/resisting/questioning all along, and take that leap of faith and just kiss each other already! But none of that's happening. Why isn't any of that happening?

Eleven o'clock cannot come fast enough.

I try to hide my relief when the volunteer chaperons start making their rounds and gently herding us toward the exit. Compared to all the buildup, the actual event was a little bit of a letdown. A mentally draining letdown, but a letdown all the same.

I can't wait to get home. To change out of these irritating clothes and be surrounded by my things. I'm going to have to decompress for an entire week, and worse still, I don't even know if all the effort was worth anything.

I quietly slink to the bench to free myself of these horribly restricting roller skates. Mona plops down beside me as I'm untying them. Somehow, she's still full of energy.

"Everyone's going to Bridge's," she announces.

"Everyone?"

She laughs. "No, Daniel, probably not everyone. But we should definitely go."

I take in a very long, very deep sigh that echoes through my bones.

"Is Gabe going?" I ask.

Mona shrugs. "Knowing them, I'd say yes."

I don't have much left in the tank, metaphorically speaking. I know myself well enough to know that I'm quickly approaching burnout territory, which is definitely bad news. I hadn't prepared for this, but I owe it to Mona and Gabe to finish what I started. The moment didn't quite happen after the crowning, but that doesn't mean this is over yet. I can still bring Gabe and Mona together. As painful as it will probably be, considering that my social battery is in the negative numbers at this point.

I suppose that settles it, then. "Count me in."

Another party right after the first party seems like over-kill. But I can't leave these two alone, not when there are so many strings left untied. Not when they aren't any closer to being a couple now than they were at the start of the evening. I have to see this thing through.

...Even if I immediately question my decision to let Mona and Gabe talk me into coming the moment I step through the front door and realize every person I've ever met is crammed into this place. But really, what did I expect? I've seen the movies. Red cups, people hooking up in dank, dark corners, loud music. The McDouglas residence is even built like one of those houses you see these types of things happening in. There's a deck in the backyard, along with a pool and a firepit. I can assume there will be drunken hijinks, a dramatic confrontation, and maybe—if we're all very lucky—a pained, slightly awkward proclamation of love. And I've got two primed and perfect candidates for that last one.

I wince and resist the urge to cover my ears as Mona, Gabe, and I shuffle through the maze of people.

"I'm gonna go get a drink," Mona says.

"I'm gonna go find the toilet," says Gabe.

"And I'm going to…wander," I say to no one at all, because they're both already drifting in complete opposite directions.

Why can't I keep those two together?

It's odd, really. Mona normally loves telling me about whoever she's into at the moment, but she's hardly said anything about Gabe. I don't know why. But until I do, I'll do what I'm good at: observing.

And there's certainly lots to see. Only I can't take pictures, because I'm reasonably sure no one wants any of what's happening here played during broadcast or plastered all over the school vlog.

Bridge finds me in the living room. He isn't wearing his crown (they stopped trusting people with them outside of supervised settings a long time ago), but he's still in the glittery suit he was wearing at the dance. "Hey, bestie," he shouts as he drapes an arm over my shoulder. "What do you think?"

"I think this may be a fire hazard…"

He laughs, even though I wasn't really joking. "So can I ask you a personal question?"

"Aren't all questions personal ones?"

He laughs as if I was joking. I wasn't. He says that a lot, and I'm not sure why.

"What's up with you and Gabe?"

Huh. That's different. But by now I'm reasonably sure I know what he's really asking. "We're only friends."

He grins and wriggles his eyebrows. "You sure about that?"

"I don't know how to answer that question." I'm being sincere. I'm way too overwhelmed to mask the way I ordinarily would, and the less I mask, the less…tactful I can come across.

Bridge only laughs. "You know, I thought I had you figured out, but you, sir, are a mystery."

"Thank you."

He walks away, absorbed into the crowd, and I'm more confused now than I was when I got here. Because if I'm being entirely and completely honest, I don't know how to answer his question, but if I dwell on it for too long, like I am now, an answer starts to suggest itself. And it's one that scares me.

But I did just spot a pool table, which is great for me because any sort of rules-based activity gives me something to anchor to.

There are a bunch of people already gathered around the table setting up a game. When I get closer I realize that Gabe is one of them, spinning a cue in their hands.

Where in the world is Mona? She should be seeing this.

I wander through the house. Each room seems more crowded than the last. But I don't see Mona anywhere.

By the time I circle back around, the game is over and Gabe has passed their cue to someone else.

"Are you having fun?" they ask.

"Yeah," I say as I scan the room for any sign of Mona. "I think so." It's probably the most dishonest thing I've said all evening. I am not having an ounce of fun.

"You only think so? We gotta fix that."

What they said doesn't really register in my head, because a sudden realization hits me. The kitchen. Mona loves to hang out in and around kitchens whenever she goes to parties like this, because that's where all the snacks always are. Odds are she's there now.

"I think I want a drink."

Gabe nods. "Yeah? Let's get you one. Follow me."

They lead the way, and I follow closely. With each step, I'm literally closing in on my objective. I can feel success, so close, so within my grasp. Gabe and I wheel around the corner into the kitchen, and Mona's name is already on my lips. I can already envision their excited reunion. And then I see her—

Tangled up in the arms of another girl.

Gabe's hand drops from my wrist. Mona and the girl break apart. Both are wide-eyed and blushing and breathing hard. Mona wipes her mouth with the back of her hand and grins. "Hey, guys!"

I can feel the tension in Gabe's posture. "I gotta go."

They whirl around and brush past me so sharply that their shoulder slaps against mine as they go.

CHAPTER 17

I've never felt this helpless. Frustration seeps from my bones, locking up my logical mind and gunking up my ability to think, to reason, to rationalize dispassionately. I hate this feeling. I am completely unmoored, adrift in this choppy sea of emotions I do not understand. And behind this mental gridlock is the overwhelming, all-consuming desire to fix this. Whatever is wrong, whatever I or anyone else has done, I have to make this right.

I mentally run through this evening's events, everything that'd led to this moment, combing through everything I've said and done, trying to pinpoint the source of this upset. But the frustration, the panic, the fear, they all cling to my mind and slow/scramble/distort my thoughts.

I'm standing outside the bathroom door, my hand hovering above the knob. I can't hear any movement from within. The knob turns. My heart stops. The door swings slowly open, and there they are.

"Hey," Gabe says.

Red-rimmed eyes. Faltering smile. They've been crying.

Possibly. Maybe. What's the protocol for this? We're only four feet apart, but it feels like hundreds.

Say something.

"Hey."

Do something.

"May I come in?"

Gabe starts. Steps back. "Oh. Um, sure. I mean, if you want to…"

"I do." I step into the bathroom. The noise from the party lingers in my ears, so I close the door behind me. With the noise muted I can focus on my immediate surroundings. It's an average full-size bathroom, roughly twelve by six feet, with the tub on the far end, and the toilet situated between the tub and the sink, on which Gabe is gently leaning with their arms crossed, looking at the ground and tapping the tile with the toe of their right shoe.

The space seems much smaller than it actually is.

I cross to the tub, slide the mat aside, and sit on the ground, drawing my knees up and resting my arms on them. From here it feels a lot like my bathroom. Comfortable. Familiar. I look up at Gabe, who is watching me. "Would you care to join me?"

Proximity. Most people will seek the comfort of others when they experience distress. I am not one of those people. At least, I didn't think I was.

For a moment I'm sure Gabe is going to say no. But they nod, and I scoot over so they can sit next to me.

Our shoulders are touching. So are our knees. Gabe leans their head back and rests it on the edge of the tub. I concentrate on breathing. Slowly. Evenly. Naturally. I steal a sidelong glance at them and realize their eyes are closed. I relax a little, and study their profile. Gabe is unreadable, as always, but I wonder now if it's only me, or if other people find them so as well.

"Is this alright?" I ask.

Gabe nods without opening their eyes, and it fills me with relief.

"I'm sorry about Mona." The words can't begin to convey the feelings behind them. This is my fault, of course. What did I miss? How could I have not seen this coming?

"That is so weird," Gabe says.

"What is?"

"I was literally about to tell you the exact same thing."

I frown. "Why would you be sorry for me?" Could they have been onto me? Gabe is smart. Maybe they figured out what I was trying to do. Maybe they knew all along.

Gabe chuckles. "Again, I could literally ask you the exact same question." When I don't respond, they shift to face me. "You really aren't into Mona, are you?"

Again with this? "I told you that a long time ago," I say, without doing much to strain the annoyance from my voice.

"I know. I'm sorry. I should have believed you. I mean, I did believe you, mostly."

I know what I want to tell them, but I'm not sure how to go about it. Until I decide to just say it.

"I thought she was into you. And," I add, reluctantly, "I thought you were into her."

"Where'd you get that idea?"

I shrug. "You two seemed perfect for each other. I thought you had a lot in common." I don't feel like recounting the specifics, because I don't quite understand what isn't working between them, but I don't think it's necessary anyway.

Gabe breathes deeply. "Daniel, the only thing we really have in common is you."

Me? It's a strange concept. I can't possibly be the only glue that binds two such dynamic and incredible individuals. It's nonsensical. And yet, if Gabe is to be believed—and why would they lie—it's somehow true. Which simply adds another layer to the rapidly mounting tangle of confusion that is currently taking over my gray matter. I need to sort through this mess. I need answers.

"So," I begin, the question still formulating in my brain, "if you're not upset about Mona hooking up with someone else, why are you here…" *Crying* is the word I leave out of my question.

"Because the 'someone else' is my ex," Gabe says.

Oh. Shit. Wow. "I'm sorry. That sounds—"

"Horrifying?"

"I was going to say uncomfortable, but horrifying sounds better. Or worse, actually."

Gabe laughs humorlessly. At least, it sounds humorless. I couldn't imagine they'd find anything about this situation remotely funny.

"I ran into someone I wish I hadn't recently, too."

Gabe gives me a look that seems to indicate that they might want to hear more. "When we were LARPing. His name is Will," I continue. "He went to Sandburg."

"From the basketball team?" Gabe asks. "I know him! Did you—" Their eyes widen. "Did you used to date?"

That almost makes me laugh. "No. We were friends back in middle school. Best friends. Although, if I'd thought he'd had any sort of romantic interest in me, I probably would've asked him out. I was definitely into him."

"What happened between you two?" Gabe asks gently. "Unless you don't want to talk about it, I mean."

"It's nothing," I begin. Which is very much a lie. "I thought we were best friends. But it turns out when I wasn't around he was talking shit about me to everyone else. Telling them how weird and annoying and clingy I was. Eventually I found out, and it was this big, humiliating thing."

I'm summarizing, of course. It isn't something I like to go into detail about. Like the fact that what really bothered me was that, the whole time we were friends, I was only being myself, or that it made me realize that I couldn't be myself if I wanted to have friends, or even exist without being ostracized. What happened between me and Will was the first time I understood how different from everyone else I was. It was the first time I understood what it meant to be neurodivergent.

"That sounds shitty," Gabe says.

"It was," I reply, with a practiced lightness to my tone that I hope conveys that it isn't a big deal and that I'm totally, a hundred percent over it. "But, you live and you learn."

Gabe nods, and suddenly this odd sense of connectedness sweeps over me. Here we are, hiding from people. Holed up in the sanctuary of Bridge's bathroom. It's…nice? But still, a bathroom.

"We should get out of here."

Gabe glances questioningly at me. "And go where?"

"I don't know. I hadn't got that far in the thought process, honestly. Somewhere your ex isn't?"

"You wanna bail on Bridge's party?"

"I don't mean to brag, but I am the master of leaving parties early. If leaving parties early was a sport, I'd be an Olympic-level athlete."

"Fuck, you're a nerd."

I laugh. I like when Gabe calls me that. "How about it? I mean, why stay if we're not having fun? Isn't that the whole point of a party?"

"I cannot argue with that logic." Gabe nods. "Okay."

It takes a second for it to register that they've agreed to my half-baked idea. "Cool. Um…let's go."

We shuffle out of the bathroom and ease back into the thick of the party. We weave our way through the gyrating bodies on our way to the front door.

We're almost at the front door when Mona catches up to me. The girl she was with—Gabe's ex—is nowhere to be found.

"Hey! Is everything okay?" she asks.

The concern is plain on her face, even in the low light. I glance back over my shoulder. Gabe is hovering at the door, their hand clutching the doorknob.

"Yeah," I tell her. "It's all good. We're just going to go get some air. We'll be right back."

"Oh. Okay," Mona starts, as if she's about to come with us, but then she stops and backtracks. "See you later, then."

"Yeah," I say, trying not to linger. "See you."

A strange feeling comes over me as I turn and walk out the door with Gabe and without Mona. I can't put my finger on the feeling, but it seems to increase the farther away we get. By the time we reach my car, I'm certain I've missed picking up on something important.

"Any idea where we're going yet?" Gabe asks as they slink into the passenger seat of my truck.

I look up at the night sky while Gabe types on their phone with their knees drawn up to their chest. Like a bird. A crow, maybe. Or some kind of stork. It looks like it might rain soon. And that gives me an idea.

"I got a place," I announce as I key the ignition. "It's exactly what we need."

Gabe doesn't ask any questions. Just buckles their seat belt. "Cool. Let's bail."

The 32nd Street Beach is gorgeous tonight.

It's close to midnight. The sky is dark save for the distant glow of the city lights across the water. I'm sitting with my knees drawn up to my chest and my arms wrapped around them watching the waves and it feels like a dream. The wind is warm and sweet.

Gabe seems to be in better spirits. They've spent the last few minutes absently skipping pebbles across the surface of the water. I want to be doing more to comfort them, but I just don't know how. Comforting people, even people I've known my entire life, is not a strong suit of mine, and it doesn't help that it's impossible to know what's going on in Gabe's head. Right now I'm not so sure what's happening in mine, either.

This reminds me of something I read about called liminal space. A liminal space is a location of transition, or a point where something is changing, or about to change, but it hasn't quite happened yet. That transition can be totally physical, a place between two real locations, like a train or a bus station, or it can be completely metaphysical, like a point between two states of being. Most people get uncomfortable in liminal spaces, which is why they're so popular in the horror genre. Because they're places we aren't meant to linger in. We can sense their temporary nature, and we naturally leave them as soon as we can. But not me. I love places like that. And this beach, dark and silent and empty save for the two of us, is perfect.

Gabe comes over, kicking up sand, and plops down right next to me, wriggling their toes into the sand.

"What's up?"

I give them a rueful smile. "Nothing," I say. But it's a lie. I can picture Mona and her friends here, splashing around in the shallows, chasing each other around, or playing chicken. All the screaming and laughter. There's no way she wouldn't try hoisting me onto her shoulders to play. We'd almost certainly lose, and it would definitely be my fault.

Gabe shoves my shoulder with theirs. "Come on, Daniel, I know that face. You're thinking about her, aren't you?"

"Probably not in the way you're imagining."

"Sure." Gabe groans. "You know you can be real with me, right?"

They shift to look at me with such unexpected intensity that I feel suddenly naked. "Sure," I croak.

"Not just about Mona," Gabe goes on. "About anything. You don't have to hide who you are from me. Not if you don't want to."

I swallow slowly. "Thank you."

Gabe nods lazily and falls backward onto the sand.

"Why aren't you dating anyone?"

The question is so abrupt that it crashes my entire thought process. "What, like now?"

"Sure," Gabe says again. They're looking up at the sky, and there's a strange casualness to their tone that seems wrong. "I mean, it seems to me like there are people who aren't dating because they don't want to, and people who aren't dating because they haven't found someone, and you seem like part of that first group."

I dig my toes into the sand. "Lots of reasons, I guess." My tone, by comparison, is cautious, measured, calculated. Because I'm not sure where this topic sprang from, and therefore have no idea where it's leading. That makes me nervous.

Which Gabe doesn't seem to notice at all. They prop themselves back up onto their elbows and shake sand out of their hair. "What about a crush?" they ask. "Got one of those?"

"That depends on how you define a crush."

I realize almost immediately that it sounds like I'm being coy, but I'm not. It was a sincere statement.

I watch the expression on their face. Their eyes narrow, like they're trying to figure out if I'm messing with them, but then they break out into a laugh and shove my shoulder. "What do you want, Daniel?" they ask. "Right here, right now, in this very moment?"

Gabe waits for my answer. I look at them, with their messy hair full of sand, the warm, salty breeze making it even more messy than it usually is.

"I want to be here. With you." I'm staring at my knees as I say it. When Gabe doesn't respond I chance a sidelong glance their way. They're looking off at some point across the shore, with a contented smile on their face.

"I want to be here with you, too," they say.

They sit up and rest their chin on their knees, and we watch the waves together.

The party seems to be still going on when we pull back up to Bridge's house, despite the fact that we've been gone for at least an hour.

"Thanks a lot," Gabe says as they prop the passenger-side door open. "For tonight, I mean."

"Oh. Yes, of course. This was...fun."

"Just fun?"

"Was it supposed to be something else?"

They grin at me. "I dunno. Are you going back in?"

I glance past them, at the house and all the people and the noise coming from within. I'd rather go anywhere else in the world.

"Nah. It's late and I'm tired."

Gabe nods, and taps the door. "Okay then. In that case...
I'll see you Monday."

"Hey, Gabe?"

They stop and wait for me to go on.

"Good night."

"Good night, Daniel." They smile at me, and the look on
their face is one I don't recognize. But it makes my insides
warm all the same.

CHAPTER 18

My entire family wants to know how the night went the next morning. Their questions feel invasive somehow, even though I'm sure they aren't. I guess there are parts of last night I don't want to share. Parts that feel too personal. Too intimate. And none of them happened at the actual dance.

The second I'm able to escape after breakfast, I retreat to my room. I boot up my computer and connect my camera so I can start downloading the images from last night. Before long I've fallen into a familiar pattern. Spot-cleaning images and adjusting the white balance, changing the exposure and the contrast, the vibrancy and the saturation—it's exactly the kind of mentally demanding and stimulating work I need to help me decompress and forget about everything else.

The interesting thing about being behind the camera is that very often I see things that other people don't. Things everyone else misses. The right light, the right angle, can show a person things about themselves they've never seen.

Why do I feel like I'm the one who missed something last night? And what could it possibly have been?

About an hour into my work I get a text from Mona.

Riverside tonight? They're screening Total Recall.

Honestly, I'm not feeling up to going out. Not after the dance. If it was anyone else, I'd say no without a moment's hesitation. But it's Mona, and I almost never say no to her.

I don't retain any of the movie. Not a single scene. I'm completely checked out throughout the whole runtime. My mind keeps wandering back to the beach, when I was with Gabe, and how it felt. And how great it would be to feel that again.

After the movie Mona and I do our usual thing, but I just can't seem to focus. I don't know if it's because I haven't fully decompressed from the dance, or because Gabe is swirling around in my mind for some reason, or a combination of both.

"So, can I ask you something?" she says. We're sitting on the swings, idly rocking back and forth. "About last night, after the dance?"

Uh-oh. The last subject I feel like talking about right now. "What's up?"

Mona tilts her head back and looks up at the clouds before speaking. "So...what was up with Gabe? They seemed, I dunno, frazzled? So did you."

I freeze in the middle of rocking. My eyes drop to my shoes, and it feels like all the blood in my body has crystallized.

Mona reaches over and rests a hand on my thigh. "Hey!

What's up? What's wrong? You can tell me anything. For real. Anything."

I steal a quick glance at her. She's right. I know that.

"The girl you were making out with was Gabe's ex," I say tersely.

Her mouth falls open. "Shit! I didn't know! Is Gabe okay?"

"Yeah, I think so."

"Fuck," she says, hanging her head. "I feel like an asshole."

"Why?"

"You're asking me why I feel like an asshole?"

"Yeah."

"Maybe because Gabe and I are sort of friends, and I'm not the kind of person to make out with sort-of-friends' exes."

"So you and Gabe are just sort of friends?"

"Why are you being so fucking weird?"

"*I'm* being weird?"

"Yes, Daniel, you are. I don't know what's going on with you lately, but I really think—"

"I thought you liked them!" I blurt. I'm so sick of being confused. I throw up my hands. "And I thought they liked you, but it turns out they don't, and now I'm guessing you don't like them romantically either, right?"

"What in the world gave you the impression that I did?"

"I…" There's so much. How do I even begin to explain everything I've thought, or felt, in the past few weeks? "Forget it."

I hop off the swing and trudge across the sandbox. I feel like such a fool. Nothing makes sense right now. Mona doesn't have romantic feelings for Gabe. I was wrong about that. Clearly. But now my sister's words come ringing back in my ears. She was sure *I'm* the one Mona has those feelings for. I'd been just as convinced about how wrong she was as I was that Mona and Gabe were perfect for each other. If I was so wrong about one thing, who's to say I can't be wrong about the other? Who's to say Mona *doesn't* have a crush on me?

In an instant she's crossed the sand and closed the space between us. "Hey! It's me, remember?" She squeezes my shoulders, smiling warmly. "You can tell me anything. I mean that. I always have."

She lets go of my shoulders, and I'm completely thrown when she takes my hands in hers. "Go on," she says softly. "Tell me something."

She's so bright and pure and strong. How could anyone not love her? Why don't I?

"I…have autism."

If there's even a chance Mona really does have any sort of romantic feelings for me, she should at least know the truth. And if that changes anything, so be it. At least I will have cleared the air between us. Which, incidentally, is another of my favorite idioms.

She frowns. "Wait, what?"

"I'm autistic," I start to say, and once I've started the words just spill out of me. "I know I should have said something a long time ago because you always say I can tell you anything and it's probably uncool of me to have kept such a secret from you for so long, but it's not something I tell anyone anymore because once people know they act differently around me and I don't like it. And I don't want you to act different around me." I pause only because I've run out of breath. When I start again, I try to speak slower. "You. Mona. Are important to me. I value your opinion. I didn't want you to see me as some... I don't know, as some freak. I'm sorry."

The ensuing silence is almost unbearable. But I wait, desperate for her response.

"Yeah," Mona says at last, running a hand through her hair, "I...already knew that."

All at once the entire world grinds to a halt. "Hold on. You knew? How is that possible?"

Scenarios run through my mind. If she knows, who else does? Who told her? Did she figure it out herself? Is it that obvious? Am I that obvious?

Mona sighs. Her expression is all bunched up. She seems uncomfortable with this, too. I'm not sure if it makes me feel better or worse. "Before we met, I guess your mom told my mom, and then my mom sat me down and gave me this weird prep talk. I thought she was gonna give me the sex talk—"

"What did she say?"

This changes everything. Everything I thought I knew about Mona and I, and our friendship.

"I dunno," she says, far too casually. "Just that, the boy you're about to meet has autism, so even though I'm sure he'll be really sweet, he might be a little...intense."

I feel like a deflated balloon. "Intense..." The word rolls around in my mind. I can't make sense of it. "Is that all she said?"

I steal a quick glance at Mona. She looks confused. And

maybe worried. "I thought you knew that. And anyways, what difference does it make?"

"It makes all the difference. Is that why you've always been so nice to me?" All this time I thought she was the one person who didn't see me as different, as the one person who accepted me the way I was. "Is that why you've always acted like I was just like anyone else to you? Is it because your mom told you to?"

"Daniel," she says. "I barely remember that conversation. And I treat you like you're my friend because you *are* my friend. Do you seriously think all this time I was just hanging out with you because I felt bad for you? Like you were just some pity case? How could you think so little of me?" She stops, relaxes, and waves a hand. "Wait. Wait. Let's not do this."

"This?"

"Yes, let this little misunderstanding drive a wedge between us for no reason. It's such a cliché."

She's right. It makes sense for Mom to have given Mona's mom the heads-up, just like it makes sense for Mona's mom to have done the same for her. If everyone acted logically, do I have any real grounds for being angry?

No. So this is an emotional response, pure and simple. Which means it will pass. I just need to allow space for my rational mind to overrule the animal part of my brain. The part that wants to wallow in this shitty feeling.

"I thought you…" *Might have a crush on me. Or at least, other people thought so, which was making me start to wonder about it, too.*

"You thought I what?" Mona presses.

"Never mind. It was dumb."

I should have known I was misreading things. That's what happens when I second-guess the facts. When I let emotions interfere. When I try to be one of them.

Mona doesn't like me like that. How could she? Why would she?

"Are you sure you don't want to say?"

For some reason I feel like she's disappointed. But now I can't imagine why she ever would be.

"It's nothing."

She sighs. "Okay. In that case, we're cool, right? We're still friends?"

"Yes. We're friends."

I've never meant that more than I do now.

CHAPTER 19

It takes me longer than usual to get to sleep. My mind won't stop wandering. My thoughts seem to always settle on Gabe, and on things I can't recall ever having daydreamed about. Like the shape of their lips, and the way they move when Gabe talks.

What the hell is happening to me?

Mona goes to school on her own the next morning. Her text mentions wanting to take care of something, but she doesn't give me any specifics. Not that she has to, I suppose. I suspect, however, that it might have something to do with her still feeling bad about making out with Gabe's ex right in front of them. It would make sense. The few times I've seen Mona genuinely upset, she tends to withdraw until she's over it. Which means by the time I see her today she'll be right back to her usual bubbly self.

When I pull into the lot I'm surprised to see Gabe posted up next to my spot. They take a step back as I ease my truck in. I'm almost too distracted to remember to gather my things out of the back seat. Once I do I come around to meet them.

They push off the curb. "You really do park in the exact same spot every single day, huh?"

"I try to. So...what's up?" I'm assuming there's a reason they're hanging out here of all places right now, given that they've never done it before. I'm also sensing some hella tension in the air here. I could be wrong; it's early in the morning, I'm not all the way turned on to the day yet, and their being here has kind of thrown me off my rhythm, but I sense it either way.

Does Gabe seem nervous?

"I think we should talk about the other night," they say, wiping their palms on their pants.

If they aren't nervous, I definitely am. "Okay. Which part?"

Gabe laughs. "All of it, dude. Look. I need to make sure of something, and I hate to bring this up again, but...you don't like Mona, right?"

"Not romantically, no. She's my best friend."

"No shit. I knew that part. Everybody knows that part. And you're not together?"

"No."

"And you don't like each other, like that?"

"No."

"Okay. Well...do you like me? Like that?"

"Yes." The word seems to come out of my mouth all on its own.

Gabe's face breaks into a wide, bright smile. "Really?"

My heart is beating in my throat. "I don't understand. You like me?"

"Yes, Daniel. I do. You don't get it. You're always acting like you expect me to pretend you're not there, but Daniel, I can't do that. You're always there to me. Sometimes it's like you're the only one who's there. And… I think we should be… I dunno, a couple, a duo, a pair?"

"Okay."

"Okay?"

"Yeah. To all of it. All of the above."

I say it before I realize I'm saying it, but to my intense surprise, once I do, I don't regret it. In fact, I feel relief bloom inside me, because in that moment I realize that this is what I want. This is what I've wanted for longer than I've admitted to myself.

"Cool. So, um…can I kiss you?"

"Yes." The word is hardly out of my mouth before Gabe presses their lips against mine. My whole body tenses, and my breath catches in my closed mouth. At first the surprise and shock of their lips moving against mine completely overwhelms my other senses, but then some deep-rooted instinct emerges from somewhere inside me, and my body moves and responds all on its own, and suddenly I'm kissing them back. It isn't just Gabe kissing me anymore. We're kissing each other. The two of us. Gabe and I. And not Mona.

Not Mona.

I break away. Gabe instantly pulls back, and we're staring at one another, breathing hard, pushing plumes of air into the cool morning sky. "What's wrong?" they ask between deep breaths.

This is all happening so fast. I need time.

"Actually, this isn't a good time."

Damn, this is bad.

Did I see this coming? How could I not have?

Were there signs I missed? Things I didn't notice?

No, that couldn't be possible, could it?

I was so careful!

I was observant. Watchful. Diligent, even.

This doesn't add up. This is out of character. Unless it isn't. Maybe it isn't.

What if it isn't?

"I just...there are things I need to figure out."

It's a technical truth, but it feels like a lie, and I hate it.

What have I done?

What are we doing?

What's supposed to happen next?

This is too much. I need to be somewhere where I can sort through and make sense of it all.

There is a trick I've reserved for these, the most dire, desperate occasions when I simply must escape *immediately*. I've rehearsed it hundreds of times, though I've used it sparingly. It requires subtlety, nuance, and absolute commitment.

The Fake Emergency Text™.

First, the surprise jolt. You have to twitch the leg whose pocket your phone is in, to indicate that it buzzed. It should be the same reaction as if someone tapped you on the shoulder without warning.

Then, the puzzled frown, followed quickly by the apologetic shrug as you reach into your pocket and retrieve the phone. Something to note here: unless your phone has actually gone off, the screen will be blank, so it's important to angle it so that the other person can't see that, or else it becomes obvious that this is all a ruse.

Thirdly, and this is where you really have to sell it, you have to glance at your phone and pretend you're disappointed at being interrupted. It helps if you can infuse your performance with a sense of urgency, like the sudden message you've received is of a serious nature, something you have to respond to immediately. Something important enough to warrant interrupting whatever it is you're doing. That part is actually critical. My go-to, for example, is typically that I have something to do with my camera.

"Oh, wow. They need me to help set up something in the production room," I announce. "I'd better go, or else they'll end up burning the place down or blowing it up."

This is only half a joke. One time Solo had all the lights plugged into the same surge protector and shorted it. There were actual sparks.

Gabe lifts their chin, but doesn't call my bluff. "Oh, yeah, no, totally. You should...figure stuff out. Definitely."

"Are you mad?"

Gabe scoffs. "Mad? Nah. Why would I be mad?"

"I just—"

"Hey." They clap my shoulder and give me what I think is a reassuring smile. "It's all good, okay? We're good. It's not that big of a deal. If, however," they raise a single finger—

the Harrison Ford—"you change your mind, after you've figured your stuff out, let me know. Deal?"

I nod. I'm already inching backward, as if my body is determined to get me out of here even if I'm still talking.

"Deal," I say. But I have no idea if I mean it. Heck, I don't know what anything means anymore.

Bridge locks eyes with me from behind his desk the second I set foot in the newsroom, and he's grinning like a madman.

"I want to know everything," he demands. His voice rings out so loud that all activity grinds to a halt, and suddenly all eyes are on me.

Coming here may have been a bad idea.

"What's he talking about?" Destiny asks.

Panic bubbles up like bile in my throat. I don't have an answer for her. I want to believe that there's no way Bridge could already be asking me about what just transpired between me and Gabe in the parking lot, because there's no way he could possibly know about what just transpired between me and Gabe in the parking lot, but this is Bridge we're talking about here. I couldn't be a hundred percent certain of that even if I were thinking clearly, which I so *am not* right now.

Somehow the turmoil that's roiling inside me must translate to my expression, because Bridge softens, the grin on his face melting away. "Oh…" he says sheepishly, "maybe I wasn't supposed to have said anything…"

"Said anything about what?" asks Solo.

Everyone is circling now, closing in, looking impatiently to me for answers. And I just…

Can't.

"I can't." My feet are moving on their own, backing me out of the room. I don't try to stop, and before I realize it I've turned on my heel and fled back in the direction I came from. My feet don't stop moving until I've wound around the corner and ducked into what I realize is a restroom.

Generally speaking I try to avoid public restrooms because every surface is my worst nightmare, but it's the only place I can come up with to hide. And that's all I want right now. To escape. To be someplace I can regroup.

It's pretty common in movies for characters to talk to themselves in mirrors, especially when they're losing it. I don't know if other people in real life do it, but I do, and it helps. So I plant myself over the sink farthest from the door, lean forward, and stare at my reflection like it belongs to another person. It almost feels like it does, because I don't quite recognize myself. My eyes are wide and anxious. There's a vein pulsing in my right temple. My skin is flushed. This is not good. I've got to get a hold on myself. Got to gain some control. I close my eyes and take a slow, deep breath. Then another. *That's it. Focus on breathing.*

What the hell am I doing? I spent all this time trying to get Gabe and Mona together, and now I'm taking Gabe for myself?

No, that's ridiculous. People aren't objects you can take or give. But I feel gross. Machiavellian, but not in the cool supervillain way, the sleazy dirtbag way.

Someone kicks the door nearly off its hinges, and I just about jump out of my skin.

"Yo, Daniel, are you good?"

It's Bridge, hovering behind me, watching me with a look of concern and worry.

"I'm fine."

Another lie. I'm a goddamned liar now. And a hypocrite. Because it used to annoy me so much that Bridge was determined to set me up with someone, but now look at me, doing the exact same thing.

Only I'm worse at it.

I let go of the sink and move to a urinal. I can't even tell if I actually have to pee, but it doesn't matter, because I'm just going through the motions so my body is occupied.

Bridge pivots. "I'm so sorry, I assumed... I mean, seeing you and Gabe sneak off the other night..."

"Wait, you saw us leave?"

"Yeah, under cover of darkness, you were very obvious about not wanting to be seen."

"We *didn't* want to be seen."

"Yeah, I'm gathering that now."

I go back to the sink and wash my hands. "So, you were asking about the party, not this morning?"

"What happened this morning?"

"I don't know."

Bridge looks as if he's about to ask more questions, but doesn't. "I'm sorry," he says instead. "I'll go do damage control."

"What does that mean?"

"I made a mess for you out there. People think something's up. People are gonna talk if they don't have answers. I'm gonna go put out the fire, as it were. Make it so they don't bother you. Trust me, I'm great at it."

"Thanks?"

A part of me wonders if he isn't just going to make this worse, but only a small part. Because I don't know how this could actually *get* any worse.

Making my way to Statistics feels like walking myself to my own execution.

Gabe said to let them know if I changed my mind, after I had my stuff figured out. Was there an implied deadline for that? Did they expect me to have sorted myself out before we next see each other?

I check my phone to see no new notifications. God, where is Mona? She'd know exactly what to do.

It takes another impromptu trip to another random restroom for me to decide to go about my daily routine as ordinarily as I can. Which means showing up on time to Statistics like I usually do.

I'm sitting at my desk with my hands planted firmly in my lap when Gabe comes in. My spine straightens, and my muscles tense, and oh god I know I'm making this awkward.

But if I am, Gabe doesn't acknowledge it as they slide into the seat just like they always do.

"Hey," they say by way of greeting.

Hey? What the heck does that mean? God, I *hate* this!

Should I worry that they didn't say more, or be grateful they even said that? Where do I go from here? How do I respond?

"Hi."

Was that too little? Am I supposed to say more? Should I have said something else? God, I hate this. I am completely, utterly, inescapably *lost*.

I can't do this. I cannot. I'm going to make everything worse, and on the off chance the situation between me and Gabe is even remotely salvageable I know deep in my mind of minds that I will destroy it beyond all hope of repair.

You know what this feels like? It feels like dealing with raw film. The barest exposure to light, or moisture, or anything, really, can do irreparable and catastrophic damage. The difference, though, is that I know how to handle film. I'm totally out of my depth here and now.

I feel horrible. I feel like my soul has food poisoning. There's nothing I'd rather do than retreat to the safety and solitude of my Fortress. But of course, because that's the only thing I want to do, the universe decides to make sure it puts as many obstacles between me and that happening as it possibly can.

I have to work after school.

"We're short-staffed," is Phoebe's only explanation when she calls me between sixth and seventh period. Phoebe never texts; it's always calls. She says texts never give her enough information.

I can't say no. I want to. But to say no would be to admit that something is bothering me, and I don't think I'm there yet. Besides, working might be just what I need to put my mind at ease.

So after school, rather than being at home, surrounded by all the things I've carefully curated specifically to help me relax and relieve my anxiety, I find myself at the boutique, up to my elbows in a mountain of retro polo shirts.

Fortunately, I love folding shirts, because it's the exact same routine for each one, and if I fold each shirt perfectly, I'll end up with displays of precisely aligned, crisply folded shirts that look impeccable. That is, until someone picks one up to try on.

I do like Gabe. That much is clear…ish. But I learned a long time ago that it's best to keep people at a distance. A polite, impersonal distance. You can't do that if you're dating. Okay, I suppose you technically can absolutely do that, but I'm fairly certain that would make you a crummy significant other.

As much as I don't feel like talking about what happened today, I know it's only a matter of time before Phoebe picks up on the fact that something is off. I turn out to be correct, when half an hour into our shift she drifts past as I work and says, with obviously rehearsed care, "Hey, so I could be, and most likely am, completely wrong about this, but you seem upset."

"So, you remember Gabe, right?"

"You mean the Absolute Unit? Who has the workshop I *still* have not seen? Sure, why?"

"They like me. Romantically."

Phoebe nods like she's impressed. "Holy shit. That's incredible. You're a lucky man. Unless I'm misreading that. Your tone seems to indicate that I am, in fact, misreading it."

"Gabe and I cannot date."

"Why not?"

"Because I'm me."

"That is vague, and does not at all answer my question."

"I don't know how to explain it. We just can't."

Phoebe frowns. "You're not making sense. None of this makes sense. I'm so glad I was homeschooled. Hold on. Are you ashamed of your autism?" she asks. "Because if you're ashamed of *your* autism, it kind of sounds like you're ashamed of *my* autism, which is like you're ashamed...of me."

I've completely forgotten about the pile of unfolded shirts I'm supposed to be folding. "Come on, Phoebe, you know I would never be ashamed of you. The issue isn't the fact that I'm autistic, it's how people treat me when they find out."

"Do you think Gabe is that kind of person?"

"I don't know. I hope they aren't."

Phoebe's words make me think of Will. I don't want to believe that Gabe could be anything like him. But back then, I didn't think Will could be anything like Will. I'm not sure I can let someone else in like that. Even if I want to. It's too much of a risk. I've been screwed over once; wouldn't it be foolish, illogical, even, to open myself up to the chance of it happening again?

"You know, I'm not what anyone would consider well-versed in these kinds of things," Phoebe says, "but if Gabe is someone who would treat you worse if they knew, are they really someone who deserves to be with you in the first place?"

A strong argument and a valid point, two things I can always count on Phoebe to make.

CHAPTER 20

For someone who is, by his own admission, "not into parties," I'm finding myself going to a lot of them lately. Today it's a wedding shower. Or, rather, *the* wedding shower, according to my mom, who I seriously suspect believes this is literally the only wedding shower in history, or at least its most important.

We've rented a room in a rec center that's big enough for a few hundred people. It feels a lot like the cafeteria at school, what with its shiny rubber floor and circular, industrial tables and chairs. It smells faintly of bleach, which I suppose is the least worrisome when it comes to scents you could encounter in a rec room.

From what I've gathered (read, very briefly googled), the wedding shower should take place between about three weeks and about three months before the wedding, which to me is a wide enough window to be essentially meaningless. It's the beginning of October, only a little more than a month before the date.

Unlike the nuptials, this is a casual affair, which means

I don't have to dress up in all those pressed, starched, and stiff layers. And wearing a tie? I'd rather someone actually strangle me, because at least then there would be an end in sight. A tie, on the other hand, won't kill me—it'll just make me suffer the entire time it's around my neck.

I've got my trusty Nikon D90 with me today, with a blank memory card and a freshly charged battery. I could probably shoot for an entire year and still have space and a charge, but as always I'd rather be over- rather than underprepared.

Fortunately, I'm not expected to talk much. I also learned during my very limited, very brief research into the topic, the purpose of the shower is, traditionally, to shower the couple with gifts, love, and attention. Because they aren't gonna get enough of that at the actual wedding.

Sorry, that was mean. I think I might be in a mood. This is a lot for me, and I may be a tad bit overwhelmed.

But today isn't about me. It's about Miles and Shante, so I've got to keep my own personal issues to myself and focus on doing what I'm here to do, which, as always, is document.

In a way, this reminds me of a pre-LARP workshop, which is basically a meetup that happens before the actual event. It's a chance for players to familiarize themselves with the environment and the rules, build their characters, and meet each other. Workshops aren't mandatory, but they can be fun. I don't usually attend. I already know the rules, and I can build my character on my own.

Thinking of LARP makes me think of Gabe, and I really shouldn't be thinking about Gabe right now. It's been an entire week since we kissed. Oh, sorry, I meant, since we kissed, they asked me out, I said yes, then said no for vague reasons I still don't yet fully understand myself.

Shante and Miles haven't let go of each other since they got here. It's incredibly sweet. I've been quietly stalking them, trying to capture all the little moments between them without being noticed. The stolen glances, the hand squeezes, the reassuring touches. I wonder if they even realize how in love they look. I wonder if I ever looked like that with Gabe.

No. Stop. No thoughts about Gabe today. Focus.

I consider my usual two questions. *What am I trying to say?* Today, I'm trying to say that these two families are going to merge perfectly into one, and what binds each of its members together is the love they have for Shante and Miles. *How am I going to say it?* By capturing unplanned, spontaneous moments of joy and love between as many different family members as I can.

This is also a potluck-style event, which for me means extra stress, because of the exposure to so many smells, textures, and flavors that I have absolutely no time to prepare myself for. There's no worse time to be a picky eater than at a potluck surrounded by family and soon-to-be family. It feels like there's always someone who notices what you do and don't eat, and since none of the dishes are labeled I can't know who I'm offending if I don't try something, or hesitate to try something, or worse, try something and hate it.

My mom brought *croquetas de jamón*, which are Cuban ham croquettes. She let me sample a few after she'd made them, so I know I like them. But I also know that it might come off as rude if I *only* eat my mom's cooking, so I make a quick sweep of the food table to see if there's anything I recognize enough to trust that it won't make me gag. Unfortunately, lots of foods make me gag, and most of the time it doesn't have anything to do with the quality or the skill of whoever made it. But that doesn't mean people don't get offended anyway, which I learned the hard way a long time ago.

Simone is there, by herself, pouring soda into a plastic cup. She reaches into her purse and discreetly plucks out a silver flask. "Want in on this?" she asks as she unscrews the top and starts pouring its contents into her drink.

"Are you joking?"

She screws the cap back on and drops the flask back in her purse. "Yes. Totally joking. Obviously. You seem melancholy, brother. What vexes you?"

I pour myself a cup of strawberry Fanta—the greatest soda flavor ever created. "Someone asked me out."

"Someone that you're into?"

"Yeah."

"So...you said yes, right?"

"No."

She sighs for a full five seconds. "Okay, I want to ask why, but I'm afraid of the answer."

"I guess I'm worried that once they get to know me—the real me—their feelings will change."

"What's wrong with you?" She says it like I said it about her.

"Nothing's wrong with me."

"Well, you sound like you think something is wrong with you."

"I do?"

"Yes, you absolutely do."

Mom waves us down, with a cup in one hand, and the other arm linked with Dad's. She's been all smiles since this morning. He's been...less so, but I can tell he's still enjoying himself. I gesture for them to stand next to Simone so I can take a picture of them together.

"I'm so glad you're here. I wasn't sure you'd show up," Mom says to Simone. "Did you...come alone?"

"Yeah, sorry," Simone says dryly, "none of my eight wives could make it this time."

"Only eight wives now? Last I heard it was nine."

"Yeah, well, I went through a divorce. It was messy."

"My condolences," Dad says with a twinkle in his eyes. Simone grins. "Thank you, Father."

Mom clicks her tongue in annoyance, but Dad guides her away, winking at Simone as he does.

"He gets it," Simone says as they shuffle away to continue making their rounds. "Anyways, where were we?"

"You were saying that I sound like I think something is wrong with me."

"Yeah, right! Listen, anyone, and I mean anyone, would be lucky to be with you. You're smart, you're thoughtful, you're an artist, the list goes on. Now, I would never pressure you to date someone if you don't want to, but if you do want to, and it sounds like you do, you shouldn't let yourself get in your own way. Feel me?"

Strangely, I think I do "feel her."

"What should I do?" I ask.

Simone finishes adding more of the contents of her flask to her drink. "Be honest," she says around a long swig. "With yourself *and* the people you care about. That's the only way any relationship can survive. Now, if you'll excuse me, I see some ceviche with my name on it."

Simone's advice rattles around in my brain. It's odd how similar it is to what Phoebe said, even though they couldn't have been more opposite in their delivery. I feel like I'm trying to mentally solve a Rubik's Cube.

By Monday I don't feel like I'm any closer to solving the Rubik's Cube than I was before. Mona and I ride to school together, like we usually do, and Gabe sits next to me in Statistics, as per usual.

Things are, in general, the same as they always have been, on the surface. But I can't figure out if it's more uncomfortable to go along with it or acknowledge that all is not what it seems.

I spend all my lunches in the Chem lab, developing film alone with just my thoughts and John Williams's score from the 1978 *Superman* movie. The lab is a holdout from the most recent renovations that doesn't see much traffic or use. I prefer to do my work either before or after school, so I don't have to worry about having to stop midway through and go to class, and I like the solitude. But every so often I like to spend my lunches here, too. Miss Mounce, who is the unofficial custodian of this place, had entrusted me with a copy of the key so I can lock up my equipment overnight, on the condition that I don't lock the door until I leave (it's a safety hazard, she said). It's a fair trade, and I'm not worried about being bothered in there.

On Wednesday, in Statistics, Gabe slaps something down on the table in front of me.

"What's this?" I ask.

"An envelope," they reply, which is true.

"What's in it?"

Gabe laughs. "Open it and find out!"

They're standing over me with their arms crossed, waiting impatiently. I tear open the shiny blue envelope and carefully remove a letter on glossy card stock with blue embossed lettering.

"An invite to your birthday party?"

"Yes! And you can't say no."

To be completely honest, I'd been thinking about Gabe's upcoming birthday for some time. Prepping for it. Trying to come up with the perfect gift. Giving people gifts is freakishly difficult. I just assumed that recent events precluded my being invited. "Do you want me to take pictures?" I ask.

Gabe plants their hands on the table and leans forward. "No. I want you to come and celebrate my birthday with me. No camera."

I feel the automatic tension in my spine. "Are you sure?"

"Positive."

I can't say no. They said as much.

On Friday, Mona and I go to Riverside after school to watch *Star Trek II: The Wrath of Khan*, which is widely considered to be the greatest of all the Trek movies, even to people who aren't hard-core Trekkies. Which Mona happens to be.

"I'm such a slut for Spock," Mona says as we make our way to the park.

It's cooler outside now. The fall air is chilly but not cold. You could get away with wearing a windbreaker, like Mona is, or a thin jacket, like mine, but it's definitely the time of year when you have to start layering. And since I'm probably the only person in the Midwest who can't, and won't, wear flannel, I have to layer a little more than most people.

"You and Kirk, both."

She laughs. "I don't know that they're in love. I do think they're soulmates. Like, they belong together, but I don't think they're fucking."

"No?"

"Not canonically, anyways. I have read tons of fanfic that would say otherwise. Written some, too. You know who would make a great captain? Harrison Ford."

"As in he could play a great captain, or that he would just be one as he is?"

"Either, honestly. He is a pilot. Hey, are you going to Gabe's birthday party?"

"Yep."

"It sounds like it's gonna be a fun time."

I'm glad one of us feels that way.

"Gabe doesn't have to make things weird between us, you know," Mona says.

I frown. "Why would things be weird?"

"Forget it," she says quietly.

I don't know if that means she wants me to actually forget what she just said, or if she wants me to press her to elaborate. The only thing I am sure of is that I'm definitely not going to forget. In fact, I'll probably still be hyperfocusing on this moment days from now.

CHAPTER 21

Valley Lanes has been around since before my parents were born. In fact, they've made a point of telling me and my siblings how they used to come here as teens themselves, and from the looks of the place not much has changed between then and now.

I can tell right away which lanes are Gabe's because they're the most crowded. Also, there are a bunch of balloons tied to the stools and a great big banner with their name written on it, but I notice those things after.

I don't mind bowling, but bowling alleys, like skate rinks, require that you exchange your shoes for footwear that belongs to the establishment, a fact that's better forgotten. I'm particular about where I put my feet, like most other parts of my body.

It smells like lacquer and rubber. The lights are too low and it's way too noisy. My hands automatically reach for the camera that I know isn't there. I feel its absence like a missing limb. I don't know what to do with my hands, so they just hang there, velociraptor-style.

I have been here for sixty seconds.

There are dozens of people here, which I anticipated given that Gabe is just as popular as Mona, who I can see already playing on one of the lanes with a bunch of others.

Bridge and Erik-with-a-K are the first to wave me down. "We were wondering when you were gonna grace us with your presence," Bridge says. I don't know if it's sarcasm, but I don't care.

The plan now is simple. Show up, find Gabe, give them my gift and tell a joke, then get the hell out of here. It shouldn't take more than fifteen minutes, tops.

"Where's the other half of the dynamic duo?" Bridge asks.

I point at Mona's lane. "She's right there?"

"I was referring to Gabe."

Huh. Now *we're* the dynamic duo? "I was gonna ask you that, actually."

And then Gabe appears, from around some corner, and when our eyes meet I feel like I'm floating and free-falling at the same time. It's almost an out-of-body experience.

"I wouldn't have pegged you for a bowler," I admit.

Gabe smiles. "Yeah, well, cosmic bowling kind of reminds me of Silo City."

Interesting. I look around, at the swirling, dancing neon colors, and the glowing pins and balls, and the colors popping on everyone's clothes and shoes, and realize they're right. This place is marginally cleaner, but the vibe *is* similar.

"You look different, what's different about you?" I ask.

"I'm wearing a binder, and it feels amazing."

"I'm glad."

"What do you think?"

"I think you look amazing."

Full disclosure, I don't often find myself thinking about Gabe's chest. I couldn't tell you what it looked like before this very moment, but that isn't what I mean. They're wearing a Rolling Stones T-shirt, checkered pants, and a pair of chunky old sneakers—nothing different from their typical attire. But they're standing taller, yet their posture seems more relaxed—something I hadn't thought possible. They seem...comfortable? At ease?

"I can't stay long," I say. Because unlike Gabe, I can never be completely at ease, and I'm definitely not right now.

"Oh. That's too bad."

I'm surprised at how genuinely disappointed they seem. Surprised, and maybe just a little bit flattered?

"Yeah..." The urge to offer up some excuse is almost overwhelming, but I hold my ground and refuse to elaborate. Because if I start doing that, I might end up getting convinced to stay longer, and if I'm honest I don't think I can handle being here for much longer. "But I wanted to give you your present."

It's then that I realize that Bridge and Erik-with-a-K have somehow disappeared. In fact, everyone seems to be giving Gabe and me a purposeful amount of space. All the better. What I want to say, I prefer to say without an audience. If I can work up the nerves to do it, that is.

Simone said I need to be honest. With myself and everyone else. I need to start with the people closest to me. I'm beginning to suspect that it might be okay to be myself, my real self. But there's only one real way to find out.

It took me a very long time spent on YouTube to figure out how to wrap the gift, but in the end I prevailed. So admittedly watching Gabe shred the paper to get to what's beneath it is a little jarring. But that turns to gratification when I see the expression on their face once they see what it is.

"You got me drumsticks?"

"It's a pack of customized ones. They've all got your name on them."

"And they're in my favorite color! This is dope, how did you even know?"

"I pay attention."

"Thank you," Gabe says quietly. "And thank you for coming. I'm glad you're here."

Something in their voice and the way they look at me makes my insides dance. I drop my gaze to the ground. "Right. Size eight."

"Come again?" Gabe says.

"Your shoe size. It's eight. I remembered."

"What are you doing?"

"Trying to demonstrate that I know intimate details about you. Because... I like you."

Gabe seems taken aback, but then they give me a wry grin. "Oh. You do, do you?"

I respond with my most practiced casual nod. "Yeah. I do. And I wanted to ask, if...maybe...do you want to come over to my place?"

Gabe raises an eyebrow. "What, right now?"

"Well, no, not in the middle of your party. Maybe when this is done?"

Gabe crosses their arms. "You're asking me to come over to your house. Today. On my birthday?"

"Yes. Is this a bad time?"

"If you were anyone else, yes, it would be. But I like you too, so yeah, I'll come by. *If*, and only if, you stick around for a bit."

"Those terms are fair." Besides, I'm suddenly feeling a lot less anxious being here.

"You bowl much?" Gabe asks as they lead the way to their lane.

"Much? No, definitely not."

"Well, in that case, come here, I'll give you some tips."

Bridge once said that in order to attract someone, you need to let them see you at your best. Where is that for me? The newsroom, probably. I know that it's definitely not here. I study the balls for a moment like I know what I'm looking at, and then grab the lime-green one because it's the color that caught my eye the most.

Gabe nods approvingly. "You're right-handed?"

"Yeah."

"Cool. So you'll start with your right foot. Bring it back just a little."

I do as I'm instructed. Gabe is three feet away from me, but it feels like we're the only two people here.

"Now, bend your knees a little bit. Lean forward at the hip. No, like this."

They close the distance between us, and suddenly they're right next to me. I feel one hand gently at my waist.

"Is this okay?"

Their mouth is right next to my ear. I can hardly manage a strained "Yeah."

"Keep your forearm parallel with the floor."

My mind is completely blank as they move my arm into place.

"Good. Now, line up with the pins, and let it fly."

They let go of my arm and step back. Suddenly I feel very cold and very alone. It takes my brain a second to reboot itself, and then I remember where I am.

Suddenly, I kind of like bowling.

"Daniel, sweetheart, are the note cards really necessary?" Mom bemoans as I pass them to everyone at the kitchen table.

"Yes."

This is a big deal. A huge deal. Tonight I'm both the director and the cinematographer. I've assigned everyone their roles and done all the set dressing. Gabe is coming over, and I have got to make sure they feel safe, comfortable, and welcome. None of which is likely to happen if folks use the wrong pronouns.

"This could've been an email," Miles says with a chuckle.

"Ha-ha. As far as jokes go, that wasn't one of your better ones," I note dryly, which makes him laugh even harder, even though Shante is shaking her head in agreement with me.

"So, Gabe is a they/them?" Mom asks.

"No. Gabe is *nonbinary*. Their *pronouns* are they/them. Not he/him. Not she/her. So, no fem-rooted compliments. Don't call them pretty, beautiful—anything you would typically call a girl, please kindly refrain."

"What if they're pretty in a manly way?" Mom asks. "Like, Tenoch Huerta is absolutely gorgeous."

"No gendered compliments. Can we all agree on that?"

Everyone nods.

"I have tons of enby friends," says Shante.

"Yeah, dude, at this point I have more queer friends than cishet ones," Miles adds.

That's mildly comforting.

"What kind of music does Gabe listen to?" Dad asks.

"All kinds. They're very discerning. You'll get along just fine."

"Do you think Gabe will like the *ajiaco*?" Mom asks me.

Ajiaco is a Cuban stew made with beef, chicken, pork, and assorted root vegetables like corn, plantain, and yucca. It takes a couple hours to make, but it's totally worth it.

"Maybe?" I answer. It didn't occur to me to ask if they'd eaten, or would be hungry, because I'm kind of bad at this.

"Relax, *mijo*, you look so stressed," Mom says. She comes over and squeezes my shoulders. "Don't you think you should give us more credit? We did very well when you introduced us to Phoebe—the one time we got to meet her," she adds dryly.

"Your mother does have a point," Dad adds. "There was no misgendering, no deadnaming, no weirdness at all, and do you know why?"

"Because we aren't terrible people, and this is a household where we respect people," Mom answers. It's weird when they finish each other's sentences like that, even though I'm grateful for the sentiment. I do suppose they're right. My parents have always taught us that love is love, and even though Mom is a firm believer that all of her children should get married, settle down, and have a family, she's never insisted on what kind of family that should be.

When the doorbell rings, my heart feels like it's leaping out of my throat, and I'm instantly hit with the sense that I'm very underprepared for this.

"Places, everyone," I mouth. I remind myself that this was all my idea as I go to answer the door.

Everyone pretends to be doing something. Mom gets up to check on the stew, Miles and Shante both pull out their phones, and Dad opens his laptop.

God, I hope this looks natural.

When Gabe steps into the house there is a strange half second of silence when we're all just looking at one another. And then I clear my throat and start rattling off the introductions.

"It's great to meet you, Gabe," Dad says when it's his turn. "Say, do you know how the moon cuts its hair? Eclipse it. Get it?"

"You don't have to laugh at that," Miles says, shaking his head.

"I'm a dad," he says. "You know I have to do this."

"Okay, now that you've met everyone, we should go somewhere they aren't."

"Good to meet you," everyone says at the exact same time as I lead the way out of the kitchen.

"Good lord, my family is cringe," I say apologetically under my breath. We flee to the safety of the hallway, where we can talk in relative privacy.

But Gabe laughs. "I like them. What was up with the cards, though?"

"Oh, I gave those to them. I wanted to make sure they didn't forget your pronouns."

Gabe smiles. "That's sweet."

By now I've almost succeeded in convincing myself that this was a horrible idea. But Gabe is here now, and I've already rehearsed what I'm going to say. I'd hate for all that to go to waste.

"I'd like to show you something, if that's alright with you."

Gabe levels a skeptical look my way. "If it turns out you've been a vampire this whole time I'm gonna lose my shit."

I laugh, and lead the way downstairs. My door is closed, as it always is. I pause in front of it to gather myself.

"You know, I've never actually been in your room," Gabe says. "How weird is that?"

"It isn't," I said. "No one else has ever been in here, either."

"No one?"

I shake my head. "Aside from my parents, no. I'm a little particular on that point."

"But you're bringing me here, now? Oh my god, is this your secret sex dungeon?"

My mouth falls open. "What? No! Wait, do people have those?"

"I do."

"For real?"

"No, you nerd."

"Oh. Cool." With a last deep breath, I open the door, and we step inside.

It's surreal, watching them take it all in as I hover in the doorway. They make a slow lap, going from the bed to the desk, checking out the posters on the walls like this is a museum.

"What do you think?" I finally have to ask.

Gabe stops next to my desk and nods. "It's...definitely a bedroom. Hold on. Why exactly did you want to show me your bedroom?"

I step inside and lean against the foot of the bed. "Because I want to be completely honest with you, and this is the most honest place I have."

"Oh—okay. What's this big secret you want to tell me?"

Here goes nothing. I slip the note card out of my pocket. I decided already that it didn't make sense pretending I don't have it, so I might as well use it now. "I kept thinking about what you said, about hiding who I am. And, well. I'm autistic."

I've practiced how I wanted to say it. Quickly. Casually. Like it isn't a big deal. Because it isn't. Hopefully.

Gabe's face goes blank. "Oh. Alright."

I sit down on the edge of the bed. "When I was younger my parents compared it to having superpowers. It's kind of true. At least, it feels like it sometimes."

Gabe carefully comes over and sits down next to me. "How so?"

"Lots of ways. Like... I can hear things other people don't."

"Like what?"

"Like electricity? In the light bulbs, in appliances, different ones have different pitches and frequencies."

"You can hear the electricity in appliances?"

"It gets on my nerves, but for the most part I can tune it out. I'm also hyperempathetic. Which is the opposite of what most people think we're like. I can taste the vibes, you know?"

"That sounds hella useful."

"It would be if I knew what to do with all that data."

Gabe smiles at me. "Not gonna lie, that is not what I thought you were going to say. But this is great, too!"

"Do you think so?"

"Of course I do. Thank you."

"For what?"

"For trusting me. For telling me. I know it isn't easy, but I'm glad you did."

Relief washes through me. "That's good. Because actually, that wasn't...the only thing I wanted to tell you..."

"Oh? You're just full of surprises. What's up?"

Deep breath. Take a deep breath. Remember what you rehearsed.

"You remember how I said I had stuff to figure out?"

"Yeah..."

"And how I told you I'd let you know when I figured it out?"

"Uh-huh..."

"Okay. Well... I did. Figure it all out, I mean. It's all sorted."

Mostly. Being honest with the people around me won't do

anyone any good if I'm not being honest with myself, and in order to do that, I have to acknowledge that this, Gabe, is what I want. That's the simple truth.

"Anyways. What I'm trying to say is, if you're still open to it, I would love for us to be a couple, a duo, and a pair."

I shove the card back into my pocket, and then angle myself so I can look at Gabe. I can feel my face burning from my chin all the way to the roots of my hair. My heart is pounding so hard I can hear it.

Gabe is fighting a smile. I'm not sure why. Maybe it's a grin. Maybe they're trying not to laugh. Are they laughing at me? Did I screw this up that badly?

"You asked me out with note cards?" they ask.

My heart drops. I totally did screw this up. "Yeah, I guess I did," I admit.

But their mouth breaks into a smile. "You're adorable. And yes. To all of that."

It isn't until then that I realize I've been holding my breath this whole time.

And then Gabe touches my hand. "So. Seeing as we're dating...can I kiss you again?" they ask in an almost whisper.

My skin tingles. "Only if you want to."

"Always," they breathe as they lean in toward me, and even though I know that isn't true—nobody wants to kiss someone all the time, literally—right now, for just this one moment, I believe it.

"Wait." They stop with their lips so close to mine that I can feel their breath on my mouth when they say it. "Do you want me to kiss you?"

"Definitely." And I mean it. In fact, I can't think of anything I could possibly want more right now. And then they do. And it feels…strange, but strange in the best way. Strange in a way that makes my stomach flutter and the hairs on my arms tingle.

Philematology—the science of kissing. I read once that a single kiss can transmit up to ten billion bacteria from one set of lips to another. There's debate as to whether the urge to do it is biological or psychological in nature and origin, but at this exact moment I don't care either way. I may not know why we humans do this, but I do know that it feels right. Maybe that's all that matters.

"Wait," I ask, pulling away midkiss, because if there's one thing I can count on my anxiety to do, it's kill a mood. "Just for clarification, my being autistic…doesn't change anything?"

"Do you want it to?" Gabe asks.

"Not really."

"Cool. Then no, it doesn't change anything. You do realize you aren't the only person at this school who has autism, right?"

"I—what?"

"Yeah, dude, Aisha was talking about it the other day. I thought everyone knew."

"Aisha was talking? About who?"

"About *herself*."

Aisha? Autistic? How had I not known?

"Hey." Gabe cups my face in their hands. All thought flushes from my brain. "Are you sure about this?"

"Of course I am," I breathe.

Gabe smiles, and brushes their nose against mine. "Cool. Well. Then. I guess this means we're dating, then."

"Yes. I guess this means we are."

CHAPTER 22

Mona goes to school on her own again the next day. And aside from the text she sends me letting me know, I don't hear from or see her much during the day.

Gabe, on the other hand, is waiting at my usual parking spot again when I pull in.

"Good morning, cutie," they say as I meet them on the curb. They pull me into a tight hug that lasts just longer than I anticipated it would.

This is different.

"What's up?" Gabe asks. "You seem on edge."

"I've never done any of this, so I don't really know what I'm supposed to do." It's more honest than I'm used to being with people, but I've decided that I want to be as honest with Gabe as I can be. We are dating, after all, so I feel like that's the bare minimum.

Gabe extends their hand and waits for me to take it. "Don't apologize," they tell me, giving my hand a reassuring squeeze, "And don't worry. I'll show you everything you need to know."

Their hand finds my waist. Pulls me in so that we're con-

nected at the hip. Ordinarily such sudden, unexpected physical contact would freak me out, but now all I feel is the
warmth of their fingers and the firm grip of their hand and
the pressure that anchors us together. I feel safe, protected.
Right now I have no doubt that Gabe can protect me from
anyone and anything.

"By the way." They clap my shoulders and lean forward
to talk in my ear. "I was thinking that, now that we're like,
dating, we should have our first official hangout as a couple."

My heart jumps. I'm still trying to conceptualize this
whole "dating" thing, and I know that dating and going
on dates are different, but related. Phoebe and I never really went on actual dates. We just hung out a lot. "I like the
sound of that."

Gabe grins. "Maybe…tonight?"

I nod slowly. "Tonight's schedule happens to be wide
open. What do you want to do?"

"I dunno," Gabe says with a laugh, "I'll think of something."

A tremor trickles through me. Vague plans. The worst
kind. The kind I can't prepare for. They make me nervous.
And yet, I can't help but notice that I'm a little excited as
well. Our first official date as a couple? If it's anything like
being together on the beach, then I can't imagine I have
anything to worry about.

I'm dating Gabe.

Gabe and I are dating.

Dating! Like, officially. For real.

Dating.

I don't know what to do with myself. I want to tell everyone and no one at the same time. I want to scream about it and keep it our own special secret.

How do these things work? Do we make some sort of formal announcement? A joint statement? I've never paid much attention to the early stages of new couples; they just sort of emerge, and everyone seems to simply know about them somehow.

But if there's one person I can count on to already know, it's Bridge. Bridge knows all, somehow, and he doesn't disappoint this time.

"I prayed, I manifested, I pleaded with the universe," he says when we cross paths in the hallway, "and now God, in all her infinite wisdom, has seen fit to finally, finally, lead you to love." He's almost in actual tears.

"You are so extra. How did you even find out?"

I'm assuming he couldn't have heard it directly from Gabe, but then again, I could be wrong.

"Did you forget who you're talking to? I am the eyes and the ears of this school, baby."

"Okay, Eyes and Ears, who did you see and/or hear this from?"

"Now, now," he says, wagging a finger coyly. "I never reveal my sources."

"Did Gabe tell you?"

"What? No! That would be too easy!"

I think I'm relieved. If Gabe is telling people and I'm not, I'd feel terrible.

I'd say I have a certain…sensitivity to when people are talking about me. People are smiling at me a lot. I didn't notice it at first, but once I do I can't not notice. I feel like I'm in the first act of a psychological or conspiracy thriller, when the protagonist is just starting to sense that all is not normal in their world.

Aisha is the next person to directly ask me about it.

I run into her in the Student Council room, where I know she'll be at this time of day. Fortunately, when I get there, a meeting is just wrapping up, and everyone is filing out of the room. I squeak past them and make a beeline straight to Aisha, who's too busy on her phone to notice my anxious approach until I'm right in front of her.

"I am so happy for you!" she exclaims before I can say anything.

"For what?"

She laughs as if I've said something clever instead of only asking an honest question. "I gotta say, of all the people you'd end up with, I would have never guessed it would be Gabe."

"Oh, that. You and me both."

I glance over my shoulder to make sure no one else is lingering.

"Listen. I didn't know you were…" I lower my voice automatically, out of habit. "Autistic."

She nods. "Yeah…?"

I can hardly contain my excitement. "I have—I'm autistic, too."

A slow smile spreads across Aisha's face. "I'm not surprised."

I do a double take, unsure whether to be relieved or affronted. Aisha seems to read this from my expression. "I kinda had a feeling," she admits. "A hunch, I guess."

I suppose I understand. I myself can usually sense when someone else is on the spectrum. If you know the signs as intimately as I do, they're easier to notice. Except apparently I'm not as good at it as I thought I was. If I can sense other autistic people—most of the time—then it only stands to reason that other autistic people can do the same.

"How long have you known?" I ask. "About yourself."

"Years," she says. "I was diagnosed during the summer after ninth grade. I'd been…struggling, with a lot of different things, for a long time. So my parents took me to a couple of specialists, and an entire summer later I had my answer. Autism."

It's odd hearing the word come out of her mouth, and even more odd that she says it like it's nothing.

"There's nothing wrong with being autistic, you know," she adds.

"Yes, of course I know that."

"But do you? Really?"

"I guess I'm afraid people will reject me if I'm, you know, me. If I don't act like they do."

"I think you should give people more credit."

I shrug. "It's happened before."

Aisha sighs. "Daniel, everyone gets rejected. That's just part of being human. No one and nothing is universally liked, but that doesn't mean there's something wrong with you, or that you have to change who you are. Besides, people here really like you."

I scoff. "I doubt that."

"They don't hate you."

"That doesn't mean anyone likes me."

Aisha raises a brow. "Aside from Gabe, you mean?"

"Well, yeah—"

"And Mona?"

"Two people out of how many that go here—"

"Bridge, Solo, Omar, Destiny? Me?"

"Okay, so maybe more than two people—"

"Daniel. Face it. You have lots of friends. And we all like you. The common consensus around here is that you're a pretty cool guy, and who better to know that than me?"

I frown. I have no reason to think she'd lie to me, but I just can't accept that this is true.

Aisha groans. "Just what do you think other people think of you?"

That's easy. I know the role I'm supposed to play here. "I'm the Loner," I answer. "The Outsider. The guy everyone recognizes, but no one knows well. Someone who's just passing through, who's not popular enough to ever be in or near the spotlight, but who isn't dorky enough to be picked on or messed with. An introverted drifter, a casual acquaintance at best."

Aisha looks at me with a disbelieving expression. "That's not accurate at all. Here, I can even show you."

She sits behind the desk and starts typing on the computer. After a few seconds she flips the monitor my way.

"Take a look. This is the tally for all the people who were suggested for Homecoming nomination. Even if a person was suggested once, they were added to the tally, and the ones with the most nominations were the ones who made it to the final list. As you can see, there were fifty-three total names. Of those, eighteen had multiple votes to their names, and from there we took the top eight. See anyone you recognize?"

"Of course I do," I say as I skim the page. "Every name on this list."

"I meant *yours*, Daniel. You are on this list. In fact, you were one vote away from making the final nominee list."

"No way." Even as the words leave my mouth I confirm on the screen that it's true. Somehow.

"Doesn't look much like someone who's just passing through, to me," Aisha points out.

I have to admit, she's right.

It doesn't feel right having not seen or heard from Mona at all today. During passing time between classes I find myself searching for her, something I've never had to do before. Something seems off between us. At least I think it does. It's hard to say. There's so much going on in my head, and I can't keep my mind off Gabe.

Gabe and I are dating.

About that specifically, I'm happy. More than happy. It feels right. It makes sense in a way I can't believe I hadn't predicted. I like Gabe. I like how I feel when I'm with them. I think about being with them when I'm not.

But this fact also surprises me. Because I never imagined that someone like Gabe could ever be into someone like me.

Happiness. Uneasiness. Surprise. Great. Now I know the base ingredients, the root cause of this emotional turmoil that's currently churning inside me and making it hard to concentrate. So much so that I don't realize it's Mona across the hall from me until I've nearly walked right past her.

She's surrounded by Athletes. Charmaine, Heidi, Victor, even Juanita. They're all talking and laughing, half a dozen conversations happening all at once, and Mona's right in the center of it all. I don't want to interrupt, but she lights up when she notices me, and just like she always does she rushes toward me without a second's thought or hesitation. Relief flushes through me. She's fine. I'm just getting myself worked up over nothing.

"Is it true?" she asks, wide-eyed and excited.

"Is what true?"

"You and Gabe are dating!" she shouts with a laugh.

"Oh. That. Yes."

Saying it sends a rush of warmth through me. I don't think I'll ever get sick of saying it.

"Oh my fucking god!" She pulls me in and squeezes me in a tight hug. "I'm so happy for you both!"

"You are?" I ask once she's let me go.

"Of course I am! I'm honestly a little surprised it's taken this long."

"What do you mean?"

"Well, you've obviously been into each other for a while now."

"Obviously?"

"Yeah, Daniel, obviously," she says with a fond eye roll. "Gabe's all you've been able to talk about since you met them."

I study her face. She genuinely looks excited. She actually seems happy for me. That's good, right?

"Are you sure you're cool with…this?" I ask cautiously.

"Yeah, of course I'm cool with it, why wouldn't I be? Don't be weird."

"I'm being weird?"

"Yeah, you kind of are. Listen, I gotta run. I'll see you later?"

Just like that, she's gone. Back with the Athletes. Her world, and she looks happy in it.

This was what I wanted, wasn't it? For Mona to do her own thing, without me? Is that what's happening now? It definitely feels like that. So why aren't I happy about it?

I retreat to the safety and comfort of the Chem lab in the hopes of easing my nerves. When I first got into photography, I'd felt like Andy Warhol, running around snapping candids at school or taking pictures of squirrels and trees. It had still been my new special interest then.

I've cleared the long countertop that lines the left wall in order to house the supplies I'll be using today: the tank, thermometer, sleeves, scissors, chemicals, and paper towels are lined up in careful order. I've run a clothesline across the back wall, in front of the floor-to-ceiling supply shelves, where I stash the rest of my equipment. Now I'm all set to work.

The door creaks open, and I whirl to see Gabe strolling into the room. They nod when they see me, and they look... glad to have found me here?

"Hey. I was looking for you."

Odd. "You...were?"

"Yeah. Mona said I'd probably find you here."

I'm not sure which I find more unsettling: that Gabe is here, right now, in a space that I've only ever occupied alone save for one exception, or that Gabe and Mona have had a conversation about me without my being there to have heard it. Granted, I use "conversation" loosely, because it could have been as simple as Gabe asking the question and Mona answering it, but even so, the idea of people perceiving me when I'm not around has always made me feel a little uneasy.

Gabe hops onto one of the old desks. "What are you doing?"

"Developing film."

Their eyes light up. "You know how to do that? That's awesome!"

"Thanks," I manage bashfully. An odd sense of pride wells in my chest. No one's ever complimented me for this before. To be fair, not a lot of people know this is something I do. But it's a good feeling. Like being seen for the first time. Good, and a little strange. Especially coming from Gabe.

"Can I see?" they ask.

I look up, trying to hide my surprise and most likely failing. "Really?"

"Sure. If it's cool with you. I don't wanna mess up your work."

"Yeah, no, you're good, you won't. It's gonna be cramped, though," I warn, "and dark."

"I'm not afraid of the dark, if that's what you're implying."

It wasn't, not at all.

Gabe follows me into the closet, and it feels like they're breathing down my neck, which is ridiculous given that they're not that close to me. We are about the same height, however, which means even though I'm probably imagining it, there's a small chance I'm not. They close the door behind us with a definite click that seems so much louder than it usually does.

"Wow," Gabe said quietly, "it's like Frankenstein's lab in here."

They aren't wrong. "I'm only developing the film now," I explain as I inspect everything a last time before I start. "Later is when I do the photos."

"Cool." They sound genuinely impressed. It makes me want to say more. So I do.

"Okay, what I'm gonna do, basically, is wind the film around the reel and put that in the tank. That's the part I need the lights off for. After that I put the developer in and shake it up for a few minutes. Next is the stop bath, then the fixer, then I can hang the film up to dry."

"Sounds straightforward enough."

"Yeah, until you have to do it in the dark. But I've run through it a few times now, so hopefully I don't fudge it up."

"Well, good luck," Gabe says with a smile. "I'll try to stay out of your way."

I glance at them. I'd been so focused on explaining the

process that I hadn't realized how close we were. I'm not imagining that this time.

Once the light is off, it's easy for me to pretend Gabe isn't here with me and focus on the task at hand. Hyperfocus, I should say. I can't count how many times I've practiced this, like so many other aspects of my day-to-day. It all comes down to repetition. As long as I have a script, I can follow it completely.

Before I know it I'm finished, and the light is back on and I remember that I'm not alone in here.

"You make this whole thing look easy," Gabe says as we shuffle out of the closet. They take one last look at my handiwork before I close the door.

"I can show you how to do it sometime," I hear myself saying. "If you'd like."

"I think I would," Gabe answers.

"Hey," I ask. "When you talked to Mona, did she seem… I don't know, different?"

"Different how?"

"I'm not sure." Of anything right now, honestly.

"She did apologize for hooking up with my ex, which was cool of her but unnecessary. It wasn't seeing them together that freaked me out, it was just running into my ex unexpectedly."

Right. Because Gabe's being upset didn't actually have anything to do with Mona being with someone else. It's baffling how obvious it is now that Gabe and Mona never liked each other. If I'd seen that sooner I could've spared us all a lot of confusion.

"Do you think there's anything we can do to help?" Gabe asks.

"I think she'll be good. She usually deals with this kind of thing on her own." Besides, I've spent the last few weeks trying to help and getting absolutely nowhere with it. I wonder if I've actually been making things worse.

In photography, sometimes the shot you want to take doesn't work out. Maybe the lighting is off. Maybe it's the lens, or the aperture settings. Maybe it's the subject itself. Or maybe, it's the way you're looking at it. Sometimes a shift in perspective is all it takes for everything to fall into place.

CHAPTER 23

"So, wait, you really think Batman is better than Superman?" I ask as I scan the side street for a free space to park.

Grand Avenue, or "the Ave" as it's known locally, is what you might get if Dr. Seuss had been an architect. It's one of the oldest residential avenues in the state, although most of the old cottages and Victorian homes that are nestled between the maple and birch trees on either side of the street were redone in bright pastels in the sixties and converted into businesses—locally owned cafés and bakeries, a vegan deli, three boutiques, and a bike tire shop that also, for some reason, serves the best pie in the city. The street itself is made of clay-colored cobblestone, and the branches of the trees weave together overhead to form a leafy, latticework canopy.

Gabe throws their hands up from the passenger seat. "I really don't see how you could not. Batman uses smarts, ingenuity, psychology, and hard-earned skills to take on criminals. Superman uses brute strength that he didn't even have to work for."

"So, because he was born different he has no right to use his gifts to help other people?"

"He has an unfair advantage."

"So does Batman. He's a billionaire. Who wastes his resources beating up the very clearly mentally unstable criminals of Gotham instead of investing in things that might actually help the city, like education, or housing, or infrastructure."

"I don't see your boy Supes doing any of that, either, and he'd be way more capable of it than Batman. He could very easily make himself just as rich if not richer than Batman, but he doesn't, because he's a big dumb jock."

I finally find a spot, and slowly back my truck into it. I don't come to this side of town often. The Ave is a tourist trap during the summer months, but now, with autumn in full swing, those numbers are starting to recede.

I turn the car off. "Agree to disagree?"

Gabe smirks. "Agreed."

Gabe directs us to a place called the Haven, a tiny record store run out of an old asymmetrical Tudor home with ugly stone walls half covered in moss, planted between Floyd's Frozen Yogurt and Carlyle's Crafts and Café. Gabe works at the Haven during the summer, and according to them, the home had been converted into a duplex back in the seventies, and the Haven splits the place with Miss Flanagan, who runs a tarot card/palm reading operation out of her side. "Believe it or not," Gabe explains as we arrive, "she sometimes does more business than we do."

I've never been inside this place. This area is a little outside of where I typically travel, but I'm immediately both impressed and intimidated. Musty cardboard boxes held together with duct tape. Creased posters of bands and singers I've never listened to tacked to the walls. Mismatched blue, black, and pink plywood display cases with the paint chipping. Wooden crates and plastic bins crammed full of vinyls in worn and tattered sleeves. The black-and-white checkered linoleum floors are scuffed and scratched. String lights and CDs dangle from the ceiling. These surroundings are entirely too foreign and way too cool. I don't fit in here at all.

But Gabe does. Of course.

There's lots to see here. Gabe starts thumbing through the records, and I follow suit, although I'm paying less attention to what's in front of me and more to the person beside me.

"Question," I begin. "You get one superpower. What is it?"

"Easy. Shape-shifting."

"For real? Any conceivable ability out there for grabs and you'd go with shape-shifting?"

"Hey, fuck you."

I freeze. Did I go too far? Gabe's tone was harsh, and I can't tell if that harshness was genuine or not. "I'm sorry. It sounds like this is something you've put a lot of thought into, and I didn't mean to make light of that."

"It's all good, man. I was joking."

"Sorry. I can't always tell." It's easier to admit that aloud now. "Why shape-shifting?" I ask.

"I dunno," Gabe answers. "I guess it'd be kinda cool to be able to change whatever you want to about yourself, and be whoever you wanted to be without being stuck in the same..."

"Body?"

They nod. "Yeah."

"Like, if you woke up and hated your nose you could change it?"

"Or not have one altogether."

Interesting.

"What about you?" they ask me as they thumb through more records.

That's easy. "Telepathy."

"You'd really want to know what other people are thinking all the time?"

"You wouldn't?"

"Hell, no."

"Why not?"

"Because people suck! It's bad enough everybody says shit that's fucked-up, even when they try not to. Imagine the stuff that goes unsaid. Besides, if I need to know what someone's thinking I can figure it out without having to read their mind."

"Must be nice."

"For the most part," they amend. "I actually have a pretty hard time figuring out what's going on in your head."

"So do I," I say with a dry laugh.

"Have you always been into film?" Gabe asks as we move toward the books.

"Not always. It's kind of a..." *Special interest.* "...a hobby that I've been into for a while."

"Is that what you want to do, like, career-wise?"

"Maybe." That is, unless I lose interest. That's the thing with special interests—they tend to burn bright and burn fast.

"What's your favorite book?" I ask. I feel like I'm keeping the rhythm of our conversation going, but there's always that worry in the not-so-back of my head that I am horrible at this. Like I'm interrogating them.

"*Frankenstein.* You?"

"*The Adventures of Sherlock Holmes.*"

"Nice."

Another piece of information I didn't know. I feel like I'm beginning to piece together who they are as a person, but I want to know more. It's so much better to be able to just ask what I want to know instead of trying to figure it out based on clues. "How did you know you were nonbinary?"

I almost regret asking the question. But it's something I've wondered for a while, and this seems like the best opportunity to ask.

"I always knew, I think," Gabe explains thoughtfully. "In my heart, or in my soul, or whatever. That sounds cheesy. Even before I understood or had a name for it or could articulate it, and even now, as hard as it can be to try to explain to other people, I know."

"None of that sounds cheesy to me."

"Thanks."

"So what's it like?" I ask as we wander. "Like, day-to-day?"

Gabe laughs joylessly. "Imagine if every time someone saw

you they made a point to tell you how you were 'grandma's little girl,' or how pretty you are, and how much of a young woman you're becoming."

"That would be ridiculous. I'm obviously not a girl."

Gabe stops and throws up their hands. "Exactly. And what if there were people, lots of people, who insisted that you were, and that there was nothing you or anyone else could do to make them see the truth? That's reality for me. People are so obsessed with putting everyone and everything in these tiny, easily digestible boxes, and if you don't fit in them they act like you're some kind of abomination. That doesn't mean I should hide who I am or pretend to be something I'm not. That isn't fair to me. It isn't fair to anyone, honestly."

"Do you think there are exceptions?" I ask. "Like, situations when it is better to hide who you really are?"

We're shoulder to shoulder now, and we're moving at a snail's pace. "Well, sure. Not everyone has the freedom or the privilege to be out. For a lot of people it isn't safe. But that's because the world is a crappy place sometimes, not because something is wrong with them. Everyone deserves the right to be themselves, no matter where they are on the spectrum."

"Spectrum?"

"Yeah, you know, the gender spectrum, or the sexuality spectrum?"

"Right. Yeah. I know that."

And I did. But when I hear the word *spectrum* my mind automatically fills in the word *autism*. Call it force of habit.

Gabe nudges my shoulder with theirs. "For what it's worth, the people who truly matter the most will embrace you for who you are."

The warmth of their touch resonates through my body. "You know, I think for the first time in a very long time, I'm actually starting to believe that."

CHAPTER 24

In film, a montage is a series of separate images, scenes, or shots that are edited together to form a continuous sequence.

The next two weeks of dating Gabe feel like a montage. All of these moments I never would have imagined experiencing myself happen one after the other. Like hanging out with Gabe's band.

Which, as it turns out, actually is a garage band, because they rehearse out of a legit garage.

"Hey, it's the guy Gabe just will not stop talking about," one of their bandmates shouts as we enter. "So glad I finally get to meet you in real life."

"I hate you so much," Gabe grumbles.

"No, you don't." He kneels to adjust the cuff of his pants. They're pill-rolled halfway up his calves, and underneath he's got on striped socks and old-school Adidas that have definitely seen better days.

"This is Max."

"The voice," he adds with a laugh.

"You can pretty much ignore everything that comes out of his mouth," Gabe stage-whispers to me.

Their other two bandmates wave vaguely at me before going back to tuning their guitars. I recognize them from their show, but I don't know their names, and I don't want to ask. I recognize a fellow introvert when I see one, and these two fit the bill.

Inside the garage, thick tangled wires snake across the dusty Persian rug on the ground, and a massive drum kit takes up a corner, gleaming like a giant spindly spider. Against the opposite wall is a wood desk that's covered in equipment and surrounded by a quartet of fancy-looking speakers. I recognize some of the stuff on the desk—a laptop and a desktop and a miniature keyboard—but there's a lot I don't, like the things that look like thick servers that have dozens of wires plugged into them. There are microphones everywhere, and a bass guitar leaning against the back wall next to a ratty old couch. At the center of it all is a single microphone stand with a sheet music stand in front of it and a folding table beside it. There's an incense burner and a pile of charred sticks on the table.

"Make yourselves at home," Max says as he tosses his backpack aside and shrugs out of his jacket. He pushes the sleeves of his striped sweater up, shakes his dreads and rolls his shoulders, and starts absently lighting and rearranging the incense sticks on the table, and it's like he's forgotten anyone else is even here.

Gabe guides me toward the couch against the far wall. I feel like I've trespassed onto sacred ground. There's a spirituality to the way they lovingly inspect their instruments and equipment. It feels like something I'm not supposed to be privy to.

Gabe doesn't seem to notice any of that. Instead of taking their seat behind the drum kit, they plop down and curl up on the couch and pat the old cushion next to them for me to sit. It's not a big sofa; there's barely enough room for another person when we're both sitting. It doesn't help that Gabe never really sits, they lounge. "This is where the magic happens," Gabe says, and it feels like they're shouting in the hush that's fallen over the garage.

"You told them about me?" I whisper.

Gabe squirms. "I mean, a little."

"What did you tell them?"

"Why are you so curious?"

Now it's my turn to squirm. Time to change the subject.

"How does a jam session work?" I ask.

"It usually doesn't," Max says with a wry chuckle. "Most of the time Gabe will just start driving and I'll take my cues from them and just riff until we hit on something we like. Or else I'll spit something and Gabe will come up with a beat that matches the rhyme pattern. Sometimes I'll just freestyle until I say something we both think is dope. It's pretty organic."

"Organized chaos," Gabe adds as they slide off the couch and move toward the drums. "Emphasis on the 'chaos.' Sometimes we jam with other musicians, but when we're trying to come up with new material it's usually just us bandmates."

And then Gabe kicks off a quick drum solo and I jump. "My bad," they say with a smirk as they grab the hi-hat. "Just getting warmed up."

Despite being in a place I've never set foot in before this moment, and surrounded by people I know next to nothing about, I'm...good.

According to Joseph Campbell, a critical step in the mythic Hero's Journey is called Apotheosis. It's the point where the hero realizes what it is they truly needed to understand all along. It's the moment they transcend, realize what it truly takes to become what they were meant to be all along.

This feels like apotheosis. Gabe has been metaphorically right in front of me this whole time, but I couldn't see that, because I wasn't ready to see it before. But I'm different now, at least a little. Even with a live band literally playing just a few feet in front of me, I'm comfortable here, with Gabe.

I sort of feel like I'd be comfortable anywhere, as long as Gabe is there with me.

Mona doesn't ride with me to school at all during the week. I catch glimpses of her in the hallway sometimes, but she's always on the move, even more than she typically is. During one of the few times I manage to catch up with her, she tells me that she's been helping clean up the highway the athletic department adopted. It must be a filthy stretch of road, because I don't see her at all during lunch or in the afternoons.

On Wednesday I go straight to Gabe's house after school. We end up in their tree house, lounging with our legs dangling out the open door while we stare at the roof and the color-changing LED lights Gabe's lined it with. Until a gentle pitter-patter begins.

"It's raining," Gabe announces gleefully.

We both sit up and watch as the downpour picks up.

"It's really coming down out there," I say. It's another space-filling phrase I used to hear my grandpa say all the time. It's good to have a few variations of that one on standby, and most people do without even realizing it. Like, my dad says, *it's raining cats and dogs*, but my mom will say, *it's raining men*, and both amount to the exact same thing.

Gabe stretches out on the floor and I scoot over to perch next to them.

"Isn't this great?" they ask as they stare out at the sheets coming down around us. "I love rain. Especially when it's a bad storm like this. It's sensory overload, but in a good way. It drowns out everything else, and I feel this weird kind of clarity, y'know?"

"I know exactly what you mean!" And I do, which is why I probably said that a little too loudly. "That's why I take forever in the shower."

Gabe laughs. "Same here. My parents hate it."

"I imagine mine do, too." Not that I've ever thought to ask.

We sit in silence for a bit, listening to the harsh static of raindrops crashing through the branches and the leaves, and cascading off the thin tin roof above us. I love the numbing noise, but my favorite part is the petrichor—the smell of rain. If anyone figured out how to distill, bottle, and sell it like a fragrance, I'd wear it for the rest of my life.

"This reminds me of this thing called parallel play."

Gabe reaches over and intertwines their fingers with mine. "That sounds kinky."

"It can be, in some contexts. Not this one, though," I add, because I can feel myself blushing. "It's a pretty common thing for autistic and neurodivergent folks. It's basically just existing together. Like, two people can be in the same place, doing their own thing, and it's just fine."

I don't get to do it often. Most allistic people get weirded out by instances of prolonged silence. Even Mona can't go for too long without talking if we're together. But, for instance, I'm perfectly content to simply be in the presence of another person without having to engage with them. Their proximity is enough. But to most other people, the silence is strange, or even off-putting. It seems to be a societal expectation that if two people are together, especially on purpose, they're expected to interact with one another.

Working with Phoebe is nice, for example, because I don't have to worry about any of that. We sometimes go for hours without saying a word to each other.

The wind picks up, and we listen to it tugging at the branches just outside. Gabe glances at me, but doesn't say anything. Only smiles at me and closes their eyes.

I like this.

"What are you thinking about now?" I ask.

Gabe sits up and leans back on their elbows. "There's this thing Bruce Lee once said that really stuck with me. He said, 'Empty your mind. Be formless, shapeless, like water.' I think about that a lot."

"What does it mean?" Philosophical quotes like that are sometimes difficult for me to decipher. The language is too vague, too flowery, for me to make much sense out of it.

"To me? It reminds me of the fluidity of it all. Like, why try to force myself into a box I don't fit in? I'm water. I can be anything. I can be nothing. I'm less concerned with trying to be this one thing, and just going with the flow. If people don't like it, that's on them, not me."

It occurs to me that I have never, ever, felt this way before. I want to show Gabe parts of me I've never shown anyone. They are the last thought in my mind before I go to bed, and the first image in my brain when I wake up. I think about the heat of their skin and the smell of their breath and the weightless breathlessness that comes over me when our eyes meet, which I actually really, really like, and I just... can't form a coherent thought.

I reach over, carefully, and place my hand on Gabe's. This isn't me following Rule Number Two: Press the Flesh. I'm not doing this for anyone else's sake. This is for me. And when Gabe flips their hand palm up and closes their fingers around mine, and I feel like I could stay here forever.

With Mona, I feel like in a lot of ways I can be myself, or at least the closest thing to being myself I can be. But Gabe makes me want to push my own boundaries. If Mona is safety and security, Gabe is risk and danger, and the rewards that can come with them.

It's only when I'm not with them that things feel different. Less than stellar. Less certain.

What I need is good, solid advice for handling this. And I know just the person. Two people, actually.

Miles and Shante are home when I come from school the next day. "Hey, guys," I say as I come up the stairs from my room. It looks like they're on their way out. "Where are you two headed?"

"Dinner," says Miles. "We're gonna grab sushi, I think."

"Can I come?" I'm already grabbing a jacket. "I love sushi."

I hate sushi. The textures are too conflicting, too incongruous. It's such a confusing food item, and I truly don't understand why it's so popular.

At least the venue is nice. It's a place called Wakame Sushi & Asian Bistro, on the western shore of Bde Maka Ska, in Calhoun. Intimate, minimalist design, soft lighting, rich, mahogany wood floors, and neatly groomed bonsai trees in pots.

I went with nigiri, because I know from experience that it's the flavor profile I can handle most easily.

"So. How are things?" I ask.

It's a ridiculous question, and I feel equally ridiculous asking it. One of those questions that isn't really asking anything specific, but is broad enough to give the other person the space to talk about whatever they want. I don't usually like asking it, or being asked, because it's so open-ended that there's no way to anticipate how the conversation will unfold. But it's my brother, whom I know fairly well, so I take the chance.

Miles shrugs.

"Can't complain," Shante says vaguely as she sips at what I think is sake.

This isn't working. I need them loose and ready to spill the beans.

Okay. Let's try a different tactic. "How's wedding planning?"

That does the trick. "I have never looked at so many flowers in such a short amount of time," Miles says with a chuckle. Shante sighs in agreement.

"Are you sick of those now, too?"

"No! That's the problem! They're all lovely. I can't decide which arrangements I like more than another."

"I'm sure Mom will be more than happy to help you choose."

That makes them both laugh.

Okay. Enough pleasantries. "I need advice."

They exchange glances, like neither of them are sure who should answer first. "About what?" Shante asks cautiously.

"Well, as you're aware, I'm dating someone."

"We are definitely aware," Miles says.

"Cool. Anyways. How do you deal with…the changes… that come with dating someone? Specifically, the changes in your other relationships?"

"Like with family, or friends?" Shante asks.

"Friends. Specifically, close friends."

"I mean, I think it's understood that when you're in a relationship with someone, that person becomes your priority," Miles says. It seems like he's choosing his words carefully.

"So, people just naturally know to stop hanging out with you?"

"I don't think it's that cut-and-dry," he clarifies.

"You can still make time for your friends," says Shante.

"Okay, but what if your friends start avoiding you? Is that part of the whole deal?"

"Are they really avoiding you, or do you just feel like they are because your focus has changed?" Shante asks. "Could it be that you're reaching out to them less?"

No, that isn't it at all.

"Sometimes people drift apart," Miles adds. "It happens. People change."

"Is that what happened between you and Dove?"

Miles frowns, and Shante sits straight up, and it dawns on me just a little too late that maybe Dove isn't a topic I should bring up when they're together.

"I'm getting the sense that I shouldn't have said that. My bad."

Miles quickly shakes his head. "No, it ain't that. Can I be completely honest? Dove and I, I guess we aren't as tight as we used to be because it felt weird being so close with another girl. Not that there was anything like that between us," he adds, reaching over and resting his hand on Shante's. "It was a mutual thing. Sometimes you just gotta decide who's more important to you."

Interesting. And frustrating. But why the hell am I so worried about Mona anyways? Maybe it's the change in the nature of our relationship that's bothering me. Change is historically not something I handle well, after all. Why should you have to lose someone you care about because you care about someone else, too? Especially if the way you care about them isn't even the same? It's nonsensical. I thought that's how it had to be, but now I have my doubts.

Shante squeezes Miles's hand, and now they're making sappy faces at each other like I'm not even here. "Should I go somewhere else until you two are through?"

"Hey," she says with a laugh as she leans over and plants a kiss on Miles's cheek. "This is technically *our* date, remember?"

"We're actually glad you came," Miles says. "There's something we've—I've—been thinking about asking you."

"Oh. What's up?"

He shifts in his seat the way Dad does when he has to broach a touchy subject. "I know you wanted to be the videographer. But…"

Oh, no. The dreaded *but*.

"I was thinking, and I was hoping, maybe, you'd want to be my best man instead."

"Oh…"

I know this is a big deal. The position of best man is an important one. I assumed he'd already asked one of his friends. He's always had lots of friends, so there are plenty of options. But me?

"Are you sure?"

I'm much better suited to filming what's going on rather than being an active participant. There's much less of a chance for me to mess something up.

"Of course I am. But you don't have to make a decision

now. Take your time. Think it over. Let me know what you decide."

Great. More decisions. That's exactly what I need right now.

CHAPTER 25

As always, I find it useful to get a second opinion, specifically Simone's. Besides, I am due for a haircut, so I stop by her shop after school that Friday to pick her brain.

"What's on your mind, little guy?" she asks once I'm in the chair.

"Something is wrong. I'm with Gabe, but… I miss Mona. And I know I'm not supposed to."

Simone frowns. "Whoever said that?"

"Everyone? That's how it works. Isn't it?" Miles practically said so.

"Well," Simone asks, "are you happy with Gabe?"

I think about it, and decide, "Yes."

"Good. But why do you have to lose your best friend just because you're dating someone else?"

"Because the person you're dating is supposed to be your best friend. Aren't they?"

"Who told you that?"

"Society?"

"Let me tell you something about society. It's almost always wrong."

"Miles and Shante said basically the same thing. That sometimes you have to choose."

Simone clicks her tongue and smooths the cape over me. "I'm gonna be really real with you. People are a fucking mess. We love to complicate simple shit, and simplify complicated shit. Sometimes we get so caught up in trying to follow the rules that we forget to question whether or not the rules make sense. What works for Miles and Shante won't necessarily work for you, just like what works for Mom and Dad doesn't work for me. Remember what I said about being honest."

I do remember. And if I'm being truly, one hundred percent honest, I don't want to lose Mona, but in order to find out how to stop that from happening, maybe I need to find out what happened with the people who already lost her.

The irony of what I need to do is sharp. All this time, I've always been especially annoyed whenever people would ask me things about Mona's personal life, as if I had some special insight. Now I understand that as her best friend, I did, and yet now it's me who's reaching out for information.

And to get it, I'll need to venture to places I historically avoid. Like the weight room. A musty, sweaty place where everyone speaks almost exclusively in grunts. Right away I feel like I'm on a different planet, one I am not physiologically designed to exist on. I am by far the smallest person here, and the only one wearing a shirt with sleeves.

Marcus is using the free weights, and even with his Air-Pods in I can hear the music he's listening to. He doesn't notice me until I'm directly in front of him.

"I need to ask you about Mona."

He sets the weights down and pauses his music. "Actually, I'm with Lilly now, bro," he says, holding up his enormous hands.

"Okay. Congratulations. What happened with you two? You and Mona, I mean. Why'd you break up?"

He strokes his chin. As if it happened that long ago. "We were never dating. I wanted to! I asked her out like three times. I even tried to introduce her to my mom."

Yikes.

"I thought we had a good thing going, but then, she just called it off, you know? I wish her the best, though. It's all love."

Yeah, cool, whatever. "So there was no specific reason?"

"Not that I know, bro."

Great. So I came into this smelly place for no reason.

Heidi's story is similar. "Okay, so this is embarrassing, but I think I fell too hard and too quick," she explains when I find her in one of the computer labs. "I guess it felt a little one-sided when we were together? Not that I think Mona did that intentionally! She's great. So kind. And we're *totally* cool now, FYI. We just…didn't connect on an emotional level, if that makes sense."

It does not, at least not to me, but it does sound like the makings of a pattern.

Juanita is the last person I decide to bother, and she's the hardest one to get anything out of. "Why don't you just ask her?" she says when I catch up to her at the vending machines later that day. "I'm sure she tells you everything already."

"To be honest, I'm just trying to understand something. I don't mean to pry into your business, I'm only looking out for a friend."

Telling the truth appears to soften Juanita somewhat, because she sighs and relaxes her shoulders. "Mona and I never got past the flirting stage," she admits. "We were gonna go out to dinner once, but she bailed at the last minute. Still not sure why, but it is what it is."

Huh. So, there's definitely a pattern. I just don't quite know what it means. I'm still missing something.

It's raining hard when I get home from school. The forecast says it's supposed to storm all day, and so I've migrated to the front porch so I can work and enjoy the weather at the same time. Ours is a covered porch, and there are two outlets, so I can bring my laptop and keep everything dry.

I keep thinking about Mona. I understand now that I don't want to let her go. I can't imagine not texting back and forth, or going to Riverside. I can't imagine not being able to tell her things, or her randomly showing up at my house, or just randomly going over to hers. Mona is too important to me. Our friendship is too valuable.

My phone goes off. It's Gabe.

Wanna FaceTime?

Ordinarily I don't, but I could use a familiar face right now, so I send back a Sure ☺.

When they come on-screen they're in their workshop, the bright lights and a wall of weapons behind them.

"What's up?" I ask.

"Not much. Just working on upgrading my gun and wanted to see your face. You?"

I feel myself blush. "Editing photos."

"Are you outside?"

"On my porch."

Gabe nods. "This weather is perfect, isn't it?"

I nod and prop my phone on the table next to me so we can talk while I work.

"So, I've been thinking about the next campaign," Gabe says. "I think I want to upgrade my armor next."

"That sounds like a project."

"Yeah, it'll keep me busy for a while."

By the time the next session starts, Gabe, Phoebe, and I will all be eighteen, meaning we no longer automatically have to be Urchins, meaning we have a lot more freedom and options to play with. It's an exciting prospect, one I've been looking forward to for a long time. But now that it's nearly here, I have no idea what I want to do. I could keep playing as a Grifter. It's a fun archetype, and versatile, but it's also the one I always choose.

And then, in the distant mist, I can see someone coming toward the house. I can tell that it's Mona, and I can tell that something is wrong. It's the way she's walking. Faster than she usually does, with her shoulders hunched forward and her chin tucked. Of course, it could be because of the rain, but I doubt that since Mona loves being in the rain. For a moment I'm sure she's going to walk right past the house, but she veers off the sidewalk and marches up to the porch.

I hop to my feet. "Hey, can I call you back?"

"Oh. Uh, sure?"

I shove my phone into my pocket as Mona swings the screen door open and ducks inside. She snatches her hood down and shakes her hair out.

"Hey," she mutters. She's breathing hard, and frowning, and staring at her shoes.

I can both feel and hear my own heartbeat. "Hi. Mona. Are you…okay?"

What a stupid question. Of course she's not okay. Even I can see that.

"Talk to me. You can tell me anything."

Her eyes meet mine, and I fight the urge to look away. Because she needs this. I can tell. I only hope she can somehow find the reassurance and sincerity I'm aching to convey somewhere in my eyes. Maybe it works, because she smiles.

And then she backs away from me. The smile falters and morphs into a firm line. This feels wrong, in so many ways. I've never known Mona to speak anything less than her mind.

"Daniel," she finally says.

Something in the way she says my name fills me with inexplicable dread.

"I love you."

My heart stops. I'm grateful for the noise of the rain, or else it would be painfully silent.

"I love you," she says again. "So much. I would do any-thing for you, and I want to spend the rest of my life with you, but when I say all that it sounds like I'm *in* love with you, and I'm not. I can't be. Now you've got this chance to be in love, and I don't want to get in the way of that."

There are a dozen questions I want to ask, and a dozen more things I want to say to her now that she's here, but I don't know where to begin, or even if I should.

"What do you mean? I don't understand."

She huffs. "I'm aro. Aromantic. It means I don't experi-ence romantic attraction. Not the way other people do. And I thought—"

Her voice catches. I take the time now to speak.

"Mona, I... I love you, too. But I have never been in love with you. Not like that. I used to think I was supposed to be. Everyone expected me to be. But I'm just...not. But I can't stand the thought of losing you, even a little bit, and I hate that I'm supposed to act like you suddenly don't mean as much to me. I hate that we aren't supposed to be friends anymore."

Her eyes meet mine. "I've been going through the same thing. I mean, everybody says I'm supposed to be jealous, but seeing you two together just makes me...happy? I just... I don't want to lose you, but I know I have to. So I guess I've been trying to figure out how to let you go."

"Do you?" I ask. "Do we have to do this? Just because it's what everyone thinks is supposed to happen?"

All she does is shrug. "I don't know," she says quietly. "What do we do now?"

I can't say anything, because I don't have any answers. My head is swimming. And then—

"Do you hear that?"

It's almost like a tiny, shrill voice. If I didn't know any better I'd think it was coming from...

My pocket.

Oh, no.

I carefully reach into my pocket and confirm what I already know. I never hung up the phone. And Gabe is still on the other end.

I hold the phone up numbly. "So, I'm guessing you heard all that..."

Gabe nods. "You guessed right. We should talk. All of us. I'm on my way over."

CHAPTER 26

I know Simone said that people are messy, but is it possible for a mess to make sense? Because this one is sure as hell starting to. Why none of Mona's romantic relationships worked out. Why so many people, myself included, misread our friendship. Why she never seemed interested in Gabe, but started avoiding me after we started dating. And me, trying to force her and everyone else around me into the boxes I thought we all were supposed to fit in. I was so preoccupied trying to make everything abide by the rules that I lost sight of the simple truth that sometimes the rules don't apply. Sometimes the rules shouldn't even exist.

Could this Rubik's Cube finally be solved?

Gabe arrives twenty minutes after we end our conversation. The rain has relented slightly and the sun is parting the clouds. Now it's only a gentle mist shot through with rainbow light. I would like to shoot it, but right now I'm not sure I could even hold a camera, let alone use it. I'm so anxious that my entire body is trembling. I can't settle on whether to sit down and try to relax or stand up and walk some of the tension out, so I end up switching between doing both the whole time.

Mona is sitting cross-armed in one of the wicker chairs, staring out at the street. Neither of us have said a word to each other. We both stare at Gabe's truck as they pull to a stop in front of the house, and it feels like it takes them an hour to climb out, walk up the driveway, and step through the squeaky screen door.

"Wow, you two look…keyed up," they say as they shake out their hair. "Let me start by saying that that was both the sweetest and most disgusting thing I've ever heard."

I swallow. I can't tell where this is headed, or if they're pissed off or hurt or something else. "Secondly," they say, plopping down in the empty chair across from mine, "Daniel. Look. I like you. Alright? And it's obvious that you two love each other. If that bothered me, I would have said something by now. I knew what I was getting myself into, and I trusted you two to figure your shit out. And Mona. Being aro doesn't mean you can't have meaningful relationships. It doesn't even mean you can't find love. I had a couple A-spec buddies back at Sandburg. I can put you all in touch, if you think it would help."

"I'd like that," Mona says quietly, smiling through teary eyes.

"So," Gabe says, clapping their hands and letting out a sigh. "Are we all on the same page?"

Mona smiles and looks at me. "Yeah. Totally."

Gabe looks at me, waiting for my response. This isn't right.

It shouldn't be. This isn't how this is supposed to work. Someone is supposed to be hurt, right? And yet...

"No," I say carefully. "I have to apologize. To both of you."

I stand up and take a deep breath. I don't have a script now. But I know what I want to say. "Gabe, when we first met, I hoped you and Mona would hit it off, and end up dating. I even tried to make it happen. That's why I invited you to watch Mona's game. That's why I asked you both to the dance. I thought if you two would just get to know each other you'd have to fall for each other, because you're both so..."

I struggle to come up with the right word, while they wait, both of them staring expectantly at me.

"You're both amazing. I've always felt that, from the first moment I met both of you. You both mean so much to me." I force myself to look at Mona. "I know you kept telling me that nothing was wrong, but you seemed so upset about the whole Marcus thing that I just couldn't resist trying to help. I didn't know the full story, and I should have trusted you."

Now I turn to Gabe. "The more time I spent with you, the more I realized that I didn't want you to date Mona. I wanted you to be with me. And when you told me how you felt, I was scared at first, because I didn't think it was supposed to happen. But I don't care about what's supposed to happen anymore, because there is no such thing. And I'm sorry for expecting that from you. Either of you. It was unfair."

No one says anything for a long time.

Finally, Gabe sighs. "Thank you for being honest, Daniel."

"I need to apologize to you, too," Mona says with a deep sigh. "For the longest time I thought something was wrong with me. I would meet someone, or try to date someone, and it would be great at first. But then the romantic stuff would start. They'd want me to meet their parents, or go out on candlelit dinners, or have little nicknames for each other, and no offense to any of them, but those things always make me uneasy. I never feel uneasy with you. I never get the feeling that you've ever wanted anything more from me than what I could give. I'm never more myself than when I'm with you. But I was so busy trying to figure myself out that I didn't give any thought to how I might be making you feel. I've been selfish, and I'm sorry."

Okay, this is weird. I've never imagined Mona would ever have a reason to apologize to anyone. Just like I never realized just how idealized the version of her in my head really is. But seeing her like this, hearing the words she's saying now, feels like I'm finally glimpsing behind a mask I didn't even know was there. I think, maybe, we're seeing each other as we truly are for the first time.

I think...this is good. Or close to it.

We're sitting in this equilateral triangle (thank you, trigonometry), Mona to my left, Gabe to my right, and I feel like my brain is buffering as I process all of this. "Not to ruin what I think is a significant moment," I say, slowly raising my hand like we're in class and I need to be called on to speak, "but are we all forgiving each other? Because if none of us explicitly say that it's going to bother me for the rest of my life."

Mona shakes her head, but she's starting to smile. "Yes, Daniel, I forgive you."

"Likewise," Gabe says before leaning over and kissing my cheek.

I smile. My body still feels numb, and my nerves are ringing, but beneath all that, I feel something like relief, and the small hope that eventually, the three of us will be alright.

CHAPTER 27

Miles and Shante are married in their friends' backyard conservatory, surrounded by potted lavender plants, white roses, and yellow orchids. Lush ferns hang in baskets from the high wrought-iron ceiling, and crystalline beams of midmorning sunlight shine through the glass panel walls like diamond prisms that refract in the trickling water of the tiered fountain. It's an intimate, informal ceremony officiated by another one of their mutual friends who'd gotten ordained just for the occasion. I've only been to one wedding in my entire life, so even though I do my best to mirror the reverential posture of the family and friends surrounding me, I feel ill at ease and out of place. Until Gabe taps the side of my shoe with the toe of one of their patent leather loafers. I look over at them, and they give me a reassuring wink.

Being Miles's best man didn't end up materializing, mostly because I wasn't actually available to properly fulfill the bestmanly duties, since I have a curfew and am underage (as it turns out, many of those duties involve alcohol and being out late). I'm glad, because it means I get to do what I wanted to do here in the first place.

Take pictures.

And there's so much to capture.

Mom is crying. Dad is trying not to cry. Simone is... drunk, I think? And that's just *my* immediate family.

The reception is a much more casual affair. The entire backyard has been transformed into something straight out of Pinterest, under #rustic, #hipster, #chic. String lights twinkle like fireflies in the warm breeze. The air is heavy with the sweet scent of petrichor and fallen leaves. Picnic benches draped in pastel tablecloths and decorated with mason jar centerpieces are arranged across the lawn.

I wander around to the gazebo, snapping photos while the band sets up. I sense Gabe's presence a half second before they materialize beside me. "Here." They press a champagne flute into my hands. "It's sparkling grape juice," they add as they post up against the table and sip from their own drink.

"Thanks."

"You look nice," they say. "The bow tie suits you."

I feel my cheeks burn. "You know, I had to watch three different YouTube tutorials to figure out how to tie this thing."

"You should've asked me," Gabe says with a laugh. They point to their own tie. "Took me three seconds. It's easy."

"Everything is easy for you."

"Only easy things."

We watch Miles and Shante's first dance on the pavilion from the edge of the catering station, with its gleaming antique chafing dishes and one glorious fondue station, next to a photo display with Polaroids clicked to clotheslines with cork pins, candid shots of the two of them with one another, with friends, with family. Shante in her powder blue gown and Miles in his matching tux, and it has to be obvious to everyone just by the way they smile at one another that they adore each other more than life itself.

This both is and isn't like the movies. None of us here fit neatly into any one trope. No one really does. I understand that now. We don't need to be categorized and forced into boxes for anyone else's sake.

I put aside my camera and take out my phone. "Hey, let's get a selfie. Just the two of us."

The Riverside plays *Soylent Green*, a dystopian sci-fi film from the seventies that not only features shocking relevance to current events, but also Charlton Heston's single greatest (and most unintentionally hilarious) performance. Mona and I see the movie together, just like old times.

"Do you think you could eat another person?" Mona asks as we swing. It's too cold out for frozen yogurt, but we still hit up the park. "If the situation called for it?"

"How on earth would a situation ever call for that?"

"Okay, what if you didn't know it was people? What if you had the most amazing meal you've ever had in your entire life, something that makes everything else you've ever eaten seem like crap in comparison."

"And then the chef tells me what I just ate was people meat?"

Mona cracks up. "Well, yeah, and here's the thing! He tells you that halfway through the meal, but it's totally cool, like, legally. Like, the person wanted to be eaten."

"You're asking if I'd, what, finish the food?"

"Would you?"

"Of course not, that's disgusting! Would you?"

Mona shrugs, but she's giggling.

It's been a few weeks since our little heart-to-heart on my porch. Gabe isn't here. They're jamming with their band, rehearsing for a gig they have this weekend. Mona and I will be there, and after the show, we'll all probably grab pizza. That's the plan, at least.

In Joseph Campbell's Hero's Journey, one of the final steps is called Master of the Two Worlds. It's the point where, after all the fighting to triumph over all the challenges their story has pitted them up against, the hero has achieved what they set out to accomplish, and now they get to return home. But home is different now, because the hero has evolved. They've changed for the better, and because of that, home, the place they started their story determined to escape, is better, too.

Every good story has this moment, and right now, I think I'm having mine.

Today's broadcast promises to be unlike any I've ever been a part of. Because this time, I won't be behind the camera.

This time, I'm going to be right in front of it.

"I gotta say, it's weird seeing you in my spot," Bridge tells me as he circles the desk, taking pictures with his phone because this is, as he says, *a historic moment for my bestie!* "But you don't look half bad."

"Thank you." I'm nervous, but in a good way. I think. I'm wearing a blazer and a tie, both of which feel like medieval torture devices that have been grafted to my body. This room is about ten degrees too warm. And I have to constantly fight the urge to pick at the microphone clipped to my collar. But I'm ready. I've rehearsed about a thousand times, and this time I've got a literal script in front of me.

It also doesn't hurt that Aisha is right beside me, and she doesn't seem the slightest bit nervous. "We're going to be great," she assures me. "Just imagine that you're talking to your best friend."

"That'll be easy," says Mona. "I'll be standing right next to the teleprompter."

That was part of our agreement. Mona and Gabe would both be on either side, which will give me something to look at without having to look directly at the camera. In theory, it'll make this easier.

"Would it help if we make funny faces at you?" Gabe asks.

"Probably not," I say with a nervous chuckle. "I still can't believe I let you all talk me into this."

"You could still change your mind," Aisha says, suddenly serious. "If you don't feel a hundred percent up to this, you don't have to."

I shake my head. "I got this."

This segment is important, to me personally, but also just in general. A few weeks ago, Aisha asked me to speak about what it's like to be autistic. She told me she wanted to help debunk some of the stereotypes and misconceptions out there about it. To fight some of the stigmas. It's been something she's been wanting to do for a long time, and now, she believed, was the time.

How could I say no to any of that?

"Also, not to stress you out, but try not to blink too much," Bridge adds. "It weakens your presence on camera."

"Seriously?"

"Yeah, but don't worry about it, bestie. You'll do great."

I used to think I was destined to be a spectator. An observer. An outsider. But here I am, surrounded by my friends, in front of a camera, about to speak to the entire student body.

I suppose you could say being behind the camera isn't the only way to tell your story.

★ ★ ★ ★ ★

ACKNOWLEDGMENTS

For me, writing has been such a solitary thing for so long that it's still strange and new to have and be a part of such a supportive community. But I am grateful, and I have so many people to thank:

Everyone at Inkyard Press who has continued to believe in me. My editor, Olivia Valcarce. This book would never have become what it is without you. My agent, Emily Forney, a literal genius.

My agent siblings and my Arizona Avengers family, two of the most inspiring groups of people I've ever known.

Everyone at Brick Road Coffee, where I wrote at least half of this novel. Thank you for creating such a safe and welcoming space for the community.

My cats, who tried tirelessly to delete huge chunks of this book while it was still only a Word document on my very fragile laptop.

The queer and neurodiverse folks and all the nerds in my life, for being who you are, and encouraging me to be who I am. This world would suck without you all in it.

The friends I've made along the way, fellow authors, editors, voice actors, booksellers, and readers. Thank you all from the very bottom of my dorky little heart.